A man who can predict the fall of a roulette ball.
A magician whose illusions break the laws of physics.
A brotherhood whose art hides the map to another world.
When Hans Winters crosses paths with the enigmatic Augustin Flamel, he's pulled into a web of danger, cosmic secrets, and a power inside him he never asked for.
And someone will kill to control it.
Some men chase fortune.
Others chase immortality.
Hans Winters is about to discover why they're chasing him.

DEMIGODS

The Hellish Road to Paradise

By Koos Verkaik

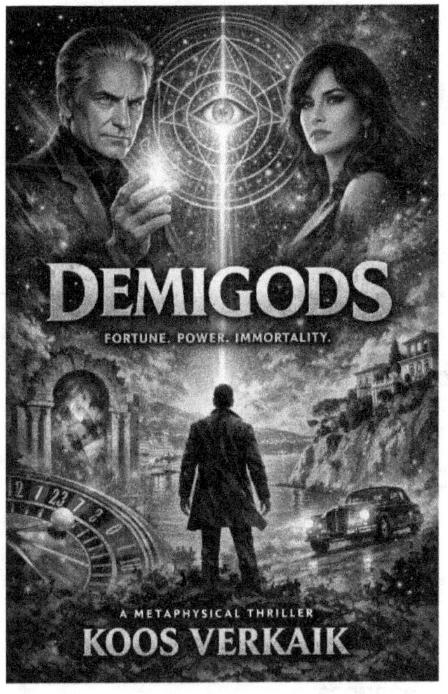

Outer Banks Publishing Group
Raleigh/Outer Banks

 Published in the United States of America by Outer Banks Publishing Group - Raleigh/Outer Banks.

www.outerbankspublishing.com

For information contact Outer Banks Publishing Group at

info@outerbankspublishing.com

FIRST EDITION - May 2026

Library of Congress Control Number: 2026939267

ISBN - 979-8-9937092-4-6
eISBN - 979-8-9937092-3-9

FOREWORD

This story had already been written, when I read a remarkable excerpt from a book by Peter Kolosimo entitled 'Shadows On The Stars'. He quotes, among others, Robert Charroux, who talks about the marvellous paintings of Jeroen Bosch (1450 – 1516).

In his painting, 'The Temptation Of St Anthony', a mysterious airship is visible, aboard which there is an instrument known as a goniometer, which was only to be invented three centuries later. The conclusion, although somewhat far-fetched, might be drawn that Bosch could have been a time-traveller who arrived in The Netherlands from another dimension. Other historical figures may also have reached us from unknown, parallel worlds and been stranded here – doomed to live out their lives on planet earth!

But it was Bosch especially who attracted my attention. As a young boy I was lucky enough to have seen an exhibition of Bosch's paintings, which was on loan from art museums all over the world, in the town of Den Bosch. It was bewildering to see what swarmed about on those paintings! At the time he created them, no one had yet heard the term 'surrealism', but the supernatural images Bosch depicted on his canvasses took turns that insisted the onlooker step outside the paths of the familiar world.
The total absurdity of those monsters and fantastic creatures is overwhelming.

Just where did Bosch's otherworldly ideas originate?

After having considered all the various options which Kolosimo put forth I purchased a book which contained copies of all of Bosch's work and went to Den Bosch to see St. John's Cathedral. This enormous, grand old church was very well-known to Bosch, and equally admired by his contemporary, Albrecht Dürer. I strolled around the statue of the insignis pictor (renowned painter) and gazed upon the face which looks so much like his putative self-portraits.

F.E. Farwerck, the author of 'North European Mysteries', was a great source of inspiration for my own novel, *All-father*. Does he also have an opinion about Bosch's work and it's origins?

Indeed he does!

He writes about one of the master's paintings, 'The Prodigal Son', and points out the fact that a man in the painting is wearing one shoe and one slipper. A sore foot, an injured heel and a limping gait, perhaps indicates an escape from the underworld. Just before the doors of Hell are slammed shut, the last fugitive could jump to freedom, and be lucky enough to escape with merely a wounded foot.

With a bit of imagination we can view this as a flight from another dimension.

The seed of an idea to write a fantasy novel as a successor to Demigods, in which Jeroen Bosch would play a leading role, was thus quickly germinated.

As I continued my investigation, I discovered countless books about his grandfather, father and brothers, who had all been painters. I learned of his admittance to The Brotherhood of Our Lady in 1480, about various prestigious people, such as Philip the Fair, and Margaret of Austria, who greatly admired and purchased his work, and about how sedate his life actually was.

It is not possible to establish with certainty if he ever undertook a journey to Italy, and he may have only visited the town of Utrecht once, staying in his native town for ever.

The puzzle of his life becomes even more mysterious when we consider the sense of security which he deemed so important to his life inside the city ramparts, opposite the terrifying demons he was compelled to depict in his paintings.

The book which I desired to pen had already began to take shape in my head. A book which show Jeroen Bosch as a traveller in time who's cradle and base resided in a dimension that is unreachable for normal mortals.

I decided to write another book, instead.

In literature, there are rules which are allowed to be broken. We high-handedly like to refer to this as 'poetic license'. This allows us to manipulate names and characters to suit our purposes without being called out-and out prevaricators. In light of this I so named one of the principal characters in 'Demigods' Augustin Flamel, after Nicolas Flamel, a man who lived in the fourteenth century who attempted to become fabulously wealthy through the ancient science of alchemy. He desired to transform quicksilver into gold.

But Jeroen Bosch is a too great a personality to cast as a central figure in a fantasy novel. The supernatural dimensions of his paintings were not a reproduction of any particular reality, they existed only in the mind of the creator himself. Researching Bosch, my respect for him grew and grew, and that is why there will be no sequel to Demigods in which he repeats his role.

Can you dedicate a book to an enigmatic painter who lived so very long ago?

Well... I just did and thank him for the inspiration.

Fantasy bridges all time.

Just imagine that everything that has been written in speculation about Jeroen Bosch is, after all is said and done, true. That he came from another world to which he could return if he so desired. And that, with the alchemistic knowledge of someone like Flamel, a man could also live forever as I put forth in my novel 'Wolf Tears'.

Then perhaps one day a man will enter a bookshop and selects 'Demigods' from the shelf with multi-colored fingers. He shall look at the cover, browse the pages, smile and proceed to the counter to purchase it.

"I have never seen you in here before," says the pretty little clerk behind the cash register.

"That's correct," he says. "I'm a newcomer. I've just found a room here for my studio."

"Are you a painter? May I ask you your name?"

"Yes, Ma'am, I am indeed a painter... and my name is Jeroen Bosch..."

Koos Verkaik - 2026

DEMIGODS

Ars longa, vita brevis

(Art is forever, life is short)

Sic itur ad astra

(This is the way to the stars)

After the completion of his work, the perfectionist always sees how he could have done it better.

He renews his efforts to improve the prototype and this becomes the beginning of a train of changes, renovations and additions.

The perfectionist clears all obstacles from before him until he finds himself standing in front of an insurmountable wall.

It is according to his spirit, and his definition that his Gods are created.

Their only limitations lie in the nature of his thinking. For the god who masters the entire scale of ability must also must be able to create a problem he cannot solve...

Even while perched upon the shoulders of gods the final obstacle shall still be too high.

Ne Jupiter quidem omnibus placet

(Even Jupiter cannot please everyone)

This logical contradiction shows the limitation of perfection and omnipotence.

It is only for the solitary adventurer that the gates open and a path is shown to the stars. He who succeeds in returning from that journey rightly deserves and is given the status of a demigod.

Chapter 1: Monaco's eyes

Walking along and reading, he had travelled from the cosmopolitan district of Monte Carlo to the harbor at La Condamine. Glancing up from the last page of the book he had been reading, he saw the white fleet of the elite bobbing on the azure water of the Mediterranean Sea. The book, which contained more than 300 pages, was about metaphysics, but it might just as well have been about horses or town planning, for he read everything he could lay his hands on. He had the uncanny ability to absorb, within a half-hour, the contents of anything he read and remember it forever.

Hans Winters placed the book on the gangplank of a yacht, walked on a bit farther and then stood still. This seemed like a good place to wait, on this bright and beautiful early morning, for the two men who had followed him from the pastry shop where he had stopped to buy his breakfast.

One of the men was short and fat and wore, although the heat of the day was quickly rising, a long heavy coat. The other fellow was a giant of a man with thick muscular arms that stuck out of the short sleeves of his cotton shirt. They also stood still now and seemed to be considering what to do.

It was a warm, lazy Mediterranean morning with groups of people sitting on the luxurious decks of their yachts having their breakfast. An old black dog lying on the dock pricked up his ears and looked out over the coiled rope on which he rested his head. Further up along the quay two tourists stepped out of a taxi.

Turning to the water, he watched the men shuffle closer to him. He stood there with his arms crossed and waited until they were right in front of him. He looked up and the man in the long coat and smiled at him.

"Bonjour," he said. "I suppose you have no idea who I am."

The tiny nation of Monaco, clinging to France like a pearl to an oyster, with Italy so nearby, is inhabited by people from all over the world and many different languages are spoken. The official language is French, but the man who stood before him now spoke Monegasque, an odd mixture of French and Italian.

"Oh, but I do," laughed Hans Winters. "Less than a year ago I was in Saint Tropez, Cannes, Nice and Monaco and in each place I saw you in the casinos, and yesterday, as I sat at the roulette table in Monte Carlo you were quite obviously looking over my shoulder..."

He answered him in French and now the stranger replied in the like:

"What an excellent memory you have!"

"Baden-Baden in Germany, the gaming house, the horserace... a year and a half ago. I'm sure that I saw you at all those places, but I don't think that I was the object of your constant attention at the time."

The man offered his hand to Hans and said:

"That's right, and I think you know what it is I discovered by watching you. By the way, my name is Aldo Duby."

Hans shook his hand and crossed his arms again. He was a man of normal height and apparently in his late twenties. His short blond hair and blue eyes clearly indicated that he was not of Southern European extraction; he was a Dutchman.

"Hans... Hans Winters," he said as he introduced himself. "In the course of your observations, I'm sure you noticed that I'm usually, if not always, a winner at the tables."

"Yes, indeed you are sir, but that is beside the point. You are not an ordinary winner. You seem to be satisfied with small winnings, since you seem to know full well that you can win any amount at any time you wish. Every now and then you walk out with a small fortune, and then a week later you win just enough to pay for your hotel room and a good dinner. You have a system, Hans Winters, and I never have seen it fail."

They stood facing each other in silence for a moment. Duby's dark eyes furtively looked past him towards the water, as the taller man walked up and down, calmly staring at the toes of his shoes.

"If it is a system at all," Hans said, breaking the silence, "I don't think it's a trick which I could teach to anybody else, and I don't have anything to offer in return, whether to buy, trade, or sell."

Duby grinned.

"Let me ask you something Winters. Let's say you were interested in one of these yachts here. One of these rich guys, these fortunate businessmen, has had enough of his sea-faring adventures and wants to get rid of his ship. How long would do you think it would take you to pay him, assuming that you didn't have a dime in your pocket when you made the deal?"

"Let me put it this way, Duby. I could get the entire amount together in one night, but I suspect someone would try to distract my attention away from my game before I was halfway through. I have never played that far, for that much money, which you would know if you have really studied me that closely. You have already said it yourself... most of the time I'm satisfied with small winnings. But, if I wanted to, I could win enough in one night to buy myself the most expensive yacht in this harbor."

"Someone worth as much as you needs protection."

"Which, I suppose, you are offering."

"Yes, that is exactly what I am offering. I would hate to see you join forces with someone who was going to give you false guarantees, and I really don't think you should be working alone. Believe me, I've seen most of the systems, and they're no good, but yours seems to be a perfect one. Systems are explainable and therefore saleable. I am suggesting a partnership which would reward you with all the luxury, freedom and wealth one man could desire. And you would have protection night and day. Money, cars, villa's, women, not to mention power and respect. Doesn't sound too bad, does it?"

"No, not too bad at all, but I could have all that any time I wanted, without anyone standing in my way."

"I am not the only one who watched you play. Sooner or later, someone else will want to have a talk with you and if you insist on being this stubborn, you'll end up taking a trip on the Mediterranean that you won't return from! The last spot you see will be the spot where they wrap a heavy chain around your ankles and drop you overboard!"

"Thanks for the warning. I'll be on the alert."

He was about to leave, when Duby stepped aside and motioned to the tall man who had remained in the background.

"Before you go, allow me to introduce you to my companion. We call him Minor, which is Latin for the smaller, inferior one. This kind Italian gentleman would also like to be your friend and protector. Come on, shake hands..."

Without hesitation, Hans stuck out his hand. Minor clasped it and slowly started to squeeze. His fingertips were broad and calloused and his thumb was like a steel hook.

"In a civilized world, the law of the jungle counts for nothing at all," said Duby. "But physical strength still carries a lot of weight in the eternal struggle between the rulers and the ruled. Very often it happens that, when dealing with situations that involve non-observance of agreements and breaking of contracts, it does indeed make a difference which side has the greater physical strength."

Minor was a head taller than the slight Dutchman. He tightened his grip and stared expectantly into Hans' blue eyes, hoping to see fear and pain, but Hans' reaction came slowly, and was not at all what Minor had expected. He surprised Minor by casually matching his strength and then easily applying even greater pressure, hurting him. Just as Minor made a fist with his free hand, and was about to strike Hans, he felt a burning pain course through his hand and fingers and he cried out, attracting the attention of people all around them. Minor's knees gave way as he felt the bones of his hand being crushed and heard the sound of his fingers being cracked and broken. He sat on the ground now, his chin on his chest, until Hans released his hand.

Duby shrunk back in fear and astonishment. He was perhaps in his late forties, but as Hans looked at him now, his reaction to these events and the expression on his face made him appear much older... older and tired. He bent down beside his crumpled companion as Hans continued on his way along the harbor.

Duby knew very well, that a partnership between himself and the Dutchman would be more beneficial to him than the other. It would yield him a certain degree of power and financial independence. Kind words had not helped him convince Hans, and Minor's interference had only resulted in a mutilated hand... his own. The giant was paralyzed from the fore-arm down, which to a certain extent, helped relieve the unbelievable pain that was emanating from his crushed hand. His last cry had ended in a hoarse gasp, and then he collapsed as Duby caught him in his arms. From on board the yachts and along the dock, everyone was staring at them and people strolling by stepped aside. No one seemed to be in the mood to stop and assist a fallen giant on this beautiful morning. The old, black dog continued to bark.

Hans Winters knew exactly what was going on in his mysterious life, and was not at a loss to explain it, if need be. The problem was that most people, especially a person like Duby, would never have believed the truth. He could explain himself in a few short sentences if need be:

"Picture a small steel sculpture, the size of a chess piece, crafted by one who belonged to the Brotherhood of Helgen, better known as the 'Austrian Twentiers' to art connoisseurs around the world. What was contained in the sculpture, is now in me. I walked until my muscles were as hard as steel, and I likewise exercised my mind until, it too, was forged anew. I have no reasonable explanation though, for what keeps me on my constant pilgrimage. I know that I am searching for something, but what it is, I am not sure. Predicting figures and combinations is merely a side effect of my mental acuity and I could not possibly teach anyone how to do it."

That is what he would have told Duby, even though he knew that he would never have believed him. He did know, however, that a meeting with Augustin Flamel, the famed illusionist, was imperative. On all of his stationary, and on his posters, an intriguing art form appeared. There was a picture of Astra on everything, and around the picture was the Latin text: "Ars longa, vita brevis. Sic itur ad astra. Art is forever, life is short. That is the way to the stars."

Flamel claimed Astra was a work of art with hidden meanings. It appeared differently to various people. Some saw beauty, while some saw only horror. The abstract forms and varied colors formed a pattern that told a tale and the images could all be translated into words, if one knew how. For this text Flamel offered, and was prepared to pay, a fortune. But no one took him seriously, they all thought it was no more than a publicity stunt, for no one could make any sense out of the tangle of lines and colors. No brain, nor computer could decipher it. But Hans Winters had knew what it said. It had first spoken to him when he originally saw it so very long ago. It was, just like the small sculpture, made by someone who belonged to the brotherhood that had settled in the Austrian mountain village of Helgen.

One of his pockets contained a worn, folded itinerary of performances by Augustin Flamel and on the cover was a photo of Astra, and that was the reason for Hans' journey to the sunny coast of Europe, the fact that for one week, in the city of Nice, the illusionist would entertain and amaze his audience every night.

That night, Hans Winters entered the casino of a grand hotel by the sea-side. He was accompanied by a tall man with broad shoulders, dressed in a light brown suit. The hair on his head was short, as was the hair on his cheeks and chin. He stayed close to the Dutchman at all times. They walked past the slot machines and card tables, and headed to the bar for a drink. When Hans sat down at a roulette table, the man stood behind him and watched over his shoulder.

The more Hans won, the more people gathered around the table, and not surprisingly, directly in front of him stood Aldo Duby. He looked at Hans, pointed behind him with his thumb, nodded and raised his eyebrows, as if to indicate that he knew what Hans was up to and silently asked:

"I see you're not alone, is he a body-guard or the police?"

The brilliant steel ball, spinning around and around the wheel, landed time and time again on whatever number Hans had bet on. There were times that Hans intentionally went against his instincts and placed bets which he knew would be losers. He felt that this was a good way to divert attention from himself. This however, was not one of those occasions... Hans became richer and richer with every spin of the wheel. When it got to the point that there were simply too many people crowding around the table, all trying to make a quick winning off of his bets, he gathered his chips and left the game. He was probably the only one who noticed how the croupier looked at the high ceiling as he uttered a sigh of relief and a silent thank-you.

Hans didn't actually need the money he had won here. He had more or less expected Duby to come searching for him and by gambling at the roulette table he had made it perfectly clear to him that he was not afraid. Back in the bar, he saw Duby again, so he put down his glass and walked over to him.

"I could have won the money for that yacht tonight," he said, smiling cheerfully.

The other men who accompanied Duby all looked at him quizzically. Here at the bar, soft music played, and every now and then a winning shriek of excitement from the casino reached them.

"Minor's hand doesn't look well," said Duby. "I can't help but wonder how you managed to do that, but my proposal remains the same nonetheless. You are exposing yourself to great danger if you continue to operate alone. Can we go somewhere where we can talk quietly? I will leave my men here and you leave your nosey friend at the bar. If you give me the time to paint a picture of your future, as only I can arrange it, you will undoubtedly be glad you met me."

Hans shook his head and put a hand on Duby's shoulder.

"I'm sorry, but I must be on my way... alone."

He nodded in the direction of the short-haired man. "That nosey friend of mine, as you call him, wants to discuss something with you."

Duby watched as Hans stopped on his way to the exit and talked to the man. They shook hands, and the man stood up and walked over to Duby with long strides.

"If he is a policeman," Duby said to his colleagues, "you can bet that there will be other cops around. Winters has arranged his own protection and has showed us once more how easy it is for him to make fast money."

Sporting a disarming smile, the man in the light-brown suit stood before him now. Even though Duby obviously had no intention of talking to him, the man started to speak, his voice was soft and shy for a man of his size.

"Monsieur Duby... My name is Jean-Paul Renouard. Monsieur Winters told me that you are the owner of this hotel and casino and that you would be kind enough to show me around."

"The owner?" Duby repeated in surprise. "He told you that, did he? And whom, may I ask, are you? And what is your connection to Winters?"

"Oh... I just happened to meet him on the beach today. I'm on holiday for the first time in years. I own a farm in Brittany. Winters was kind enough to invite me to accompany him tonight and he offered to show me how some of the games of chance are played. But you could show me more, he said..."

Behind him, Duby heard the others snicker. He swallowed his anger and decided to ask a question, the answer to which he already knew.

"Tell me, do you have any idea in which hotel Winters is staying?"

"I wouldn't know. We left the beach together to get a bite to eat in an outdoor cafe, and then afterwards we took a walk and came here."

Duby slid off of his bar stool and hurried past the amazed Breton. Outside the air-conditioned building he inhaled the warmth of the early evening and looked around. The Dutchman had already disappeared into the crowd of tourists strolling through the streets.

Hans Winters' only goal that evening was to catch a performance by Augustin Flamel. His long wanderings had melded his body and mind into a mighty machine, but he had no idea what to do with that machine. He was primed and ready for something that seemed to be big, adventurous and dangerous, all at once... without being able to guess what it was. He liked the comparison of himself to a machine, or some piece of equipment that looked impressive, but no one had any idea how to use.

That morning he had shared breakfast with an English couple, Mr. and Mrs. Cale, who had told him of their plans to drive to France for the day in a rented car and they invited him along. He had instead gone back to his room and read a thick book about ancient Rome before the reign of the emperors. Now, as he descended to a terrace at the side of the road, he counted the passing BMW's, Mercedes' and assorted Italian sport cars and was, all things considered, very bored. He therefore appreciated it even more when he suddenly got some unexpected company. A very attractive woman, around the same age as he, sat down beside him and slid close to his side. She wore a very short summer dress and her dark brown hair fell alluringly past her shoulders. Her jewellery was all made of gold. Seldom had he seen a prettier face and her voice was soft and clear when she told him that she was here all by herself, and that she had left all her worries and troubles at home.

"I do as I please... I want to enjoy my freedom for as long as it lasts," she said.

"What's your name and where are you from?" asked Hans.

She made some grandiose gestures with her arms, her sunburned skin and white nails reflecting the brilliant sunshine.

"When I am here, I feel wonderful. It is a big enough place that I may dissolve into the teeming masses and still small enough to for me to be able to settle in quickly. Everybody here is cheerful and the cash just simply flows like wine. You ask my name... As long as I am here, it is Monaco."

She leaned over to him and spoke in an even lower voice.

"Where I come from is a sad and lonesome place. What is the use of organizing a dinner party for fifty people when no one shows up? Or living in a house with twenty rooms and always being alone? I will delay my journey home for as long as possible, and in the mean time I will enjoy myself. I shall want for nothing. All I need is a friend to share it all with..."

Hans leaned back to have a better look at her and decided to play her game. He asked her no more personal questions and offered no information about himself. The irises of her eyes were so dark that they seemed to blend right into her pupils. She gestured incessantly with her hands as she spoke. He could not make out any particular dialect in her French.

"I rented an apartment with a beautiful ocean view," she said. "It would be perfect for two people, for us, but I would really rather not be seen going in with a man. It could get me into trouble. Do you have a hotel room?"

"Yes, not too far from here."

"If you can offer me a drink, I would love to go there with you. Let's escape from the heat of the day and have some fun. I'm sure that no woman ever gave you what I can offer you. When it's time for me to return to my lonely existence, I would like to do so with lots of warm memories."

They stood up, and as they walked to Hans' hotel she held his hand.

"Do you understand what it is I'm about?" she asked.

"I see a big house somewhere in the middle of France," he said. "Outfitted with all the very best creature comforts. A country estate with beautifully laid-out gardens. The beauty of things fades though when you have nobody to share them with."

"That does not only apply to homes and gardens," said Monaco. "It also applies to the human body."

When they were in the hotel elevator, she put her arms around his neck and pressed her lips to his so passionately fiercely that he had to grab her wrists to free himself from her embrace when the door opened on the fifth floor. They went down the hall to his room and he unlocked the door. Once inside, Monaco immediately sat down at the edge of the bed and opened the mini bar beside her. Hans went to the bathroom, allowing her time to fill the glasses, knowing that she was about to lace one of them with a fast-acting drug of some kind.

He washed his face with cold water and took off his outer clothes. Returning to the bedroom, he saw Monaco pacing back and forth, a glass in each hand. Monaco could not help but notice the make-up, the skirt hanging over the back of a chair, and a silver ring on the washbasin that was obviously much too small for a man's finger.

"Don't worry, I'm all alone... today," he said wryly.

She turned to him and shook her head.

"No one is ever what you think they are," she said. "And that is what makes every encounter so exciting."

She offered him one of the glasses and as he took a few steps towards her to take it, the pungent smell of whisky entered his nostrils. Hans Winters was lean and muscular, and she felt the hardness of his chest as she ran her hands across his upper body.

"Cheers," said Monaco.

He emptied his glass in one gulp, put it down on the mini bar and lay down on the bed. Monaco took only a small sip from hers, as she used her free hand to unzip her dress. He leaned on his elbows and watched her closely as she undressed. Once she was completely naked he thought to himself that he had never seen a more beautiful woman. She paraded back and forth along the foot of the bed showing off her fine body to him from every possible angle. She watched him closely and he saw a glimmer of panic in her dark eyes.

"You drink even more greedily than I do," she said. "Let me pour you another."

"A double dose" Hans thought to himself, but said nothing.

She took another small bottle from the mini bar and went to the washbasin where she had put her leather handbag. With her back to him, she opened the bottle, and although she thought that she concealed her actions, he knew that she had also taken something out of her purse. He gazed admiringly at her ass and smiled when he heard her say:

"I had intended to give you whiskey and water, but I have a feeling that you prefer it straight. Force of habit I suppose..."

She sat down beside him, and once again he emptied the glass in a single swig and handed it back to her.

"Your husband prefers his whiskey diluted," he guessed.

He felt a slight shock go through his body. An unpleasant pressure rose behind his eyeballs as his whole system rebelled against the sinister poison spreading through his body. His elevated heart rate pumped the blood faster and faster through his veins. The effect of the anaesthetic was blocked almost instantly and his muscles tightened as he felt his body tingling as it went on the offensive against the unwanted substances. Whenever Hans wore a wristwatch, it would stop ticking; when he was near any technical appliances for that matter, he caused malfunctions. Any infections that attacked his body were quickly eliminated and diseases were driven out just as fast as they had descended upon him. What Monaco had mixed into his drink was enough to knockout a bear, but Hans was wide awake.

"Let's please not discuss my husband," she said.

He narrowed his eyes and looked at her dreamily.

"Is something the matter?" she asked, her voice full of hope.

"I don't know... I find this entire situation to be very strange. Are we, or are we not, going to have some fun here today?"

Monaco nodded as her hand slid along his body and she once again felt the peculiar hardness of his muscles. For a moment she seemed to hesitate, but then relaxed and lay beside him, teasing him with sensual caresses. It was as if she could feel the unbelievable strength that lay beneath the surface of his skin. Touching him gave her a weird sensation and she became curious and excited. She kept looking at his half closed eyes as she removed the rest of his clothing and continued to explore his body with her fingertips.

"Is something wrong?" she asked again.

Her voice was different now. She had wanted him to doze off right away, but now she hoped he would stay awake for a while longer as she straddled his body with her legs spread wide and slowly lowered herself on his steel-like manhood.

"This is fantastic," she said.

With every step Hans Winters had taken on his wanderings throughout Europe, he had become more and more aware of a portrait of mankind unfolding before him that was far from perfect. He realized that there was an aggressive side to human nature that gave it the tendency to rush headlong into imminent self-destruction. It occurred to him that there was something missing in ordinary mortals, and this shortcoming forced them to lead their earthly lives limited to only the basic senses. He could not say how, or why, these thoughts had come to him.... it was as if they had been whispered in his ear; but at this moment there were none of those flaws present, Monaco's sexual motions were as perfect as her body.

When she had drained the lust from his body, she lay across his chest and he heard her sigh deeply. He turned his head slowly aside and closed his eyes. She must have thought that he was asleep, but she continued to move as if in a sexual trance. Suddenly, he turned his head and looked at her. Monaco's dark eyes grew wide with surprise and they seemed to have a golden halo around them. He attempted to keep her still for another few seconds to feel the last, lingering drops of heat flow from her body, but she jumped off the bed with her hands cupping her full breasts as if she were suddenly ashamed of her nakedness. He closed his eyes again and his breathing became deep and calm.

Monaco looked at her watch... it had stopped. She began to go through the closets and drawers in the room. She threw his clothes and shoes in a heap on the floor and searched the pockets of his jackets and trousers. She also looked around in the bathroom. She came back into the bedroom with the intention of searching through the clothes Hans had been wearing when they came in, but

Hans was standing at the window staring outside and he was already wearing them again.

Monaco was so terrified that she had to grasp a chair to steady herself.

For more years than he could count, Hans had spent every night at a different place. He had slept out in the open, at hotels, and more than once had forced entry into summer houses and abandoned buildings. He had also become very handy with pass-keys. Indeed, even now, he had taken Monaco to the room of the English couple who had invited him along for the drive to France.

"Now I see that Duby is serious... deadly serious," he said. "He sent you to ransack the room and find out who I really am. I hope you will clean up the room again before you leave, the people staying here are really very nice..."

He wondered if she would become angry once she had recovered from her fright. Her mouth fell open in amazement and there was fear in her voice as she stammered:

"Exactly who, or what, are you? You crushed Minors hand and..."

"Whatever that was that you put in my glass, had no effect on me," he supplied.

"Please," begged Monaco. "Give me something, anything... A name, some morsel of information. I have never returned from a mission unsuccessfully."

"Tell Duby to leave me alone."

"You don't understand. I have nothing to do with Duby. He is a nobody. If I come back without a good story, all I can expect is a terrible beating. Where I come from, a hard regime rules..."

"So, there is no country house in central France, no green gardens..."

"Did you already know what my plan was when I first approached you?"

Hans passed her on his way to the door. She tried one more time:

"Name a time and place for a meeting. Let me arrange for you to meet someone with more authority than Duby. I can guarantee your security."

He went down the hallway and took the stairs down rather than use the elevator. On the floor below he entered his own room. There he packed his few belongings and clothes in a rucksack. Half an hour later he returned to the room of the English couple and saw that Monaco had gone. The three little bottles, empty now, lay in the washbasin. He had brought three full bottles from his own room and put them in the mini bar. Except for that oversight, Monaco had cleaned the place up well. He left with the empty bottles in his pocket and locked the door behind himself with a pass-key. He went downstairs, paid the bill, and walked out into the warm Mediterranean sun.

Hans had taken a taxi, hoping to get out of Monaco as quickly as possible. Much to the driver's consternation and confusion, at almost every traffic light his motor died. The chauffeur continually blamed it on defective wiring. Once out on the highway, heading towards France, the various warning-signals on the dashboard lit up making the control panel look like a demented Christmas display. The driver desperately wanted to look for a garage, but Hans simply said:

"Drive along or a while, there's a good chance everything will soon return to normal. That will save you the cost of a mechanic who wouldn't find anything wrong anyway."

He spent the night in a small hotel and woke early the next morning. He had planned to take a walk inland and enjoy the beautiful landscape of the Haute-Provence. If he'd only had more time, he would have liked to cross the wild mountain country and enjoy the wide vistas and deep ravines, but he didn't want to stray too far from Nice, where Augustin Flamel would soon arrive with his entourage to perform his wonderful feats of magic.

A dark red Peugeot had sped passed him when he was barely fifteen minutes into his trek and then, a little later on he saw the car again, parked alongside the road. When he left the road, following a steep uphill path, the Peugeot came slowly up beside him. He stopped, and stood on the right side of the road to let it pass. The man at the wheel looked straight ahead, and in the back seat, at the left side-window, sat a man with short black hair and puffy face. He had never seen either of these two men, but he had no trouble at all recognizing Monaco, who was also sitting in the rear seat. Her long hair cascaded down her face and she was wearing sunglasses, which unfortunately were not big enough to conceal the dark marks around her eyes. The brief glimpse he got of her was enough for him to know that, as she had predicted, she had received a furious beating after reporting that she had found out nothing important about her lover of the previous night.

The brake lights lit up as the car came to a standstill in front of him. The motor remained running as the man in the back turned his head to look around. There was no one else was in the surrounding area. The crowded coastal palaces and hotels, and the beautiful Mediterranean Sea could not be seen from here. With long strides Hans walked on, coming up on the right side of the car. At the precise moment he was even with the shining hood, he dropped his rucksack and in the same fluid motion rolled himself over the hood and past the windshield.

He landed alongside the driver's door and wrenched it open. He grabbed the driver, pulled him from the car with incredible strength, and hit him in the jaw so hard that the stunned man was unconscious before he hit the ground. He then opened the other door and the man with three chins and black hair shouted something in Italian and then repeated it in French.

He made wild gestures with his hands in an attempt to ward off Hans as he reached in for him. Monaco screamed as he grabbed hold of the man and took a few steps backwards. He dragged the heavy, ponderous body over the ground and then released him.

"Wait!" shouted the man, as he kneeled on the ground with both hands in the air over his head.

He wore a dark, well-tailored suit and black shoes. Above his thick eyebrows small drops of sweat quickly formed. Hans had already begun to disregard this obviously weak player. He ran to the back of the Peugeot and picked up his rucksack. Returning quickly to the front of the car, he pulled open the front door, threw his backpack inside, and slid in behind the steering wheel. It had been a very long time since he had actually driven a car himself. The engine roared as he accelerated, leaving the fat man and the chauffer covered in a rain of dry dust.

"You've been badly beaten, Monaco."

"Take me back!" she screamed.

"Do you know what you have done?"

"I thought I was doing you a favor by getting you as far away from there as quickly as possible," Hans said, his speed and bewilderment increasing simultaneously. If the motor did not fail him, he planned on driving along for about a quarter of an hour and then parking the car somewhere out of view and throwing away the ignition key.

"You are kidnapping Andrea Carandini's future bride!" she shouted.

He turned his head and saw that she had removed her glasses. She had been so viciously beaten that she looked like a raccoon, with its black mask across its eyes. Her lower lip had also been pretty badly torn up. When he turned his attention to the road again, she continued:

"The man who was sitting beside me was Andrea Carandini. Now that you have seen how he treats me when he gets angry, imagine what he will do to you after he has caught up to you. He is the boss of Aldo Duby, Minor and a hundred more men. Hans Winters, you have brought the curse of the Mafia down upon your head, just when he was about to offer you a helping hand. I really don't think you have much time to live."

Although he kept his attention on the road in front of him, his thoughts were of Monaco's eyes.

"Don't you worry about me, Monaco," he said.

Chapter 2: Like a Fish Under the Ice

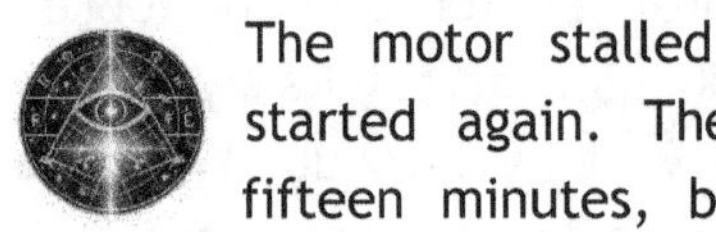

The motor stalled and Hans could not get it started again. The ride had not even lasted fifteen minutes, but he had driven extremely fast, and was thus able to put some distance between themselves and their starting point. During the last few miles they had been losing speed despite the fact that he had kept his foot pressed all the way down on the accelerator. As if it had a mind of its own, the Peugeot had rolled on in silence for a while and then finally came to a complete standstill. Hans knew he was to blame, although every now and then this prospect seemed so absurd to him.... ascribing a living, stubborn will to a hunk of metal. He grabbed his rucksack and stepped out.

Monaco followed him and took a deep breath. The whole time that they had been driving she had cursed him and beat upon his rock-hard shoulders with her clenched fists. At one point she even threatened to jump out of the speeding car, but thought better of that idea when he had shown no reaction to any of this. Now she was wondering why he had stopped so suddenly after such a wild ride. There was no town or village in the immediate area, there wasn't even a house or building in sight.

"The key is still in the ignition, Monaco. If you'd rather go back, the car is yours... Maybe your friend Carandini is still sitting on his knees, praying to the heavens that you'll come back to pick him up."

Irresolutely, she played with a lock of her long hair.

"I would certainly like to do so," she finally said, "but I know how he is when he has flown into a rage. Yes, he was in the dirt... he sat there on his knees, the great Andrea Carandini!"

She pronounced his name as if it were an incantation and somehow it made him think of stolen riches begotten by violence. He also thought about the fact that there was no way on earth that she had considered him powerful enough to make a man of that calibre kneel down.

"I suppose he'll vent his rage on you, and when he's done, he'll promise once again that soon he will marry you," Hans remarked.

"I suppose it's wiser for me to stay with you for a while," said Monaco. "Shall we drive on?"

"I'm afraid that's not possible. It's hard to explain, but as long as I am sitting inside, the Peugeot probably won't start. Come over here..."

He beckoned to her and she took two steps towards him. He pushed her dark sunglasses to the top of her head over her thick, dark hair. He put his hands on her cheeks and gently ran his thumbs over her eyebrows and eyelids without actually touching them. On his many long journeys he had often suffered from blistered feet, sore toes, or bruised ankles.

He had learned that by concentrating hard enough, he could banish his pain and make his injuries disappear, simply through the power of his mind. All that was grazed and bloody, he could repair on himself in a few seconds time, but he had never attempted this on anyone else.

It was not until Hans saw the ugly black bruises around Monaco's eyes disappear under his nurturing thumbs, that he knew he was a healer.

He slid a forefinger across her sensual mouth and her chapped lips became sound and soft once again. A drop of clotted blood broke into thousands of small particles that were instantly spread by the warm wind.

Monaco touched her face, and then turned and stooped to look at herself in the mirror of the Peugeot. When she straightened up again and looked at him, her dark eyes were full of awe and a certain amount of fear.

"How did you do that?"

"I honestly can't tell you. But believe me, it is the first time I ever did this for someone besides myself."

He began walking, and immediately fell into the rhythm of motion to which he had grown so accustomed. He left the car behind with the key still hanging from the ignition. Monaco had stayed back for a moment and now ran to catch up to him. Panting, she held the inside of his arm and lay her head against his shoulder.

"Not so fast! I can't possibly keep up with you at this pace... and I don't find your answer very clear or satisfying. My face is as good as new, and believe me, I couldn't be happier or more grateful. I can't help but be a bit frightened though when I think about how you took away my bruises and swelling simply by moving your fingers across them. What I saw in the mirror is impossible. When I touch my cheekbones, I feel nothing... if I had done this a minute ago, I would have screamed in pain."

Hans paid no attention to what she said. He had questions of his own to ask.

"It was no coincidence that you came across me, was it?"

They walked along a path that led them to a road heavy with traffic. Hans intended to hitchhike the rest of the way to Nice. It seemed wiser to him to go into hiding in a big city rather than to continue roaming around the countryside.

"As soon as I left your hotel, someone was waiting for me," said Monaco. "You were followed from the moment you stepped outside, and Carandini's men haven't lost sight of you since. He had intended to be nice to you and to invite you to spend the day with us. We slept not far from you and his body-guard. The chauffeur whom you beat the crap out of was awake early enough this morning to watch you as you started out."

"I assume Andrea is an Italian, Aldo is from Monaco, and you're from France. This seems to be an organization that is spread out across several different countries. You had mentioned the Mafia. What else does Mr. Andrea Carandini do besides beat up his sweetheart?"

"He is involved in international business. He has shares in gambling palaces all along the Italian and French Rivera's, and in all other kinds of enterprises such as hotels and restaurants. The branches of his tree are as numerous as the cracks a stone causes in the windshield of a car. Lines of all different sizes going in all different directions. A maze of properties, investments and interests. He is the head of the organization and if we should call it The Mafia, well, that after all, is just a word."

"An aggressive, violent man who, for whatever reason, had decided to be on friendly terms with me today."

"Andrea can be sweet and full of patience, but when he gets angry, he knows no mercy, and there is no one who can stop him. He is so powerful that even a giant, such as Minor, would allow himself to be beaten half to death by him without ever lifting a finger to defend himself. As I have already told you... You are marked for death now, but I don't think you are at all worried about that."

Monaco stopped, took a small round mirror out of the bag that hung from her shoulder, and once again looked at her face in disbelief.

"This must be the work of the devil himself," she said, and he saw the fear come over her again. "There are not too many men like you. Andrea is a clever man, and he knows how to combine facts. He knows a man who once acted much the way you do. Someone who travelled on foot and earned his money by gambling. Andrea owned a gambling house that almost couldn't pay off one of the guests one night. That man, who left loaded with Andrea's money, became an obsession with him, and he says you look very much like him..."

They had reached the road and Hans stuck his thumb out at the passing cars. If someone would be kind enough to offer to take him to Nice, he would try to turn his mind to something unimportant to prevent the motor from dying.

"Who are you talking about?" he asked, although he already suspected that she meant Augustin Flamel.

He wanted to hear her say his name though to be sure.

A grey car carrying a travel-weary couple from Le Havre, a city at the estuary of the river Seine, stopped at the side of the road. They were using the dark, quiet, roads on their drive to the Riviera. Their final destination was Nice, where they had booked a hotel room in the old centre of the city.

Monaco knew her way through the restored districts and promised the driver she would tell him how to get around town when they got there. She got into the back seat next to Hans, looked at him and said in a soft voice:

"Augustin Flamel."

Then she started to talk about Nice. She described the Boulevard des Anglais where they would see how much bluer the water was than the grey waves of the Channel. She also told them a little about herself and it seemed to Hans that she only offered this information when she knew he was listening as well. She had led an adventurous life, without ever really having to travel too far. Her unique beauty had brought her work as a model, and a lengthy stay in Cannes had yielded her a small part in a film. She lived a life as diverse as the rocky coastlines she travelled along, but always with the same certainty of the hot sun blazing across the clear blue sky. Hans considered the fact that she took care of her cash flow by robbing sleeping men in their hotel rooms as they dreamed of her luscious body, the last thing they had seen before falling asleep. Andrea Carandini had crossed her path and had fallen in love with her.

Once they had brought the couple to the entrance of their hotel, they walked together through the labyrinth of little streets of Vieux-Nice. Hans looked around constantly to assure himself no one was dogging their footsteps. In a small restaurant they had a dish of assorted fish and lobster. Later on, they went searching for a room to spend the coming night in, and found one with a view of a blind wall in a narrow alley. There was a bed, two chairs, a small table and a cupboard. It was late afternoon and the room was hot, as there was neither air-conditioning or ceiling fan provided.

"I believe there was something we didn't quite finish the last time we were together," she said as she began to undress.

It was now evening as she stood in front of the open window, wishing a gust of air from the alley would bring her some cooling relief, but only a hot breeze wafted in and softly stroked her sweaty face and breasts. She looked at the man lying on the bed and said:

"Are you made of steel all over? How long can you go on like this with a woman?"

"I can't really say... I can say, however, that I've never been the one who gives up first and wants to go to sleep."

Monaco walked over to him, and in the brief amount of time it took to reach him, she had decided never to return to Andrea Carandini, with his unpredictable nature and his fits of anger.

The following day they remained in Nice. During the daylight hours they went for short walks around the city. Monaco needed new clothes and went out on her own for a bit to do some shopping. When she entered the restaurant where he was waiting for her, her arms full of bags, Hans gave her a silver ring. They climbed the Colline de Chateau to look out over the city and the sea.

They saw it together, and that gave it's beauty sheer perfection.

During this time the large company of Augustin Flamel had arrived. Hans and Monaco had bought tickets for the first show and that night, after dinner, they had walked over to the theatre and joined the people already in line waiting for the doors to open. After finding their seats, Hans looked around to see if they were being watched and asked Monaco to be on the lookout for Carandini's men.

"Nobody, not a soul" said Monaco.

She anxiously looked forward to the spectacular show which she had heard so much about. With Flamel, the art of magic had reached it's pinnacle. He was called an illusionist, but to many he was a magician, for illusion is always a trick, and the true magician makes use of the art that makes the impossible possible. Of course there were those who did not necessarily appreciate Flamel, but still, everywhere he went he was treated with respect. In regards to his act, everyone gave him the benefit of the doubt. What he did was real just so long as no one was able to prove that he was pulling the wool over his audience's eyes.

He did not like very much to play the part of a healer, but people everywhere searched him out to tell him about their diseases, especially the local aristocrats of whatever city he happened to be in. They all managed to arrange meetings with him where Flamel cured them and gladly accepted their money. He had a great hunger for wealth, and because everyone was aware of that fact, no one ever showed up without a good deal of cash when seeking his help.

The lights in the auditorium dimmed. An minor illusionist, the opening act, appeared on stage and commanded flames to shoot out of the front of the stage. The heat from these mystical fires could be felt almost to the rear of the hall. Then he brought out tigers, which gingerly stepped through the fire without so much as scorching their striped fur. In the next moment there was darkness, pierced by a beam of white light, making the illusionist visible.

In the darkness was heard a sound as if dozens of men had landed on the floor at the same time, and when the spotlights flashed on from all sides, the stage appeared to be filled with dancers, musicians, conjurers and animals, and props had been set-up to be used in the various acts.

What happened then was not much different from performances given by other travelling shows, with the difference being that everything here happened en masse.

It was not possible for the human eye to register everything at once... At first glance, the eye was confronted with lightning-fast appearances and disappearances, floods and seas of flames, and mass battles ending in vast emptiness. The audience found itself on a wide boulevard along the Mediterranean when suddenly, a ship sailed directly in front of them, pushing a huge wave before it that made the front rows of spectators flee in panic. But no one got wet and the very next moment the illusion was over. For an hour the settings changed in form and color along with the rhythm of the music. Then the actors split into two groups who ran headlong at each other. At the precise moment of impending collision, they all vanished into thin air, and what was left was an empty stage where the illusionist who had appeared in the beginning, bowed to his audience.

There was now a thirty minute intermission during which most of the audience remained in their seats. They compared notes about what they thought they had seen, but no one was able to remember everything or to put the events in the right order. They were overwhelmed, excited, and dizzy, all at the same time.

Hans and Monaco had left their seats and went out to the foyer to get a drink.

A man with a calling-card on his lapel announcing him as a member of the press, approached Hans uninvited and began talking to him. He was so astounded by what he had just witnessed that he felt the need to talk about it, even if it was with a complete stranger.

"This is not the first time I have seen this, but it is all so well thought out, that you begin to believe in miracles. This is overwhelming!"

"Augustin Flamel hasn't been onstage yet, has he?" Monaco asked him.

"No!" said the man. "I'm not even sure if he has anything to do with this part of the show at all. After the intermission come the truly grand illusions. On an empty stage, bathed in cold, white light, he will show us a variation on his tricks of disappearance, with everyone standing right in front of him. He is the master, who needs no frills."

"Is there anyone who suspects how he does it?"

"No a one. Not a single theory applies to his methods. Still, people like myself, who follow him and analyze his performances, are left with a burning question. Why does he never fetch back what he causes to vanish? If I knew that, I would have a major scoop. I cannot prove it, but I suspect he is unable to do so..."

Monaco asked him several questions as Hans walked, a cup of coffee in his hand, to a corner of the foyer. There was a broad staircase with a rope stretched from rail to rail across the bottom and a man close by who's task it obviously was to prevent people from ascending. He wore a grey suit which looked very much like a uniform. Hans gave him a nod and asked him if he worked for the theatre or if he was with Flamel.

"I am with Flamel," he answered.

"I know it is not easy to get an appointment with him," said Hans. "Still I would very much like to meet him, for there is something important I must tell him."

"Many people would like to exchange views with him."

"I understand... is it at all possible that you could pass a message on to him?"

The man was so tall that he had to bend to look Hans straight in the eye.

"Yes, it's possible.... You can be sure that I shall speak to him on your behalf."

"All you have to say is that Julius Caesar was murdered on the banks of a big river."

He had expected the man to burst out laughing, but he didn't. While straightening his back and crossing his arms, he said:

"I don't know much about history, but if I remember correctly, Caesar died in Rome."

"Yes, yes, of course he did," Hans replied quickly. "On the floor of the Senate on March 15, of the year 44. He was 55 years of age. What I am referring to is a hypothetical turn in history."

"Just a moment," said the man, and taking a giant step over the rope with his long legs, took a telephone out of his pocket and went up a few steps.

After speaking softly to someone, he held up the small cell phone and beckoned to Hans. As he lifted the rope to proceed, Monaco joined him. Hans reached out, took the phone from the man and put it to his ear.

"Hans Winters..." he said.

"Hello," responded a sedate voice. "My name is Pirenne. I understand that you wish to get in touch with Mr. Flamel. You mentioned a game of intellect. It begins with the murder of Caesar. Do you know the name of the river in question?"

"Probably the Rhine," said Hans. "Where the Celts and Germans were very close to each other."

"It is a discussion raised in response to hand-written books from the Brotherhood of Helgen. There are many people who can tell us all about it. Is there anything more you wish to say?"

"Only to Augustin Flamel... about Astra..."

The line was silent for a moment, and then Pirenne said:

"All right. You get yourself a ticket for tomorrow's show. Remain in your seat after the performance. I can probably arrange something for you then."

The call was cut off and Monaco gestured to Hans.

"You must hurry... We have to get inside!"

The journalist who had said that Flamel's performance would be devoid of flash and exaggeration must certainly have been a master of understatement, for the enormous stage was completely empty. The man who stood upon it though filled the space with an electric, expectant presence and tension.

He was about sixty years old and had long, wavy hair which was combed back and reached just above his shoulders. He wore tight black trousers and a sleeveless shirt which left his shoulders and arms bare. He ignored the applause, which lasted at least a full minute, staring in front of him the entire time with great concentration.

The lights above the stage and throughout the theatre remained brightly lit. Flamel remained silent; there was no microphone present for him to use even if he had wanted to do so. He raised his hand, and somewhere behind him the sound of engines starting up could be heard. Five large automobiles were driven onto the stage and parked alongside each other with about three feet between them. The chauffeurs, all wearing the same grey suits as the man in the foyer, got out, closed the doors and walked away.

A little smile crept across Flamel's face and he lifted his head. Some people from the audience stood up and approached the stage. Using the small staircases at the wings, they proceeded to come up on stage and crowd around the cars. No one had invited them, or for that matter given any indication at all that this was allowed, but it had become an unmistakable characteristic of Flamel's performances which was repeated where ever he went.

Television crews were taping the show, and two camera-men walked up with the crowd and another worked from out in the orchestra pit. Hans and Monaco remained in their places, but when everyone in front of them stood up, they did likewise so as not to miss what was going to happen on stage.

The cars were then examined thoroughly by the members of the audience who had gone on stage. They were looked at above and below, within and without. Some people even stamped around on the stage to make sure that there was no trapdoor present which would swing open and swallow the cars. Flamel made a single gesture with his hands and the crowd parted for him. He did not request that they return to their seats, he would rather they stay on stage and watch from a close proximity.

The huge room became silent as Flamel walked along the vehicles, touching one after the other lightly with his fingertips. His muscles tightened as he pushed each one down a few inches testing their suspensions. He walked around in a wide circle, finally stopping in front of the centre car. He pressed down on the hood with both hands, let out a shrill cry and as he removed his hands. The car vanished.

Moving quickly to his left, he repeated his motions with the same results. He proceeded around the stage, sometimes laying his hands on the hood, sometimes on the roof, always with the same outcome... All the autos had completely vanished into thin air, which was followed by cries of astonishment and thunderous applause from the crowd of spectators .

The men in grey suits gathered around Flamel to prevent people from attempting to touch him, not meaning him any harm, but in admiration, perhaps closer even to adoration. Surrounded by his aides, he finally managed to get off the stage.

The illusionist who had warmed up the audience with his opening act, returned to the stage, and with a microphone in his hand, began to chant the magician's name over and over again. The audience, who had been ushered back to their seats, joined in the cheering and chanting until Flamel finally returned to the stage and took a deep bow.

He participated in the grand finale, winning the audience's hearts and minds even more with a potpourri of tricks and illusions. The human mind could not comprehend what the eyes saw as miracle after miracle was performed.

As Hans left the theatre, one of the men in grey slipped a ticket for the next performance into his hand. A telephone number was written on the reverse side with Pirenne's signature just below it.

He departed early the next afternoon, leaving Monaco behind in the hotel. Stopping at a news kiosk, he bought a magazine which carried a cover story about Flamel. He read the magazine through to the end, but learned little about Flamel he hadn't already known from reading other periodicals. Walking along and reading transported him to a familiar state of mind, but he noticed that it did not give him the usual satisfaction. He had covered so many miles in loneliness and isolation, but now that he had met Monaco there seemed to be an end in sight to his solitary way of life.

When he was nearer to the theatre he went in to a small restaurant for a bite to eat, but felt lonely without her sitting beside him.

That night as he watched the opening act of the show, which was exactly the same as the night before, he noticed things that he had previously missed. During the intermission he went out to the foyer again, where a different man in grey was guarding the staircase.

Someone else similarly dressed approached him and called out his name.

"Monsieur Winters! If you wish, you can observe the wonders of Augustin Flamel from a more comfortable location. He has arranged a place for you in a van with the television crew, just alongside the director's truck. You will have the best view in the house and you can watch it all from a luxurious armchair."

As they went out together to the side of the big theatre, he caught a glimpse of the interior of a huge truck stacked with all kinds of equipment. Thick cables ran from the vehicle into the theatre.

"The director instructs the cameramen from here," his companion explained. "They shoot as much as possible every night and intend to one day compile all the footage into a documentary about Flamel. Only very special guests are invited into the van, and tonight Flamel has decided that you should be the one. After the performance, I'll return to escort you back into the theatre. Augustin Flamel is not only anxious to meet you, he has even set the remainder of his evening aside for you. And if the conversation goes the way he hopes, he desires that you be his guest again tomorrow. I have absolutely no idea what is going on, but it is obvious that he will do almost anything to please you."

A short time later he was sitting in a big leather swivel chair in front of an enormous television screen watching everything that transpired in the theatre. Periodically the screen was broken up into eight sections and he could see and hear all the different camera angles at once, the empty stage, the half-filled auditorium, the loud conversations in the foyer, Flamel pacing up and down bathed in the bright light of his dressing room and the various participants of his show walking the corridors.

The man poured Hans a glass of wine and stayed for a while chatting with him. When the audience returned to their seats, the man took his leave of Hans, saying before he departed:

"Monsieur Flamel asks that you pay very close attention. He contends that you will understand better than anyone else what is happening..."

Hans sipped his wine and watched the large screen as every now and then a little square would appear in a corner showing what another cameraman was shooting.

Flamel strutted proudly onto the stage and the five cars were brought to him. The four outer vehicles were white and the one in the middle was a black Mercedes. The camera zoomed in on Flamel's hands as he placed them on the hoods of the cars. Hans leaned closer so as to see it all even better. He concentrated intensely on the magician in hopes of discovering something which would explain these mysteries. The four white cars disappeared as Augustin Flamel raised his hands. Hans leaned back in the chair and heaved a deep sigh.

"There is simply no explanation for it," he said aloud.

Flamel walked up to the Mercedes and pushed his fingers down on the hood. The camera zoomed in on his hands and then travelled along the car to the back. The rear lights and the trunk were brought into focus. In one of the upper corners of the screen a small square appeared. Hans looked at it and lunged forward, grabbing the monitor by the sides. From a close distance he watched the smaller square grow until it overcame the image of the back of the Mercedes. What he was looking at now was the lit interior of the trunk.

A small camera and lamp had apparently been built in.

Monaco's dark, frightened eyes looked back at him.

Her mouth was covered with a broad strip of adhesive tape. No sound could be heard, except for the noise Hans himself made as he ran back and forth in fear and anger in the van, as if hoping his actions would somehow make her aware of the fact that he was watching.

Then he saw Flamel standing at the front of the car, and as he pulled his hands away from the shining metal, the Mercedes vanished.

Hans had managed to calm himself down and was using all of the power within him to stay in control of his emotions. He stepped out of the van and hurried to the director's truck.

The door was slightly ajar and he opened it a bit further and looked inside. On all the various screens he watched Flamel acknowledge the applause. The sound was turned on in here and he could hear the noise and jubilation of the crowd.

"No unauthorized person allowed!" shouted a man sitting close to the door, who stood up and was ready to block Hans' progress should he try to proceed any further inside.

Hans beckoned to him and the man came closer.

"I have a question," he said with a steady voice. "I saw someone lying in the trunk of a car which Augustin Flamel just made disappear."

The man laughed and shook his head. He was of small stature and wore a flannel shirt, jeans and sneakers.

"Seems like a tall story to me," he said, coming still closer. "You obviously have seen more than I."

"I was sitting in the van next to this truck," Hans explained. "Sitting behind one of your screens. There was obviously a camera built into the car and I could clearly see someone lying in the trunk."

The man leaned out of his truck and placed his hand on Hans' left shoulder.

"There was a van there before," he said. "But as you can see, it's gone now."

Hans turned his head and saw that the man was right.

"Are you from the press?" the television technician asked. "I will only be co-operative with those far-fetched, sensational stories when the subject is based somewhat on the truth, but I don't feel much like getting involved with something as absurd, and as fictional, as what you are claiming..."

He stepped back inside and closed the door.

Hans Winters started to walk - to where he was not sure, but he started to walk nonetheless.

He was aware of having closed his eyes and still being able to find his way through a city he barely even knew. It was almost as if he could turn over his locomotion reflexes to a central control system that worked in a manner completely unknown to him.

His spirit seemed disconnected from his psyche and physical make-up. He was lost in thought as he allowed his concentration to be overwhelmed by other things. As he went from the new district, where the theatre stood, towards the vieux-Nice, he picked up none of his unique vibrations, indeed, he felt nothing at all.

No sweet floral scents on the warm summer air reached his nostrils. He was totally unaware of the people who gawked at him.

He crossed the streets when and where his instincts told him it was safe, luckily never bumping into anyone, or getting run over by a car. He walked unconsciously up and down the narrow, bustling streets.

On his hike to Hammerfest he had stood, on a clear winter day, in the middle of a frozen lake of which the ice was so transparent that he was able to look right through it. Under his feet and through the thick layer of ice, he had seen many fish swimming around under the frozen water. He carefully knelt down, and bringing his face as close as possible to the ice, saw the fish as a symbol of the unattainable. They were like fragments of thoughts that could never be put on paper, like plans that could not be executed, or happiness, right in front of him for the taking, but still eternally unobtainable.

A screen of ice behind which Monaco had vanished without a trace.

At the hotel desk, a clerk he had never seen before was working the night shift..

He was asked to show his passport as a means of identification to get the key to his room, and when the fellow asked him where his companion was, he simply mumbled something about her taking a few days off. Hans did not ask the clerk any questions about Monaco's possible actions while he had been out and went directly to his room. The small hotel had no elevator and he took the stairs three at a time.

In the room he only found his own few belongings that easily fit in his rucksack. Monaco's clothes were all gone.

There was nothing left behind to indicate that she had ever been there at all.

The pent up emotions of this long strange evening finally took hold of him with the speed and power of a thunderbolt. Trembling all over he sunk down in front of the bed, sweat running down his face and arms. He could not recall the last time he had actually cried, but now the tears fell like rain drops, cascading over his cheeks and down on to his leg.

Monaco... She had never told him her real name, but he had read it on her passport which she took it out to sign the hotel register. Louise Verne... He never before said her real name.

"Monaco!" he sobbed loudly, and that very moment he wished that he could die right here, just sitting here, so that never again would he be troubled by thoughts of love for an unattainable woman such as she. He slowly looked up and gradually began to calm down his fiercely beating heart by taking deep, regular breaths. His thoughts were no more than fragments, like the fish which flitted away in the deep, dark Norwegian water trapped under the ice.

He focused his attention on a small picture hanging above the bed, a reproduction of a self-portrait of a master he was unfamiliar with. His eyes narrowed and he stretched out his arms as he felt an unbridled fierceness begin to build within him. He was especially angry at himself for not having taken her with him to Flamel's performance and even more so for not being suspicious when the man in grey had taken him outside and asked him to step into the van.

With thumbs held up and fore-fingers extended, he moved towards the little painting as if he were firing a gun at it.

Hans had seen so many strange things lately that he was not frightened at all, not even a little bit, when the reproduction he had been aiming at suddenly vanished from the wall.

Chapter 3: Astra

Hans sat on the bed for a while, dazed. It was the same bed he had so recently shared with Monaco, and now... she was gone. Finally he stood up, collected his meagre belongings and shoved them in his rucksack. Then he walked over to the phone that sat on one of the bedside tables, and took from his pocket the card with Pirenne's phone number on it.

He held the receiver to his ear for a moment, and then, placing it back in its cradle without having used it, he picked up his rucksack and left the room. Quickly and silently he made his way through the corridor and down the stairs. He stopped on a landing just above the lobby of the hotel, from where he could see a man standing behind the desk with one hand on the phone.

In his other hand he held a silver revolver.

Across the desk from him stood Aldo Duby and the giant, Minor, who was sporting a heavily bandaged right hand. Hans had figured that if he made a phone call it would probably have been tapped, and the sight of Duby reaffirmed that supposition. He knew that Andrea Carandini was responsible for the disappearance of Monaco, but he could not be sure whether or not Augustin Flamel had known that she was in the trunk of the Mercedes.

As the door opened and some more men entered the lobby, Hans felt the rage well up inside himself, but managed to keep it under control. They were here to get him and take him, by force if necessary, to Carandini. He slipped back upstairs and threw open the bolt of an emergency exit. Just outside the door was a metal ladder which led down to a dark alley. The backs of several different restaurants opened into the alley and the smell of a unique blend of herbs, garlic, basil, fish and meats reached his nose. There was no one outside and at the exact moment Duby and his gang knocked on his door, Hans climbed down the ladder and disappeared into the darkness.

He ducked into a pub and dialled the number on the card.

"Pierre Pirenne," came the voice from the other end.

"Hans Winters here... I..."

"The theatre was empty, Winters! You were supposed to wait for us after the show, weren't you? We searched everywhere for you."

"So you're telling me that you have no idea what happened, eh? If I were to tell you that I was escorted out during the intermission to watch the show from a TV van, you'd say you don't know what I'm talking about..."

"That's right... I haven't the faintest idea."

His voice sounded sincere enough.

"I know that it's late, Mr. Pirenne, but I would like to have a talk with you anyway. And besides, I need a safe place to sleep."

He was about to say something more and mention the name Andrea Carandini, but his thoughts wandered and he saw Monaco before him, and suddenly he was unable to form a complete sentence. It was quiet for a moment and then Pirenne's voice came again:

"Get yourself back to the theatre and meet me at the main entrance. I'll bring the car around and pick you up. Um... a question, Winters. Suppose you're sitting next to me in a car, would it be, in any way, a different experience than I'm used to when I'm driving alone?"

"The motor might miss... or even come to a complete halt," he said softly.

Now it was Pirenne who was at a loss for words.

"I'm on my way," continued Hans. "I suppose I don't have to tell you what I look like."

Without waiting for an answer, he cut off the connection and went outside. He walked aimlessly around the small streets until he was sure no one was following him and then, leaving the old centre, he returned to the theatre. A car was standing in front of the theatre with the engine running, and as Hans approached it, the driver opened the door and said:

"Monsieur Winters! Get in."

Pierre Pirenne was a lean, balding man with a sharp nose. Black hair curled from temple to temple along the back of his head and he had a short moustache. He glanced aside and grinned when the motor began to sputter.

"If you are who I think you are, there is much for us to discuss."

"There are a couple of things you must tell me, Monsieur Pirenne. For one, where are we going?"

"Not everyone associated with the show stays in hotels. We've rented a house not far from Nice. Flamel is there too, but he's tired and you probably won't get to meet him tonight. I'll introduce you to Philippe Mundy, Flamel's chief of staff. It's very important that you tell him as much as possible about yourself. You can talk to Flamel in the morning, that is of course, if you're not so tired that you intend to sleep late. We'll be there in a quarter of an hour. Now, Winters... I'll listen to you while I try to keep this motor running..."

Hans told him about Carandini's wish that he come work for him and about how he met Monaco. He told him about what had transpired after being brought to the van outside the theatre. His overwhelming sorrow returned as he related the events surrounding Monaco's disappearance, and it made it almost impossible for him to speak.

The car followed a winding road as the headlights lit up the faces of great rocks with brush growing sparsely upon them. The motor faltered just as often as his voice did.

"One of the journalists at the show was wondering why Flamel never retrieves the things that he causes to disappear. He even put forth the theory that perhaps he is unable to do so."

He looked out the side window and saw the endless, black, star-studded sky. If the journalist was right, Monaco had vanished into this great nothing for ever.

"I can't answer that. I will, however, look into what may have happened, and as soon as I know anything I'll tell you. I take this all very seriously and really do understand how you must feel..."

"Driven by curiosity, the young warrior had gone down to the river to try and see what was happening on the far shore. He was of Germanic birth and had never seen a Roman before. He did know some Celts, with whom his tribe traded. Many gods lived in his head and it was the warlike Tiwaz who now whispered to him that there was nothing to fear.

He was a strong swimmer and the cold water had no real effect on him when he dove into the river. He had left his weapons behind and carried only his knife between his teeth.

A Gaulish chief, travelling with the Roman army and a companion to Caesar, was the first to see him and was frightened by the large, half naked figure who rose up from the water. Perhaps he was thinking of the god Teutates, who demanded that the human sacrifices offered up to him be drowned first. He shrunk back, but the man beside him remained steadfast.

This man was Gaius Julius Caesar, who, with his Gaulish friend, had left the safety of the encampments to walk along the shore of the river that formed the border of his great empire.

The frightened Gaul pulled his sword and took a step backwards in preparation for his defence of the Emperor. How a fight erupted is hard to say, but the result was disastrous.

When the ensuing battle was over, the dead body of the Gaul lay across the corpse of the murdered Caesar, and the murderer had long since disappeared into the swirling waters by the time a centurion and his soldiers arrived on the scene. The bodies were removed at nightfall, and thus no sign could be found as to the identity of the offender. Not a footprint in the mud, nor a wrinkle in the river, was visible where the culprit, who was assumed to be a Germanic warrior, had entered the water. The only evidence of his existence was the knife that had been used to stab Caesar through the heart and was now pulled from the Gaul's neck by the centurion.

The people fell into panic and mourning, and looking up to the dark heavens in despair, they begged their innumerable gods for help. A dense layer of cloud drifted in from the north, and as it moved upriver, it unloaded a deluge of hailstones that fell on those who were earth-bound like stab wounds from a dagger. The sky was filled with an onslaught of gods, commanded by Tiwaz, the god of war. Wodan and Donar raced furiously on huge horses with Freyja, the goddess mother, at their side, screaming. The heavenly kingdom of the Germanic gods was emptied as the deities all streamed earthwards and whom, along with the sun-god Belanus and the god of thunder Taranis, gathered above the mourning crowd to meet their modern-day Celtic relatives.

Thunder echoed across the sky as Taranis and Donar saw each other and beat upon their shields with heavy celestial hammers. Atrio, the goddess of the woods, and Lenus, the healer, urged the gathered company to make haste. The heavens shook as the gods mingled with one another and gave vocal evidence to their presence with their booming voices.

They then headed south, joined by the tribes whom they had forced to submit to their will.

Other Germanic armies also came from across the broad river and joined the Celtic warriors.

Day followed night, but the light of day could not penetrate the thick, supernatural cloud that accompanied them on their quest, and the gods now were only visible to the believers below as flashes of lightning. The Celts, saddened over the loss of their martyred leaders, never once thought that it might have been a Germanic fist that had clenched the offending weapon and directed all their vengeance at the Romans.

The Roman oppressors were driven back, and as they fled in panic, they could be heard calling in vain for the help of Jupiter. As for Mars, their mighty god of war, he never showed himself at all. After many days of battle, the sun once again shone down upon the world, as the Germanic and Celtic gods rested. But the mortal armies continued their struggle, with the temples of Rome as their goal. They were not interested in Jupiter, the father of all gods and men, nor in Mars, Apolo, Vulcanus, Minerva, Vesta or Ceres. Their particular curiosity was in Janus, the two-faced god, who could see into both the future and the past. The Celts also worshiped gods who possessed multiple faces, but they had heard amazing stories of Janus' unbelievable strength and power. He held a key in his right hand that fit all the locks to all the gates of Heaven. In his guise of Janus Patulcius he opened them, as Janus Clusivus he closed them. The four gates to his temple at the Roman Forum were always open and whoever was privileged enough to be allowed inside, would find the answers to all the riddles of life.

The armies finally entered Rome unopposed, swarming across the squares and squirming along the procession routes that led to the temples, until they finally found the temple of Janus....but the four huge gates were closed.

Gaius Julius Caesar had stayed behind at the river eternally and his friends and subjects now grieved for him. The mighty Roman Empire was torn apart, divided and in despair.

Some tried to break down the temple gates, but all their efforts were in vain.

The benevolent Mercury, god of fair play and enterprise, descended on the area held aloft by winged feet. He implored the congregation of Romans, Celts and Germans to try and live together in peace and harmony. In his hand he held one of Janus' precious keys, with which he opened one of the mighty gates and invited all those who wished to enter to do so, and see for themselves what wonderful secrets were hidden inside. Each man wanted nothing greater than to enter and have the secrets of life revealed to him, but none dared be first.

They had come so far and had finally attained their goal, but there was something more now. There was something inside this particular temple, something special and powerful, that exceeded even the power of Belenus and Tiwaz, and would even have astounded Jupiter.

Mercury bowed, and as he invited his new-found flock to enter, he promised them all a place in heaven between the sun and the moon.

What brave soul would take the first step?

The start of every new year is symbolic of change and hope for the future. It is a new beginning, and it is no mere coincidence that the first month of the new year still honors the name of Janus: Januari."

Hans Winters set the reproduction of Astra he had been looking at, down on his knees, and stared in front of him as if in a trance. He was in a spacious room in a renovated, old villa on a large estate. He sat in a big leather armchair beside the hearth, with its warming fire burning brightly.

He paid little attention to the man sitting opposite him, who's mouth was ajar in a look of surprise. He was Philippe Mundy, whom he had been introduced to by Pierre Pirenne, shortly after their arrival. He was a short man with a round face. He had an abundance of short, curly, grey hair, including his moustache and beard, under which very pale, pink skin was visible. His eyebrows, however, were strikingly black, in contrast to the grey of his hair and his light brown eyes. He was about to say something, but held his tongue as Hans continued:

"That is what Astra has seemed to make clear to me. These are the impressions that I get when I look at it. I have, of course, put all of this into my own words, but that does not alter the substance of the story. I have thought about this every day during my travels. A new start, Januari... a place between the sun and the moon...

In the German, English and Dutch languages, we know Sunday and Monday in pretty much the same way. In both Dutch and English, the word Friday honors the goddess Freyja. The middle of the week is Mittwoch to the Germans, but to the Dutch it is Woensdag, and to the English Wednesday. They are all reminiscent of the god Wodan, while the French call that day Mercredi, which reminds one of Mercury. Astra recounts a tale filled with impossibilities, for after Caesar's death, the Roman Empire began anew and his successor was August! Also, obviously, a month of the year, something which Astra remains silent about. It is a historical falsification of the first order."

He tore up the piece of Flamel's stationary with Astra imprinted on the back, into long strips which he held over the fire until they were almost completely consumed by the dancing flames, and then let them fall into the hearth before burning his fingers. Only then did he look up at Mundy.

"What's wrong with you? Did something frighten you? Look at you... you're trembling all over !"

"Only Augustin Flamel and I know the meaning of Astra. He, because he is able to translate the colors and forms, and I, because he has shared that knowledge with me. But you also, seem to know what this work of art means. I am a man who is usually in complete control of his emotions, and am not easily shaken, but if you only knew how long we have waited for this moment, how we have hoped beyond our wildest dreams to find another who understands Astra."

He stood and walked over to Hans. Leaning over, he put his arms around his neck, the coarse, short curls of his beard rubbing against Hans' smoothly shaven chin.

"Welcome, Hans Winters! Please, give me a minute to compose myself. I thought that Pirenne was going to bring me someone who meant nothing. How wrong I was! Would you like something to drink?"

"I wouldn't mind some hot coffee."

Mundy left the room on his mission, and it was only now that Hans noticed he was barefoot. He wore a cotton shirt and worn-out old trousers. He soon returned with a coffee pot and two cups.

As he poured, he said:

"First, allow me, very briefly, to say something about myself. And when I am done, I would like to ask you some questions. As far as I can see, you are the man we have been looking for all this time. We could not be sure that another man such as Flamel really even existed."

He placed two full cups of coffee on a small table and plopped back into his chair with a sigh. There was sweat dripping from his forehead down into his black eyebrows.

"Flamel calls me The Observator. I am a listener, and a combiner of thoughts. I am a man who wants to hear all the different theories about any given subject, but will never re-forge them into a theory which would be acceptable to myself. In our sphere of existence everything we assume to be the truth, we do so only by using ourselves as a starting point. In this fashion though, not only do the experiences of a human being and a fly differ who happen, by coincidence, to find themselves in the same room, but so does that of two men who happen to find themselves face-to-face."

"Which seems to me to be a theory as well," remarked Hans, as a look of despair spread across his face.

"I had hoped to arrive at your door under better circumstances," he said. "Now, I have lost a friend, a very dear and important friend; and even stranger, I find that when I, not knowing how to deal with my sorrow, fell to my knees in anguish and thrust my arms before me, caused a painting to vanish into thin air... just like that," snapping his fingers for effect.

Hiding his face in his hands, he looked through his fingers, watching the pink toes of the Observator moving nervously up and down. Although he had not been asked, he began to tell Mundy what he had already told Pirenne. He also finally got to ask Mundy the question foremost in his mind:

"Can Augustin Flamel retrieve what he has made disappear?"

Only this time he added:

"There is no way I could get that painting back on its nail. If you really are Flamel's chief of staff and confidant, you should be able to answer me. I was content with Pirenne's answer when he told me that he was not able to give me an answer, but I will not accept the same answer from you."

The Observator sipped his coffee and curled his toes. He put the cup down and scratched his cheek.

"We have been having great difficulty keeping Andrea Carandini away from us. How strange this world can be! When science refuses to believe you, the Mafia smells a profit. It's obvious that he gave the order to lock your girlfriend in the trunk of the car. Believe me when I tell you, Hans... Flamel would never experiment with a human being..."

"Because the return trip is impossible!"

A short nod from Mundy was enough for Winters to understand that Monaco's fate had been sealed. In the silence that ensued, Hans fought to control his emotions. He would have liked to jump up, leave the house, and run through the dark night, beginning a new, endless journey. The Observator knew enough to allow him time to gather his composure again, remaining so silent that even his breathing carried no sound.

"You know, Professor," Hans finally said softly. "I abandoned any hope that the vanishing act done by that little painting on my wall was a trick. I understand that I alone am responsible for that empty spot on the wall. I miss Monaco greatly. Is Flamel here? I must to talk to him as soon as possible..."

"Yes, he is here, and he knows that you have arrived. It is by his request that we are having our little chat so that I can get the facts straight about the situation. He is a man who needs a great deal of rest. He has another performance tomorrow evening. Listen, Hans, I may not be a young man any more, but I have no problem staying up all night and talking, and you're probably better off staying up with me than being alone in bed, in a lonely room. There are miraculous things happening, and we certainly don't understand them all. And we have our very specific problems, too, as I told you. Such as people like Andrea Carandini always being on the look-out for whatever he might be able to get from us. I cannot emphasize enough how happy we are to have you here, and tomorrow you will meet Flamel, I promise. Can you tell me your story? Can you explain how you learned to understand Astra?"

"I would be glad to try, although I have never even attempted to explain it to anyone before. I've always kept everything about my life a secret, it seemed senseless to trouble anyone with matters so seemingly unbelievable."

Hans stood up and opened his belt, inside of which there was a secret compartment to hide money and other valuables in. He removed a small steel object from it and offered it to Mundy, who took it with trembling fingers.

"The Brotherhood of Helgen," he said. "The makers of Astra, were the crafters of this little statue. The Austrian Twentiers... the same statue is in Augustin's possession. No doubt, your story will be very much the same as his."

The shiny little statue, only some inches high, was conical in shape, and using a little bit of imagination, one could see a human shape in it. A globe-like head, a slender neck that gently flowed into a body that was flat on the bottom to allow it to stand. Mundy stroked it, turning it over and over again in the palm of his hand.

"How did you come by it?"

"I come from a family of antique dealers and art collectors. My parents had their own shop and there were various uncles, aunts and cousins who also made a living in the business. Every room in the homes I grew up in, was filled with antique furniture and the walls were covered with classical paintings. Someone in the family, I don't remember who exactly, learned that the work of the Brotherhood of Helgen was becoming popular among a group of wealthy collectors. I even seem to remember hearing about a family meeting being organized to raise capital to make some quick purchases. Paintings, drawings, and a great deal of wood-sculpture were obtained... and there among them was the statue. No one actually considered it art, it was more of an unsalable gem that had come in with a bulk shipment. It fell into my possession and I was immediately attracted to it, you might even say connected to it. That is why I still carry it with me after all these years, although I am convinced that whatever special powers it had, have long since disappeared. There was something creeping inside of me, something that took possession of my body and changed my life. Let me show you what I mean..."

He grabbed his rucksack and took a thick memo book with a worn cover from it. The edges of the pages were almost black. Mundy, who still held the steel object in one hand, reached out for the book with the other.

"Just a moment," said Hans, who suddenly changed his mind. "I have already told you and Pirenne so much, including what I have learned from Astra. I only hope that I have not fallen into a trap and am not about to find myself already held captive by Andrea Carandini..."

And then, in a sharp voice, Hans added:

"I want to speak to Flamel! Not tomorrow, tonight!"

"I agree with you," said the Observator, as he took the memo book and opened it. "You two must meet. As a matter of fact, there very few things which I would not allow you to do. You are very valuable to us."

The memo book had been used with no regard for specific dates indicated on the tops of the pages.

On the first page Hans had neatly written some details concerning his first grand walking tour. He had begun to add drawings to his notes and the more the Observator skimmed through the pages, the more vague and strange the drawings became, while any actual written text was left out more and more. In his later doodlings he had designed complicated line patterns, and on one page, near the beginning, there was an unusual landscape. If one had sharp enough powers of observation, they might take note of how this delicate little landscape gradually changed into an intriguing line pattern that very much resembled the work of the Austrian Twentiers at the height of their skills.

Mundy nodded.

"Yes! Yes! It's definitely time to call for Flamel. You never created any kind of artwork before you began your travels, did you?"

"I had nice handwriting, that's about it though. I had absolutely no talent for drawing...whether recognizable or abstract."

At that moment Mundy stood up, went to the door and opened it, and Pirenne came in. The smile on his face suddenly gave Hans new hope. He sat up straight in his chair and listened to his heart beat fiercely. The Observator remained standing by Pirenne and listening intently to what he had to say.

Pirenne sat down by the end table next to the coffee pot.

"You can take it from me that nothing bad has happened to your girlfriend," he said.

Mundy nodded, and with a look of satisfaction on his face, left the room. In his hands he still held the memo book and statue.

"Andrea Carandini wanted to scare the hell out of you, and I think he succeeded. If Aldo Duby had captured you in your hotel room, by the time he was finished with you he could have made you promise anything and you would gladly do whatever he wished. No doubt it was his intention to break your spirit and make you willing to go along with whatever his scheme is. They want to see you lie prostrate before Carandini."

"Monaco is alive..." stammered Hans.

"Well, we're almost certain. Let me explain it to you. You were escorted out of the theatre, but not by one of our men. The director's car belongs to a television station that has bought the rights to broadcast the show. The little van which stood behind them, did not belong to them. The pictures that were seen in there could not have been relayed to the monitors in the van. Think about it... the van drove away while you were standing in front of the director's car. The equipment in the van would have to have been connected with the equipment in the other vehicle if you were actually able to see what the cameras were recording at that moment.. Do you follow me?"

"Oh yes, sure..."

"Tapes of shows that Flamel has done previously are available everywhere. Last night he made five cars disappear from the stage again. We buy cheap cars and give them a quick repainting. This time it was two Fords, two Volkswagens and a Renault, all white. About a year ago, Flamel made some cars disappear into the great unknown for the first time, as a test. It was recorded by a television crew and one of those first cars was a black Mercedes, the only Mercedes I believe he ever used. I think I know what has happened. Around the same time you were in the theatre, or on your way to it, your girlfriend was taken from your hotel room, put into the trunk, and filmed there. An excellent job of editing was then done combining the earlier disappearing car and your beloved Monaco being locked in the trunk of another vehicle. That is what you probably saw on the monitor in the van."

Strange are the reactions of the human mind. At first Hans felt relieved as he began to understand that Monaco must be somewhere in France or Italy. A moment later he felt incredibly stupid that he had fallen for this ruse at all, and now all he felt was a great hatred growing towards Andrea Carandini. Rather than feeling joy about Monaco's apparent survival, he felt the rage and hate against Carandini well up inside him for imprisoning her in the first place. Carandini had one more enemy tonight.

"No doubt you would have been made to do many things before being allowed to see her again," said Pierre. "You were within an ace of being completely in his power."

"Perhaps I shall have to go to him anyway," sighed Hans. "I cannot stand the fact that he has her."

Before Pirenne was able to react to that, the Observator returned. He still clutched the little statue and memo book in his hands. The door remained open.

"Flamel is coming," he said, sitting down. "He was already asleep, but he is very glad that I woke him up."

Flamel appeared in the doorway.

He brushed his wavy, uncombed hair back with his hand and stared with dark, intelligent eyes at Hans. He had obviously dressed in a hurry. His pants were dishevelled and his shirt was unbuttoned. Hans stood and began walking towards Flamel, as the magician did likewise, his hand outstretched in greeting.

They both exerted amazing strength as they shook hands, strength enough to crush the fingers of someone like Minor, but recognized between themselves as a sign of a secret sect whose members make themselves known to each other in this fashion. An embrace followed, and then Flamel pushed himself away, and stood with his hands on Hans' shoulders, to be able to take a better look at him. Hans was surprised when he saw tears in the man's eyes.

"Every day we hoped for an encounter like this!" he exclaimed. "We have prayed for it! But we had lost heart and had begun to believe that there was no other like me. Welcome, Hans Winters... Welcome!"

After their greeting, they sat down and Hans repeated for Flamel all the things he had related earlier to Pirenne and Mundy. For years he had kept his silence about his life, and the things which occupied his mind, because he felt that this was best. Now however, he would have repeated it gladly, if necessary, a thousand times. When he was done, Flamel pulled his chair closer to Hans and began to speak:

"My abilities have been developed far beyond yours. After all, I have had many more years of practice, but I will try to teach you everything I know. I have never been a magician or an illusionist, just as the people of the Brotherhood of Helgen were not artists when they settled in Austria. I will initiate you slowly and with patience. That is of course, if you want to stay with us. If I tried to explain everything to you at once, your brain would reel. And besides, I have to get used to the fact that someone has finally come along who has shared experiences similar to my own."

Pirenne rose and opened the French windows at the back of the room. It was a sultry night and the flames of the hearth had made it quite warm in the room.

"What kind of creature is man?" Flamel asked aloud, but to no one in particular. "We continually look for perfection, even though we know we will never find it."

Winters glanced at the Observator, whose thick black eyebrows were raised.

"A theory," said Hans, and for the first time that evening a smile appeared on his face when he saw the Observator's expression.

"It is true," continued Flamel. "Man changes, renews himself, and constantly looks for obstacles with which to test himself, until he finally finds himself before an insurmountable wall. His limitations lie only in the nature of his thinking however. Even the gods are like us, for the god who masters the entire realm of possible ability, must also be able to create a problem even he cannot solve. This logical contradiction shows the limitations of perfection and omnipotence. There is so much that we can do, but that is not even close to what we are capable of! We are creatures bound to earth, doomed to spend eternity here; we may come and go, but there is no possibility of real escape."

He stood up and began to pace the room, his long hair falling in his face, and he unconsciously brushing it aside.

"And we are physically weak creatures, too. We have heads full of dangerous thoughts, that sit on top of vulnerable bodies."

He made a fist and rapped on his stomach.

"The puny animals of the world form their armor naturally to protect themselves, while we have to invent and manufacture such things as bullet-proof vests. We are the only creatures on earth who possess a notion of the universe being so vast, indeed, we are the only species that is aware of it at all. We are the only ones bold enough to prick the heavens with our little rockets. We gaze upon the unreachable heights above us and create a world of gods! Like castaways doomed to drown, we sit together on a raft knowing that death is waiting for us to jump."

He came and sat on his knees in front of Hans.

"Half products, that's what we are. We see, we know, we understand, but still we remain within the borders of our abilities. Endowed with as much intelligence as we are, we should be able to tear ourselves loose from this world of limitations and exceed al limits. What do we do though? We continue to creep along like caterpillars because we don't know how to become butterflies. I say we are half products because we are missing something... But you and I have experienced a process that allows us to burst forth from our earthly cocoons, you and I can escape...!"

"You are moving too fast!" warned the Observator.

"Damnit, I know that, Philippe, I know that. But how do you think I feel right now, with this young man sitting in front of me, who has also been influenced by the Austrian Twentiers? There is one more thing I want to tell you, Hans. The big house in Helgen, where the Brotherhood worked... I have managed to buy it. It is all mine now, and I want to take you there and show you something that is far too strange and much too alarming to try and tell you about. And after you have seen it," he continued, looking out of the corner of his eye at the Observator, "you will understand that what I am talking about is not just a theory. Am I right or not, Philippe?"

"Yes. It is true."

Augustin Flamel rose and walked to the door with long strides.

"Now I want to show you something that is actually outside of this matter, but is very interesting all the same."

It was quiet when he left the room. A kind of electric tension, an aura of raw power, seem to come and go with him. Then Hans said:

"We create a world of gods, he says. But Astra also tells us of so many gods. What is missing from the story that would make it clear to us, Professor?"

"We haven't figured that out yet either. You know as well as I do that it this is an implausible story. It probably was never meant to be a realistic story at all. It is another one of the Twentier's mysteries. No one, except for you and Flamel of course, understands anything about the construction of the art. We have not even found a computer system that can denote a common line in it. And we don't understand anything about your translation. It looks like, and seems to give every indication that, it is leading up to something of the greatest importance, but what that is remains a secret to us."

Flamel returned to the room and handed Hans a stack of color photos.

"Take a look at these..."

What he held in his hand was nothing new. Hans had seen photos of prehistoric cave paintings many times before and even recognized some of the pictures as being from the caves of France and Spain.

"Lascaux in the Dordogne, Altamira in Northern-Spain..."

Very realistic paintings of animals and formal human shapes clutching weapons in their hands. And the colors are amazing, even after all these eons... black, dark brown, orange, ochreous..."

"Ten, twenty, thirty thousand years old or perhaps even older..."

Then he held out a photo of a smooth stone wall, on which a tangled knot of rough scratches were cut. Without taking his eyes of it, he handed the rest of the pile back to Flamel.

He did not notice the content look of mutual understanding and relief which Flamel and Mundy exchanged.

"Yes," said Flamel, "all these photos were taken in France and Spain. Except for this one, Hans. You singled this one out immediately. It was taken by divers off the African coast. They discovered the entrance to an unmapped cave and went inside, where a subterranean tunnel led to a spacious chamber. How old do you think those scratches are? A couple of hundred thousand or maybe several million years, who can tell? Most of the world at large has already decided that these lines don't mean a thing. They figure large rocks must have rubbed against the wall and caused the scratches. There is no structure in them, they have come about purely by coincidence. But what comes to your mind when you look at them?"

Hans looked up in surprise at the man standing beside him.

"A greeting, a salutation... I mean, you can say it in many ways, but what it strikes me as is a simple... hello!"

Mundy slapped his hand hard against his knee.

"How can this be possible!" he cried out. "How I wish that I could see and think like you. I have sent this photo to every possible lab and specialist in the world. I spared no pains bringing it to the attention of the most respected intellectuals. And to all, they simply remained scratches without meaning."

Flamel took the photo back from Winters.

"And now, I really must go to sleep. I will teach you soon how to fall asleep under all possible circumstances, Hans. "I have a feeling that you don't quite feel the need of a bed yet..."

They all shook hands, and Pirenne retired as well as Flamel. Hans and The Observator remained behind, sitting together by the hearth where the flames had died out.

"Why did Flamel say that what was in the photo was outside of our current situation?" asked Hans.

Mundy rifled through the pages of the memo book and glanced at some of the abstract drawings. He held a page out to Hans on which he had long ago drawn a number of lines that vaguely hinted at the contours of several buildings.

"Neither you or Flamel are able to make something that looks like Astra. Now that you cannot see the photo any longer, do you think that you could reproduce the scratches on the stone?"

"No. I don't think I could."

"There is no doubt that there have been partial collapses in the cave in question, and there are other sets of scratches that seem to have no meaning at all. We can't go back in time to the previous hour, never mind a couple of million years... But with Flamel you will certainly discuss the future..."

They went outside through the French windows and entered a dark garden. The sky was filled with stars, and Hans could see that the garden was surrounded by a hedge of tall conifers that formed a natural black wall with softly waving, pointed tops.

"Beyond this is an extensive estate," said Mundy. "But you need not worry about a thing. The house is well guarded. How I wish this current engagement was over so that we could get back to Austria. We all live there together in the house of the Twentiers, and I'm beginning to miss my wife dearly.""

"Is Flamel married, too?"

The Observator started to grin.

"Not exactly, no, but he has never had a lonely night. There are always whispers about those performances of his also. That seems to be something you would understand better than I though. He has had a regular girlfriend for quite some time now. I'm sure you will meet her soon."

With a shock Monaco exploded into Hans' thoughts again.

"It's true," Hans confirmed for Mundy, "even Monaco, my sexual tigress, on our wildest nights, had always been the one to tire first."

The air was cool and he took a few deep breaths.

"You are in control of yourself," he heard the Observator say. "You are strong. Believe me, you are even stronger than you think. But if you want to rest now, I will show you to a bedroom."

"I saw some books on a shelf next to the hearth. Just leave me here. Until recently, I was used to spending my nights in loneliness, I'm sure I'll find something to keep me occupied."

Back inside, they closed the big French windows and Mundy bid him goodnight, but turned around as he was leaving the room.

"Perhaps there is something you would like to ask..."

"Oh trust me, I have a thousand different questions. Like... Something was in the steel and now, whatever it was, is in me. What can it be?"

"We have spent a fortune on research, but we still haven't found that out."

"You have your theories, but you couldn't make a balanced whole out of it, is that it?"

"Yes."

"A final question, although it might seem rather bizarre to you. Flamel makes cars disappear. Not in the usual way an illusionist makes it happen, but in the mode of a great and true magician. Is he able to make himself disappear?"

The Observator gave him a sharp look.

"You have started to combine, you have listened well to what has been said. We have to initiate you very carefully, because we have already extended our knowledge quite far. But that is no answer to your question, Hans, and you are certainly entitled to us being honest with you. Yes, Augustin Flamel can make himself disappear."

Softly he left, closing the door behind him.

Hans took five books from the shelf and sat down. After he had read them all, he lay down on the couch and managed to fall asleep.

His mind was ravaged by several gruesome dreams as he slept, none of which he would recall once he woke up.

Chapter 4: The Twentiers

The house had been built atop a high, flat bed of rock that gave it a strategic overlook of the rolling countryside below. The landscape was dotted with the remains of what were once proud castles. Hans, bored and anxious now, had decided to take a look behind the tall hedge of conifers and walk around the estate.

Ornamental bushes such as oleanders and bougainvilleas grew in abundance and walnut trees were scattered around the property. At the edge of the sloping rock face, a metal fence had been erected. Hans leaned over it and looked down at the green hills; far off in the distance he could see some small white houses with orange roofs. A light morning mist seem to make the background fade away as the green of the fields passed gently into the blue of the sky.

Hans felt strong, stronger than he had ever felt before, for he now knew that he could handle emotional trials as well as physical tests, without falling apart. But one fact remained unchanged by any new-found powers; he would not go to Austria without Monaco. Before he would even consider leaving with Flamel, he would have to see Monaco and find out if she still wanted to be with him; he wanted her to accompany him to Helgen.

Getting his mind back on track, Hans' thoughts returned to the Austrian Twentiers. What did he really know about them?

When he had first begun his rambling life, he was reasonably well-informed about the different directions the history of art had taken, and knew that there had been many experiments with style during the end of the nineteenth and the beginning of the twentieth centuries. Besides impressionism, also called the beginning of the modern art, Jugendstil and expressionism were also very popular. The abstract works of the Twentiers, with their vivid colors and fantastic forms, were immediately successful and few remained unsold once they were made available to the public. They were sold for what, at the time, was considered a high price, but it wasn't until decades later that anyone found them so extraordinary that every painting fetched a small fortune.

Enough had been made to satisfy collectors all over the world, but as they filled their walls and hoarded all the known pieces, the prices were driven up and every discovery of new material was like striking a vein of gold.

During his travels through Norway, Hans had been able to translate a bit of Astra artwork himself and had discovered that not all of the abstract works created by the Brotherhood of Helgen told him a tale. Much of the art remained unintelligible to him, and he never once entertained the notion that they had been made with the intention of passing a message along.

While he was in Oslo, not far from the Karl Johansgata in the city-centre, he paid a visit to a fair where art, mostly paintings were sold, and watched a young woman on the verge of buying two abstract works from one of the dealers.

Her name was Anna Gerhardsen and the man was Per Falk.

Falk held up the two canvasses for her Anna to admire. The one on the left depicted a scorching sea of flames, painted with such a ferocity, that it made the observer feel like squinting while looking at it. In his right hand was a picture of a chilly whirlpool, which had the effect of pulling the viewer's attention into the sucking maelstrom.

"The Brotherhood of Helgen," said Per Falk solemnly, "never indicated either name or date on their works, but we have reason to believe that these pieces were done around 1928 and that Wolfram Wikander was the artist."

Hans eavesdropped a little closer so he could hear the price being asked.

"My prices are always reasonable and my customers are guaranteed a high re-sale price, so if you happen to be someone who doesn't love art for its own sake, consider it a wise investment. Everything done by the Austrian Twentiers is in great demand these days, with their abstract period at the top. Especially when the masters, Ulrich von Drach and Wolfram Wikander, have wielded the brush."

This was an art fair where both well-known artists and amateur painters alike, were given an opportunity to sell their own works. Where mass-produced landscapes, still lives, or portraits were available, and where a lone art dealer like Per Falk might turn up with some more exotic and exclusive wares. The chance to make an unexpected, and perhaps even sensational discovery here was real. Per Falk's prices may have been a bit high, but compared to what a real collector would actually pay, they were fair, especially for two paintings by Wikander.

Anna Gerhardsen nodded in agreement to his price and asked if she could pay by check when they were delivered to her home. Falk had no problem with those arrangements, he simply required her signature on the bill.

At that moment, Hans came up beside her, and said:

"This is not the art of the Brotherhood of Helgen. You can take my word on that."

Per Falk put the canvases down on the table and raised his hands again, as if about to lash out in anger.

"There is not a collector in the world who would agree with you, sir... whomever you may be! The hand of the master betrays himself here with the brilliant use of flowing lines and unmistakable shades of color. Wolfram Wikander has bestowed upon it his own peculiar hypnotic aura. Touch the red and burn your fingers, look at the blue and feel as if you are drowning!"

He put his hands down and produced from his pocket a little card, which he presented to Hans. On it, in stylish letters, was printed his name and address. He came from Blindern, an outskirt of Oslo.

"You must come and visit me sometime, I have more work in my private collection, much of it by the great masters."

Anna Gerhardsen looked at Hans with hurt, begging eyes, as if she blamed him for destroying a dream.

"I happen to be very well informed about what the Brotherhood of Helgen has done," she said. "In fact, I have done an extensive study regarding the subject, but I never had the chance to buy any of their work... until now, or so I thought"

"Someone who thinks they are about to close a great deal, often finds themselves in a difficult period when objections are raised that might be considered a disturbance of the euphoria."

Having said that, Hans placed Falk's card on the table and walked away towards the other stalls.

It was freezing outside, a typical Norwegian winter's day with a strong north wind howling, so he stayed inside wandering about and looking at the wide range of offered paintings. Suddenly, Anna Gerhardsen materialized before him and touched his arm.

"Yes, yes... it was all too beautiful and simple to be true," she sighed with a smile. "A good acquaintance of mine, Nordli, is an expert in the field of abstract art. I told our Mr. Falk that I had to think it over for a bit and called Nordli, who told me that the Austrian Twentiers seldom, if ever, painted on canvas and that those which were done are all well-catalogued and every one of them was worth a fortune. Most of their artwork was made on wood. The paintings I wanted to buy are truly beautiful, but they were not done by the hand of Wolfram Wikander. I am very happy to find you still here, for I owe you a great debt of gratitude."

She lived in an apartment in town, on the top story of a nineteenth century building. She took him home with her, and when he expressed his interest in the Brotherhood of Helgen, she began to tell him everything she knew about it.

"Ulrich von Drach was a physicist, and his wife, Martha Ritter, was a very talented architect. Strangely enough though, in their daily lives, they had nothing to do with art. Together, they were founding members of the Brotherhood. Even stranger is a shadowy figure by the name of Wolfram Wikander. Not much is known about him, except that he was an athlete who excelled at running. Legend has it that he ran more than six miles in less than thirty minutes, something we only first saw accomplished at the 1972 Olympics in Munich, almost fifty years later.

What exactly happened in Helgen, will always remain a mystery. Some say a cult-like sect was born around Von Drach, Ritter and Wikander, and dedicated it's existence to art in all possible forms, with Martha Ritter, the architect, a great source of inspiration. One meditated and participated in sports and preferred total isolation to any publicity whatsoever. No one could believe that Ulrich von Drach and Wolfram Wikander had been able to achieve such a high level of craftsmanship, and skill in their art, and still not let their cerebral accomplishments prevent them from inviting in the press, and showing off in front of photographers."

Anna told him all this as they sat in her living room, the walls of which were filled with paintings. She had studied the history of art and was now working for a publishing company that specialized in books about painting throughout the centuries, and now this! It stuck in her throat that she had been on the edge of buying something attributed to the Austrian Twentiers, when in fact it had nothing at all to do with them.

"They were marvellous pieces," said Hans.

"They certainly were! But how did you know that Per Falk was lying?"

"I didn't. I suppose it was in the way he hesitated while talking about the opportunity to buy the canvases for a reasonable prize and then make a quick re-sale. By offering them to you he stood to make a nice profit. As for the rest... I can't explain how, but I knew that it was not Wikander who painted them."

That, at least, was the truth... he could explain so very little about himself.

He could give no explanation for it, but he was convinced that the Brotherhood had nothing to do with either of the pieces. The pictures, regardless of how intriguing they might have been, had not given him that special feeling which the art of the Austrian Twentiers always produced in him.

Anna continued her story.

"They were creating all sorts of things. There must have been so many talented people among them. There were highly elaborate and intricate wood carvings, huge statues, paintings filled with mystical realism, ornate pieces of furniture and everything that left their studios was of the highest possible quality. A true collector of this work could become quite wealthy, even if he were to sell off only a small part of his collection. Every now and then there were stories, or shall we say rumors, that floated around about them which no one was sure whether or not to take seriously. It was said that they occupied themselves with bizarre rituals, and that they might have discovered a way to turn an unimaginative, uninspired individual into a world-class artist; manipulate and control personalities, if you will. They did not seem to suffer from a shortage of the cash needed to fund scientific research, and Ulrich von Drach, the physicist, may have been on to something that he wanted to keep strictly secret, which would explain their reclusive way of life.

A persistent rumor made the rounds in 1929 that Martha Ritter and Wolfram Wikander had disappeared! In the course of the investigation the doors to their little world had to be opened but Martha and Wolfram were not found. No clear answers were obtained however because the sect, as one might imagine, threw a wall of silence around themselves. But it seemed that something inside the group was fermenting. Outsiders had a suspicion that Wolfram Wikander had had a sexual relationship with Martha Ritter, the wife of his best friend, Ulrich von Drach.

The press covered the story incessantly. Had Ulrich von Drach, the undisputed leader, taken his revenge and killed both lovers? We will never know, Hans, but soon afterwards it became very quiet around the big house. The shutters were always closed and the snow was never removed from the walkway. Anxiety and suspicion in the community rose and rose, until public opinion forced the authority's hand and they staged a raid on the house. They were apparently concerned about the possibility of a collective suicide, the ultimate act of desperation for a cult, when they have come to feel that it is their only remaining option to maintain their purity.

Besides, suspicions were even greater now that Von Drach and the others had vanished into thin air, just as Ritter and Wikander had done. Right before Christmas of 1929 the doors were shut and locked for the last time, and behind them were left the empty rooms, stables, attics, studios... and secrets.

The riddle never was solved, and to this day it is a source of inspiration for all sorts of articles and documentaries; and all of the mystery surrounding the case has caused the prices for any work from Helgen to shoot sky-high."

Then with a sigh she added:

"And here I thought I had a chance at a really successful bit of business, by buying those two paintings from Per Falk!"

She invited him to stay for dinner, during which, she told him all she knew about the Brotherhood of Helgen. By the time she was done it was very late and she asked him to stay the night. Hans did just that, and two days later he was back on the road, continuing his hike through Norway, on his way to Hammerfest. There was really nothing that he knew of for him to search for there, but he allowed himself to be led by his restlessness. Without ever understanding what it was exactly that he was he was doing, he felt a powerful spiritual, and physical, change getting him ready for... For what?

Anna Gerhardson cried as he went down the stairs of the old apartment. In the short time they had been together, she had begun to fall in love with him. Besides the fact that he was strong, self-assured, and quite good-looking, no man had ever satisfied her the way he had.

She definitely wanted him near.

Hans was roused from his thoughts with a start; he shivered as if the cold winter wind of far-off Norway was in his bones again. The patches of fog in the distance had lifted and a single white cloud floated high above the green landscape. The Observator was standing behind him and held out a plate on which a number of rolls surrounded a cup of coffee. He held another full cup in his other hand.

"Good morning. Did you manage to get some sleep?"

"A bit. And even though I don't feel rested, neither do I feel tired."

"You can call on special powers without even being aware of the fact that you are doing so. I brought you something to eat and the coffee is still hot."

They leaned over the fence as Hans began to eat a roll.

"We cannot tell you often enough how happy we are with your arrival," said Philippe Mundy. "I hope that you will keep everything we tell you to yourself. We must be one-hundred percent sure that we can trust each other."

"I understand, and I promise," said Hans.

The Observator nodded and slurped his coffee.

"Then we will never bring this subject up again."

"I have made a decision, Professor. I will only join you after I have found out whether or not Monaco will accompany me. I must meet with her, although it seems to me, that something like that cannot be so easily arranged."

"Let me think about it. I'll discuss it with Pirenne. He stays in touch with Carandini."

Hans was about to take a sip of his coffee, but that last statement stopped the cup right in front of his mouth.

"Are you doing business with the Mafia, then?"

"If that were the case, if we were cooperating with them, they wouldn't be playing these games with your girlfriend, would they? We have already suggested that science usually accepts things much later than the criminal mind does, but that's easy to explain. Scientists first must have proof of something, when the criminal mind has already found a way to use it for profit. The astute researcher must ask himself: How on earth does Hans Winters always win in the casinos? The Mafia however, doesn't care how you do it, just so long as you push most of the profits in their direction."

"Yeah, that seems pretty clear."

"We do, however, try to make it as difficult as possible for anyone to follow what we are doing. What do you think would happen if it was proved, beyond the shadow of a doubt, that Augustin Flamel can make things disappear... forever? The whole world would be turned upside down. That is why we always take precautions. Allow me to give you an example. For fourteen nights in a row Flamel stands before the audience in the theatre in Nice. Every night he makes five cars disappear, so that makes seventy in total. What do you tell the bookkeeper who has to explain to the taxman, that yes, seventy cars were purchased, but unfortunately they could no longer be found?

Now it begins to get complicated. We go to an auto junkyard, pick out one hundred and forty wrecks, but always insist on seventy matched pairs. Then we make a bargain with the dealer. On paper, we only buy seventy cars from him. Those cars get fixed, are given a paint job, and we get the motors running again. Flamel makes seventy of them disappear on stage.

Later on, there will be an entry in the books which indicates that the cars were bought back by the dealer. In fact, you will find right there, in black and white, that Flamel is an illusionist who makes his living through the use of tricks.

This is one of the ways we stay on the alert. If the wonder were to become a reality, panic might break out everywhere. Everyone allows themselves to be lulled to sleep so easily. Except for the Mafia. Andrea Carandini does not know much, but knows enough that he wants to incorporate us into the corps of his unquestioning, faithful followers. If we take his side, we're rich! Anyway, Aldo Duby has promised you heaven and earth, but what they want us to put in Carandini's hands in return is so dangerous, that we cannot bear to even think of the consequences should we agree. He continues chasing us though, and we try to stay ahead of him. Pirenne is our man who deals with Carandini and his men. I'm sure you will hear shortly whether or not there is anything he can do for you where Monaco is concerned."

Hans put the empty plate and the cup down on the ground. The Observator took the little steel statue out of his pocket and offered it back to Hans.

"You going to hide it away again in the secret compartment of your belt?"

"I don't think I need it any longer. What was in it, is in me now, right?"

"Yes, it is empty now, like a used battery. Besides it's really not a very good-looking object, is it? Maybe it was never anyone's intention that it should be considered art, but on the other hand, it may very well be that the Brotherhood had completed the circle from realism to abstraction. Then this is no longer a matter of design. But again, these are all theories, and they lead nowhere."

"I like the comparison to a battery. What was in it...?"

"I am a physicist," began the Observator and then stopped abruptly, looking long and hard at the expression on Hans' face.

"Just as Ulrich von Drach was a physicist..."

"So you are aware of that also. Yes, you see, Flamel came looking for me, he wanted my help as a physicist. We became friends, both obsessed by the same subject, and this quest kept us together. But you were asking a question: What was hidden in the steel? Correct?"

Thinking deeply, he stared out at the blue sky.

"I suppose I had best tell you everything we know, and perhaps even let you in on what we keep hidden from the world inside the house in Helgen. This is something which has to stay between you, Flamel and me. Pirenne is not in possession of all the facts. Come, let's go for a walk in the garden."

The plate and the two empty cups remained behind along the fence, as the Observator put his hands behind his back and walked with measured steps in the direction of two walnut trees.

"I will tell you about one of Flamel's theories which, I think, is close to reality. It is rather frightening, and believe me, Flamel is scared!

He refers to man as a half-product.

We are creatures who know their place in the universe. According to Flamel, our behavior indicates our desire to be more than creatures bound to this planet. We undertake all kinds of endeavors in an effort to rise above all earthly things. Meditation, out-of-body experiences, calling upon divine inhabitants of heaven, all these things... plus the fact that you finish a book in one hour, and you are well versed in all possible subjects. These are grand undertakings. So you must also know, Hans, that our galaxy exists of about one hundred billion stars, maybe there are also one hundred billion other galaxies. We are always talking about the stars and planets in billions, and about millions of light years. Many other planets might be very much like ours. Is it not absurd, then, that we are allowed to suspect something like that, without ever being given the possibility of reaching those worlds?

Now.... let me tell you a bit about an element which, until now had remained invisible, but is a component of that steel.

It is a fact that it doesn't exert an influence on everyone. What's also certain is that it has found its way into both you and Flamel. When Flamel told me that he had set foot on a world beyond our solar system, I would not believe him.

No matter how nervous, frightened, and insistent he was; no matter how he cried and sobbed when he told me his story. I refused to believe it and simply assumed that he was having some grand hallucination. About how he came to be there, what he saw, what he felt, and how he managed to get back again... well, he can give you all those details himself. He was so very convinced that he had been light years away from us....!"

Hans stopped, his mind reeling, and leaned against the trunk of a tree for support.

"Impossible!" he said.

"Listen, Hans, he then disappeared a second time. Right before my very eyes! He reappeared in the room from which he had left. He staggered, fell, coughed up some noxious looking phlegm and began raving like a madman. He lay there naked on the stone floor for what seemed to be an eternity. I knelt beside him and tried to comfort him - regardless of where he had been, he was back now, and in rotten shape.

I reached out, running my fingers through his hair, and something fell to the ground, which I immediately retrieved. It was a tiny little thing, that looked kind of like a straight pin, such as a seamstress uses. I'm sure you have seen them, with the tiny, brightly colored plastic nipple on the end. As soon as I put it in my hand... it began to move! My mind was racing, and my reaction was just as fast. I put it in a glass jar with a screw cap, the way a biologist in the field would do with an insect.

There is not much to be seen of the little creature with the naked eye, but when I enlarged the pictures I had taken of it, I could see that the ball is transparent and that underneath, a thick, amber colored substance is moving about with black spots that occasionally become visible.

The hind part, thin and oblong like a pin, is a marvellous shade of blue with yellow, luminescent spots. There are no paws or wings, but still the little creature is able to float and move through the air at very high speeds. I have constructed a special, extra- large terrarium for it, made out of thick, unbreakable glass. You can see it for yourself soon.

I'll tell you Hans, I was so amazed at the uniqueness of this little creature that it made me think, and I decided to give Flamel the benefit of the doubt.

It is very possible that we have at our house in Helgen, the old home of the Austrian Twentiers, a life form that did not originate on earth. I must also tell you that I suspect that whatever it is that has been absorbed into your and Flamel's systems, is also in that little creature.

Otherwise it would have remained behind when he was transported back, or burst apart like the cars Flamel sweeps from the stage! He cannot wear clothes, rings, watches, or anything of that sort either; they don't come back with him.

Augustin says that the human desire to approach divinity is normal. He also thinks that it should be normal for a creature that understands its place in the endless universe, to be able to travel through that enormous space. That's why he was talking about spacecraft pricking the sky last night. What he means is, that it is useless to search for the technology to bridge these great distances because, according to him, it all goes back to the knowledge of a process that has, and always will be right here.

It must be found in countless creatures, scattered all over the universe, and it enables them to cross the vast distances of the universe like a great bird that can fly from one mountaintop to another without having to worry about the depth of the ravine below him!

On earth life developed less dramatically, unfortunately, and what the Twentiers discovered is perhaps not earthly at all. We are dealing with a physical procedure which overshadows all known forms of techniques. Just imagine, Hans, if everything Flamel asserts is true. That would mean that during those turbulent years between the two world wars, The Brotherhood of Helgen had indeed found something spectacular!"

He saw that Hans was no longer walking beside him, but resting against the tree, so he sat down under the tree beside him and pulled up his legs. Hans sat and stared out with blank eyes.

"We have, of course, examined Flamel from head to toe," he said. "You could say that we have turned him inside out. We checked to see if his blood contained anything that did not belong there, we have done DNA tests, and his brain waves have been measured multiple times. Nothing! His muscular body reminds me of an athlete's, but except for the walking, like you, he has never trained."

Hans showed no reaction. Mundy wanted to tell him even more, but realized that there was no point since he was probably no longer getting through to him. So he left him sitting alone by the tree, and came back about fifteen minutes later with Flamel.

Hans looked up at Flamel and said:

"The Professor tells me you're scared. Believe me, so am I! I have heard much more than I can possibly digest all at once. Damn, I haven't had a headache in years and now there is an incredible pressure behind my eyes. I also feel as if I'm about to have a major panic attack at any moment."

"Do you want to just sit here calmly for a bit longer?" asked Flamel.

"No, I'd rather move. A dive into the sea would probably do me some good."

"Then let's get away from here," said Flamel decidedly. "We'll look for a nice, quiet, deserted beach behind some high rocks, where tourists seldom come. I'll come with you. I do have to get to the theatre sometime after noon to meet a group of journalists, and I have to prepare for tonight's show, but I have some time now. Shall we go?"

Hans smiled.

"How can we possibly sit in a car together without the motor refusing to work?"

"I will teach you how to guard against that through concentration. Didn't it ever strike you strange that certain machinery continues working, even if you are close to it? A television or a radio suffers no interference, while a mantle clock can suddenly stop ticking. As soon as you have learned to control it, everything will operate without failure, while if you wanted to, you could bring a plane out of the sky..."

They looked each other in the eye.

Once again Hans was overcome by terrible feelings of fear. Feelings that became even stronger when he thought he saw that same fear Flamel's eyes.

Flamel had selected a nondescript car from the big parking lot in front of the house. He drove quietly and seemed relaxed enough. They descended to a little village and came out on a winding road that led to the coast. It was already getting quite warm, so they drove with all the windows and Flamel's long hair was blowing in the wind.

"It was that strange little life form which made Mundy change his mind," he said with a grin. "First he was convinced that I was hallucinating, then he slowly became more and more interested in my ideas. Then he became really worried. He was incessant! What kind of risks do you take when you make such a journey? What can you take with you? Should you be quarantined for life in case you are infected, and could possibly be capable of wiping out all of humanity? His questions were almost unbearable!

Hans, neither one of us asked to be the way we are. We barely know what is going on with us, and we haven't had a clue as to the source of our energy until now."

"But you are sure that you did not found yourself in an disturbed frame of mind... I mean, you think that you can actually bridge these vast distances in a short time. Then you might also assume that you are dreaming, and in that altered state of consciousness, are able to create a fantasy which takes on a definite form. That could explain the life form. Hell, one idea is just as crazy as the other."

His emotions had gotten the better of him, and Flamel was so upset that he had to pull the car to the side of the road and stop. He turned to Hans and made a gesture of powerlessness with both hands.

"I sat there on a cold, dark, stone ground. Above me seven little satellites circled, and behind them was the starlit sky! I looked into the unfathomable depth of the universe and knew that I was not dreaming. Later, I drew the night sky that I had seen and the Observator did everything he could to find out where I might have been. He found no clues. Believe me, the Observator has questioned me intensely. He wanted to know every detail. There were some questions I could not answer. He asked me things like: Had I been able to see my own hands and feet? Did I realize that I could breath, or did it occur to me that I wasn't getting any air at all? Hans, I know what I have seen and there is no doubt about it. Life on earth is apparently missing one very important facet, which is so normal on other worlds that it even exists in the smallest creatures.

In other places, it has made conscious creatures into godlike beings who can go wherever they please, while man has always remained earthbound, like a worm. You and I, however, have reached, unasked and unintended, the status of a demigods.

Demigods, that is what we are, Hans, demigods!

And it is our God-given responsibility to find out what the extent of our capabilities are!"

"My brain is reeling again," sighed Hans, as he rubbed his closed eyes with his fingers.

"What do you think about that photo you showed me... the cave with the scratches on the rock..."

He shrugged and held his head to the side, like a man listening for the grenade he had just thrown to explode. He expected the answer to his question was going to hit him somewhere deep inside.

"Let's say that the scratches are a million years old... from a visitor who left a mark of his presence before he had to leave again..."

The effects of his words did not fail, Hans' entire being was filled with horror.

And Flamel drove along.

"Our bodies have adapted themselves to whatever it is that has been absorbed into us. When I was glancing through your memo book and saw the illustrations, I of course had to think about myself too. You were luckier than I."

The car accelerated and Flamel took the bends skilfully. As they approached a high point, a thin strip of the blue Mediterranean became visible. They found themselves not too far from Cannes and went in the direction of La Napoule.

"I came into possession of a little steel object by chance, when I bought a house long ago. It had been bricked into the wall above the hearth and the previous owners had left it behind. I chipped it out of the wall and soon afterwards got the strange feeling that it was radiating some kind of energy or something. I don't have to explain that to you, do I? When you started to feel restless, you began walking. If I had only done so myself! Instead of a hiking tour, I booked passage on a ship in the port of Marseille that was about to sail for South America. Had it only been an old-fashioned steamer, I would have gladly shovelled coal day and night to rid myself of this excess energy."

He turned onto the coastal road.

"I had hoped that my nervousness would disappear when I got to another continent, where I could calm down in a completely unknown environment. But the invisible power from the steel had taken hold of me, never to release me again. If I had only taken a plane! Right after I went ashore, I started to walk... Chilli, Argentina, Brazil and Peru. Fortunately, I also learned how to meditate there. I have discussed this quite often with the Observator.

When you meditate, and then afterwards open your eyes and say that you have been in another world, it is understood that you have made a spiritual journey. When you disappear right before someone's eyes and then re-emerge a couple of days later on the very same spot, well Hans, that is obviously quite something else.

While in Lima I saw, by chance, a picture of Astra

in a magazine. The people from whom I bought the house here in France, had told me that the little statue I found in the wall was made by the Brotherhood of Helgen. I found that I was able to read Astra and started, just like you, to combine facts.

Later I saw the original painting in the Louvre in Paris but by then I already had many years of self-training behind me. I also had left behind me the time in my life when I earned my money gambling. I travelled around the world with my shows, and was thus able to keep on developing my special talents. Plus I had the capital to be able to pay for all kinds of research. Philippe Mundy joined me and became my most important associate. Together we tried to find answers to all the questions, and thankfully, you are here now, too..."

After a while, they parked the car and climbed down a steep rock face to reach a little sliver of beach. Flamel took off his shirt, shoes and socks and walked into the water still wearing his trousers.

"It'll get really hot today... The sun will dry you in no time."

There was little wind and no high waves. Hans slid into the water, swam away a fair distance, and dived under. The coolness of the water did him good, and he stayed in the sea for almost an hour, making sure that he kept enough distance between himself and Flamel so that he wouldn't have to talk the whole time.

When they sat down on the beach afterward, he decided to broach another subject, because everything that had to do with the Twentiers and the influence of the steel weighed so heavily on his mind.

He told Flamel that he had already informed the Observator that he would like to come along to Helgen with them, but would not leave without Monaco.

"I want to at least ask her if she wants to come along with me. She told me that Andrea Carandini asked her to marry him, but I don't believe she still cares about him."

"Take it from me, Monaco is not the only beautiful woman he has proposed to," grinned Flamel. "But the party always seems to get postponed indefinitely. If the Observator has told you that he will have a talk with Pirenne, he will. I'm sure you know that it is not exactly the smartest idea in the world to take someone out of the Mafia camp, and bring her to a house full of secrets, but on the other hand I understand your feelings and wish you the best of luck, but even to Monaco you must remain silent about certain things and that won't be easy once she starts getting involved in everything."

"I know that. I also know that I can trust her..."

Now Flamel started laughing out loud.

"Well, damn me... You're in love! When you first met her, she tried to knock you out, twice, by putting something in your drink. I heard all about it from Pirenne, when he came to ask me for an explanation about the vanished Mercedes. Let me tell you this: Monaco will probably have some more interesting surprises in store for you!"

He gave Hans a pat on the back.

"I am on your side, my friend. We will do our utmost to get her back for you."

"Thank you. Must you leave now, or can I go for another quick swim? The sea calms me down."

"Take your time. I'll wait here quietly, we can both use the time to get a grip on ourselves."

Hans stayed in the water for an hour, and afterwards they sat on the beach, until it was time for Flamel to go and prepare himself his meeting with the press and his show.

On the return trip, they discussed the parallels in their lives. Flamel was the voice of experience, and he was going to tutor Hans until he was ready to accompany him on a journey beyond all imagination.

Flamel also told him that his people kept him informed about everything and that he had a talk with Pirenne before he came into the garden that morning. This brought him once again to Hans' desire to get Monaco back.

"You have all the freedom in the world and I don't know why you would want to limit that, but that is up to you. You are our Benjamin and we wish you as much happiness as is possible, but I must urge you one more time; conceal important matters from her. But you will find out soon enough that there is much you'd better keep to yourself. We must keep the group of insiders as small and as tight as possible. The show I travel with is an independent knot of performers, but sometimes I gather other people around me too. After the last performance, there will be a big party for all of us in Nice, and after that we will split up. I will go to Helgen then. If Monaco decides to come with you, don't tell her beforehand what your destination is. You can travel alone or with us."

"I understood it all very clearly," said Hans. "Don't worry about anything, I know all too well what is at stake."

Before they left the beach, Flamel bent down and scooped up a handful of sand. As he let it slip through his fingers, he said:

"It has been said that there are more stars in the universe than there are grains of sand on earth. And it’s true, trust me! We can look at the sand and form a concept of infinity."

He picked up some more sand and threw it in the air. The wind was calm and the sand fell back to the beach in a slight arc.

"It would be absurd to accept the fact that the universe holds so many forms of intelligent life, and that we will never get to meet them."

Chapter 5: The Ghost of Genoa

Over the next few mornings the garden behind the house became a classroom as Flamel began the education of his new disciple. Each morning they sat on the grass facing each other, while the Observator sat on a stone bench not far away. Hans was learning how to relax, and to concentrate on his inner feelings.

He delved deep within himself and tried to trace the source of the power that had crept into the core of his existence. He tried to get a spiritual hold on it and manipulate it, rather than allowing it to lead him. This effort cost him a great deal of energy, and although he appeared to be calm, the sweat was streaming down his body. Sitting cross-legged, hands on his knees with upturned palms and outstretched fingers, he looked very much like a meditating mystic who was searching out a place for his soul to rest by contacting some divinity through prayer.

"Mysticism is not a human failing," taught Flamel. "The search for a union with higher powers, for deliverance for the uncertain, desperate soul, is both a blessing and a torment. At first, the Supreme Being created itself and imparted it's being with mighty and unknown power. Then it made certain that it had dedicated mystics to worship it and be entirely devoted to it. The human consciousness brings with it so much confusion, that the search for certainty is certainly justified. The mystic gives his fate away with confidence, but you do it the other way around,

Hans! By recognizing your capabilities you learn to take fate into your own hands. For you the journey to heaven is not symbolic, for you it is not a mental task for you can leave this place which holds all others prisoner."

Because what lived inside him now was untraceable, the Observator compared it with a geometric line:

"Its length is endless, but it has no thickness. It is inside of you, squirms through you, and has taken hold of you, but is still not anything which we can see."

"Nevertheless, you must learn how to catch it," said Flamel. "Even though it is an imaginary ribbon without substance, you must coil it, knit it together and take control of it. You must forgive me if I cannot explain this clearly to you, Hans. I never had a teacher and still don't completely understand what happened to me. Together we must experiment and combine our powers."

In the depths of his soul, Hans felt the presence of something that was nestled there and reacting to his will. It concentrated itself so quickly, into a new, untested power that unleashed so many feelings at once, that it caused him to suddenly be thrown backwards and he landed on his back in the grass. Gasping for breath he tried to sit up. Flamel and Mundy were already by his side and placed concerned hands upon his shoulders.

"It took your body years to absorb it," said Flamel. "So don't expect your mind to do it immediately."

Time after time, Hans repeated his lessons; searching, holding, and manipulating.

On the day before Flamel was to give his last performance in Nice, he succeeded in getting a better grip on what was inside of him. As soon as he had hold of it, he slipped into a state of mind that made it possible for him to be open to new impulses.

In much the same fashion that he had been able to wander the streets of town with his eyes closed, he now managed to concentrate his powers and be able to keep them at his disposal. A fountain of colors exploded into his consciousness and formed a wide stream of balls of light spinning around each other. The explosion rocked his mind with lightning and he was carried away by shooting beams of light that brought him to a point in the distance that absorbed all color, and where the deepest shade of black manifested itself as a bottomless pit.

"Stop!" he heard someone cry.

He was being given a good shaking. He opened his eyes and saw the blue sky through the branches of a walnut tree. Flamel sat on his heels right in front of him, holding Hans' cheeks with hands wet with transpiration.

"Not so fast, boy, not so fast! You were on the point of leaving us. You were within an ace of vanishing into thin air right before our very eyes!"

On the last night of the engagement the theatre was full to bursting. The opening act had thrown the audience into an appropriate state of ecstasy and when Flamel finally appeared, as many people as possible moved on stage to crowd around him. Numerous cameras recorded, from every possible angle, The Master making five cars disappear. The ovation that followed seemed endless.

After the show everyone was invited back to the big house on the hill and transportation was provided. The farewell party there would last all night. In the garden behind the conifers, lanterns had been hung and there were tables on the terrace with food and drink. Inside, music was provided by a band whose members changed often, as it was made up of musicians from the theatre who all played many different instruments.

And the men dressed in grey guarded the house.

It struck Hans how relaxed Flamel was as he moved among the people.

Everyone wanted to talk to him one last time and thank him for the marvellous time they had enjoyed while hanging around with him and his troupe. He was patted on the back repeatedly and it was his voice that was heard in laughter and jovial repartee above the other voices and the music. This was the end of a long journey through many cities and many staunch friendships had been made. Not to mention the fact that with Flamel as the main attraction, much money had been made all around.

Hans Winters sat watching the crowd. He truly admired the artists from the show. They were proud of their profession and the aura created by magic and the splendour of the illusions found gleeful expression in all they did. They loved the unusual, and they showed it in the way they carried themselves and the manner in which they dressed. But no matter how different each one was, together they formed the facets of a sparkling jewel.

He was not used to loud, noisy parties. Behind him lay years of loneliness, behind him lay the footsteps of the solitary traveller. An unpleasant tightness in his chest came began to take hold of him, keeping his breath from coming calmly. He recognized this as a fear of the unknown and wished that he were one of those merry people, who were able to stand with their feet firmly planted on Mother earth again at the end of a performance. Beginning to feel really bad now, he stood up and went outside.

He took a glass from a table in the garden, put some ice cubes in it and poured some cold water for himself. It was crowded here too, so he went and sat at the back of the garden where nobody could see him. Plastic tables and chairs had been placed all about, and he sat down and looked out over the metal fence at the brightly lit windows in the houses so far below. Somewhere in the distance the lights of a car lit up in the darkness, illuminating the green leaves on the trees, and then disappeared again. The cloudless sky was filled with stars, but Hans took no notice of them.

Someone approached him whom he immediately recognized as Murielle Robin, a confidante of Flamel whom he had once or twice before in the house. He had his suspicions that she was Mundy's girlfriend, even though he had heard that she had also slept with Flamel.

She was a pretty woman, about forty years old, with thick, dark hair that did not quite reach her shoulders. She had a small face with big, oval eyes, and she was wearing a black dress adorned with copper-colored trinkets.

"You're sitting here so alone and so quietly," she said, taking the seat across from Hans. "Flamel rents houses in the most beautiful locations wherever we go. It is a pity that we must leave here so soon."

Murielle was also an initiate and seemed to know more than Pierre Pirenne. Hans knew that she had studied biology, but used most of her free time to pour over all the written material left behind by the Brotherhood. At the house in Helgen, where she also resided, she undoubtedly was engaged in observing the strange little creature living in the glass terrarium.

They talked now though about her passion for the texts of the Austrian Twentiers.

"Because they were such great artists, everyone put a very high value on everything they ever wrote. Every line, almost every word, could be left open to misinterpretation. Oracular language with multiple explanations can often lead to violent discussions. The motive of Astra has achieved quite a place in short dissertations, comments and stories."

Mireille had brought along a glass of wine and now stared at Hans over the brim of it. Perhaps she was expecting some unique reaction from him when she said that the meaning of Astra was known not only to Flamel and Mundy, like he was originally told, but he said nothing, and after she had taken a drink from her wine, she continued:

"The murder of Caesar is paramount. Then we read about Celts and Germans marching to battle, urged on by their gods, until they finally reach Rome and stand before the temple of Janus."

Now Hans looked at her with a bit of surprise evident upon his face.

"So... does that mean that many more people had been able to decipher the meaning of Astra simply by guessing that it is identical to the written stories?"

"No, no. You have translated Astra in great detail, and in a way that has never been put down on paper before. It is a fact though, that the Brotherhood used the same theme over and over again, especially in their most beautiful poems. Everything can be explained in one of two ways, and it has become an intellectual game between the two camps to try and convince the other who is correct. It is almost a pastime to those who are philosophically minded."

"You make me very curious..."

"Do you want to hear what I have to say, or would you rather rejoin the party? If I have bothered you in any way..."

"No, please stay and tell me all about it," urged Hans.

He began to feel calmer now than he had been earlier. To his left was the depth where every so often a small light would shine, and above him was the starlit sky, which he could look up at now without thinking of marvellous, dangerous journeys.

To his right, the other guests walked, talked, and laughed in the light of the lanterns, while behind the hedge was the house from where the music wafted out through the big French doors. The bass tones came sneaking along, close to the ground, while the higher tones travelled clearly through the sky and faded with every gust of wind.

"One faction starts from the principle that history never repeats itself. The earth was created and provided the opportunity for life to different physical creatures. Perhaps at the end of countless chains of existence, intelligence could manifest itself in a way that does not look human at all. Combine this theory with the possibility of an intervention in historic events, which could have a disastrous result.

Caesar is murdered and there is no Roman Empire, but Celts and Germans unite in a brotherly fashion. New nations emerge and Rome is more a trading partner than a tyrant. How do those two powers stand in relation to each other? Rome is dependent on an unbelievable amount of slave labor that forms the motor that keeps everything going, and they have everything built with the finest stone. On the other side of the coin we find the Celts and Germans, who have an entirely different outlook on slavery, and have different laws, and they build their houses from wood. So, during the time we call the middle ages, we will perhaps find no cathedrals in these regions, but instead wooden places of worship to honor Belenus or Tiwaz. Druids and seers lead the way down the spiritual path, and the rest put their trust in faith.

For arguments sake one might assume that everything will be drastically different if Caesar has died too early. It is all about the development of new hypotheses. As time goes on, the great migrations of people begin and it starts to get crowded in the regions of modern-day France, Germany, Belgium and Holland. Later, the Scandinavians come to visit their German brothers and are accompanied by all their strange gods. It is interesting to philosophize about all this, especially when there are freethinkers and historians sitting around the table who constantly add new ideas to it..."

Mireille took a sip of wine.

"And what about the other camp?" asked Hans.

"Well, in the other camp they say that the members of the Brotherhood were all atheists. According to them, the Austrian Twentiers would not have acknowledged omnipotence and would have wanted to indicate that there is a definite border that true believers should not cross. Yes, yes, I see you raising your eyebrows... Let me try to make it a little clearer for you.

Listen. A multitude of people marched on to Rome. Word spreads that there is something in the temple of the two-faced god Janus. In a poem, it is Janus himself who appears and blocks the way of the obtrusive, inquisitive crowd. Another time it is Mercury who descends from the sky on winged shoes and displays the key. There is a story, which imparts the leading role to the wild Germanic god of war Tiwaz. He approaches the doors with thundering violence, but all the variables have one thing in common; the door shall never be opened! There is no firm answer to all this and the stories and the poems stir up more questions, but give no answers."

"What does that mean to you?"

"I just don't know, but what I do know is what people say who like to discuss it. The belief in what a god is able to do, in this case Janus, is tremendous. All sorts of miracles are attributed to him and he is able to see into the past and the future as well, and can make....or break..... the life of a mortal.

But where is he? Is he on Earth or in Heaven? Is he as the sculptures have depicted him? Is he omnipotent, or does he need the help of something like the winged shoes of Mercury to move himself through the human world? The answer is not an easy one to give, but if there is anything that can clear it up for us, it must be in the temple that was dedicated to him. Behind those doors the secret must lie that would explain everything!

As long as those doors remain closed, there is still hope and belief.

But when the doors are opened, and the searcher finds nothing inside which gives substantial proof of a divine existence, not much remains to cling to in a spiritual way.

That is what the Twentiers tried to make clear, they claim. When the doors opened and the people had streamed inside, they would have found no answers to their questions and no secret waiting to be divulged to them."

"Build a temple around air and proclaim a belief," said Hans.

"Exactly. So, we have two different ideas about what the Brotherhood may have intended to tell us. A game played with history that turns the world upside down, and the story of the atheists which say that the pantheon..."

She bent down, picked up half of a walnut shell, which was lying next to her foot, and handed it to him.

"...is just an empty shell! But as long as the nut remains closed, no one can tell whether or not it contains a kernel!"

"Anyway, they are both unique ways to approach the work of the Brotherhood. If you had to choose, Mireille, which camp would you be in then?"

"Neither," she said decidedly. "Although I like to join in such discussions, I don't see how it makes the ideas of the Brotherhood any clearer. But that is all because of Astra, the work of art that could only be explained by Flamel and you. And of course there are all those marvellous things Flamel is able to. We must especially remember that Ulrich von Drach was a physicist, not a philosopher, and that his wife was an architect who made the most beautiful designs..."

"Wolfram Wikander was supposed to have been an athlete, a runner they say..."

"He remains a mystery. He was athletically built and had unbelievable sexual staying power, but he may have also not run a mile more in his entire life than you or Flamel."

"Bitten by the steel," sighed Hans.

He looked past her at the people in the garden and saw Pirenne waving and coming towards him with long strides.

"So there you are!" he called out. "I've been looking for you for quite a while and thought that maybe you had left the house to get a breath of fresh air."

"It is cool and quiet out here," said Hans with a smile. "Do you need me?"

Pierre looked at Mireille's empty glass.

"Wait," he said, "I'm going to get myself a bottle of wine and a glass. Can I get you anything?"

"Another glass of cold water with some ice would be just fine."

"I'll see to that."

He started to walk away, but stopped after a couple of steps and turned back towards Hans.

"In a little while I'm going to tell you how you can arrange a meeting with Louise Vernet, and if you play it right, well, perhaps you can bring her along tomorrow!"

"Louise Vernet?" asked Mireille, after Pierre had gone back to the front of the garden.

"Monaco," he explained.

"The little poisoner," she said with a smile, giving away the fact that she knew about that as well.

That she was actually in possession of all the facts became obvious when Pierre had returned and sat down with them again and started to talk. It didn't bother him at all that Mireille was present during this conversation. He put down a glass and poured wine from the bottle he had brought back with him.

"I have had a talk with Carandini," he said. "He is very worried about the increasing power of a certain Carlo Dordoni. I don't have much information about this man, but what I do know is that they call him the Ghost of Genoa, because he finds settlements for things that take place outside the mainstream of everyday life. Some previous misfortune has forced him to look elsewhere for his luck and now the Ghost walks around in the territory that Carandini has claimed for himself. It seems to be unusual that this breed of gentlemen ever cross each other's paths and Carandini, for his part, has never done any business in or around Genoa. He considers the Riviera his territory and concentrates on France, Monaco and a very small part of Italy. He curtails his activities where Dordoni's power begins."

Hans was listening with keen interest.

"In San Remo," continued Pirenne, "the Italian town not far from Monaco, the Ghost has opened an illegal casino. Everyone is gambling heavily there, but it is by invitation only. Of course Carandini wants him out of there. He is aware of the fact that the financial position of the Ghost is rather weak at the moment, so his plan is simple. He wants you to win so much at the roulette table for him, that he can take over the casino when the Ghost cannot pay you. Special codes of honor exist between these people, which we in no way understand. If you were to win all by yourself, you would probably never be paid off. Hell man, you would probably be happy enough simply to be allowed to leave in one piece. But, when you are work for Carandini, you will definitely get your money and if there were not enough, an exchange would settle the debt. The illegal casino would become the property of Carandini and the Ghost would go back to Genoa."

"Let's see if I've got this right... I do what Carandini asks of me and in exchange I get to take Monaco with me," said Hans.

"Yes, that's the deal. I will tell you how to get there. We know it's a tricky deal, but one that would be worth your while. Carandini won't cheat you, as long as you make it clear to him that you are on his side. He is even prepared to forgive you for pulling him out of the car and dragging him around in front of Louise Vernet, because you obviously were unaware of whom he was. I am more concerned about Carlo Cordoni, for you will be his guest and his men will be guarding all the doors."

"Does Flamel know about this?"

"Of course he does. Both he and Philippe have been completely filled in."

"And what do they think about it?"

"Flamel says that you are free to do as you please. He is convinced that you will go. Philippe thinks it is too dangerous, but agrees with Flamel where your freedom of choice is concerned."

"Of course I will go, but only under the condition that Monaco must be present. If Carandini has her stashed away out of sight, the whole deal is off. I want to see her and talk to her. Besides, before I agree to anything I first have to know if she is willing to come with me at all."

"According to Carandini, she does and that's a fact. What else can I tell you? Oh, yes, Carlo Dordoni has said quite often that he wants to part with his casino, but the price is high. Now that it is obvious that Dordoni needs money, Carandini smells his chance. If you win more than the Ghost of Genoa can afford to pay, you have won everything for Carandini. I will call him and make an appointment with him for you. You will get all the information from me that is necessary once it is all arranged. Tomorrow night, in San Remo, you just may win a woman at the roulette table. We will all pray that you return sound and safe."

He emptied his glass, rose, and headed back up to the house, leaving the open bottle of wine on the table.

"Tomorrow we will still be here," said Mireille "We leave in a couple of days, so it is not a sure thing that you will be returning here. I will give you all the information about the house in Helgen, including the directions for the drive. It's so nice to work with you and Flamel, you remember everything so easily. I will give you a few different phone numbers so that you can always reach us and I'll give you a cell phone for yourself."

She leaned towards him now and said in a much softer tone of voice:

"I will take good care of Monaco when she is with us in Helgen, and you are busy with things that she does not have to know about, you leave that to me."

Then she tilted her chair back a bit, and leaning with her hands folded behind her neck, she stared at the starry sky.

"Come out of this one unscathed, Hans Winters," she said. "For you have journeys ahead of you that are much more dangerous. Finally, Astra has given us a second Flamel! Astra was displayed everywhere imaginable, on the posters, on the stationary, on the pamphlets... Flamel was convinced that sooner or later someone like you would turn up. Astra was an utilized in an ambitious, well organized publicity campaign with posters in all the towns where he performed, and fortunately it has produced results. You mean a lot to us."

She left him alone now, while Hans remained sitting there, staring at the stars for hours.

The next morning, he got directions from Pirenne. Just before he was to get into an old, rebuilt car that looked like something that Flamel would choose to make vanish, August came up to him.

"I hope you're not going to try and stop me?" laughed Hans.

"No, I come to warn you," said Flamel. "Not about Andrea Carandini, nor about the Ghost of Genoa either, but about yourself. Listen carefully, Hans. You're like a half trained puppy right now! You only know half of your power but still you do not hesitate to show your teeth. I am afraid that there's no holding you back once you have started biting, like an attack dog that no longer responds to its commands. Please, try to keep your temper, do what Carandini asks of you and he will release Monaco. It is very important to Carandini that he can get Dordoni away from what he calls 'his territory'. It is all a matter of power and honor and he will do anything where that is concerned. If you don't come back to his house, I will see you later on in Austria. In Helgen."

"Yes. I know how to find it by car, I have a cell phone and I know all the numbers I might need by heart. Goodbye, Augustin."

"Goodbye, Hans. I wish you all the luck in the world."

Hans spent that afternoon walking through the town of San Remo in the Italian region known as Imperia.

The old part of the city lay on a hill and the newer part was built along the coast. Nestled under the lee of a high mountain, Monte Bignone, this was the most popular seaside resort at the Riviera di Ponente for generations. Here the winters were mild, especially for Northern Europeans who fled from the cold.

Yet this day was exceptionally warm and just before evening, Hans searched out a cool café, where he could get a meal and escape the heat for a while. Over his dinner he read book about the excavation of human fossils that were more than two million years old in East Africa. When he left the café, he left the book behind, finished.

It was getting late when he walked back to the old part of the city, and it was dusk by the time he reached the San Siro church, built in the twelfth century, where Aldo Duby and Minor were waiting for him. Remaining silent, they gave him a nod of recognition and escorted him to a station wagon with darkly tinted windows. He was pushed down on to the back seat and Duby pulled a hood over his face, so that he could see nothing.

"The casino is a private place," he said. "Someone who will only be going there once doesn't have to know exactly where it is."

The car drove off with the two men sitting silently in the front seat. They were probably under orders not to have any conversation with him, no matter how much he, or they, desired to do so. And now that Hans sat here helplessly in the dark, with this hood over his head, he also had no doubt that Minor would like to lay a couple of heavy blows on him.

The silence last for almost twenty minutes, and then Hans finally had to speak.

"I think that it must be you sitting behind the wheel, Duby, since Minor is not capable of driving very well with a bandaged hand. Now, do me a favor and go straight to our destination if you don't mind. We've already driven along the sea twice and now you're heading back into the centre of town. A couple of more blocks and you'll be back at the church where you picked me up."

Duby began to swear and Hans felt a hand adjusting the hood.

"He can't see a damn thing," said Minor. "Drive fast, Aldo, I find it scary to be in a car with this guy."

Hans concentrated on the sound of the motor and was proud of the fact that he hadn't caused it any stress. Another twenty minutes passed before the car stopped and his mask was removed. It was dark out now and Hans found himself on a gravel path with tall palms growing on either side. He was outside of San Remo, and at the end of the path he saw a low stone house where bright lights shone from behind glass doors.

"Go inside," said Duby. "Someone is expecting you."

"You're not coming?"

"We're not invited," was the sour reply. "Probably because we don't get along so well with Dordoni's men."

Hans walked up to the glass doors, which were opened for him by a man in a white suit, who searched him and then escorted him down a long corridor. Together they descended a flight of stairs and Hans realized that the house must be built on a hill or a large outcropping of rock.

At the back of the house were several stories situated against a slope.

A door of thick, dark wood opened into a spacious room with chandeliers hanging from the high, vaulted ceiling and a floor of black stone. There were roulette tables, and along the entire back wall a walnut bar, all of which were crowded with men and women in expensive evening attire.

The door closed behind him and with his hands in the air and a smile on his swollen face, Andrea Carandini came up to him and embraced him. Hans felt the disgustingly greasy, short hair slide past his cheek as the man pushed himself against him and patted him on the shoulder.

"So there you are! I have already warned Carlo Dordoni about you. He is my dearest friend, but he attaches no value to anything I have told him. He says that you will undoubtedly win a bit, but you will not earn a fortune here."

He shook his hand once more and remained standing there smiling.

"We're all men of honor here, Winters! You get me this house, with everything in it, and I will reward you with the beautiful Louise Vernet. Dordoni will allow you to leave and always have nothing but the utmost respect for you, I guarantee it. He will want you to be his friend as much as I do, and we are already old friends, aren't we? Let that be so for always..."

Behind him a narrow, little man loomed up, wearing a suit the trousers of which were too wide. Small brown eyes peered at Hans from under frowning eyebrows. His nose was twitching and a thin moustache danced up and down when he grinned. He made Hans think of a sly, little weasel as he shook hands with the man.

"This is Carlo Dordoni, the Ghost of Genoa," said Andrea in a jovial tone. "If we were both hunters, I could say that his hunting ground adjoins mine. Carlo arranges his businesses without so much as creating a breeze. Which explains his nickname, The Ghost. Many people have done business with him without having actually met him, for Carlo knows very well the fine arts of manipulation and intrigue."

Dordoni showed no reaction to Carandini's introduction of him, and looking at Hans, said:

"Any friend of Andrea Cordoni is my friend as well. To keep the game honest for everyone, it has to be played at all the tables. Which means that you will have to switch tables from time to time."

"That's fine with me," said Hans and then turning to Andréa, added: "First I want to talk to Monaco."

"That goes without saying," replied the fat man. "It was promised to you through Pirenne, wasn't it? Come with me to the bar, we'll have a drink together and Louise will join us shortly. What an absurd idea of hers, by the way, to call herself Monaco all of a sudden!"

They walked slowly across the big room while Dordoni remained behind.

As they neared the bar, a place immediately opened up for them. Two men bowed courteously, took their glasses and moved away. One man in particular remained at the bar seeing to it that everyone kept a respectful distance from Hans and Carandini. Andrea paid attention to no one and talked to his guest.

"I have known Flamel for a long time. He had just returned from a long journey, to South America I believe, and he immediately started to gamble. That's how he mainly filled his pockets, but he was also an inspired artist. As a matter of fact, I have some paintings hanging on my walls at home that I once bought from him. What can I offer you to drink, Hans? The wine cellar here is very good and after this place, and everything in it, belongs to me, I'm going to take the best bottles with me!"

Carandini did not say a single word about the incident outside Nice, when Hans had dragged him out of the red Peugeot so violently. Instead, he drank to Hans' health and kept on talking. He did, however, bring up the subject of Hans' meeting with Minor.

"That incredible strength in your hand! Minor understands as little about it as I do. How is it possible that a slender young man like yourself can have so much power? You also healed Louise's face very mystically. You and Flamel have something that is very special. Join me, Hans, and you and I will own the world.....together!"

He smiled again, but Hans remained serious.

"I want to speak with Louise. Right now!"

Carandini said something in Italian to the bartender, and Hans correctly took it to mean that he go get Louise. He watched as the man walked to the corner of the bar and opened a door in a panelled wall. Monaco appeared, looked around, immediately saw Hans and ran to him. She was wearing a long, tight dress that hugged her sensuous body. She threw her arms around him and kissed him passionately.

"Give me a straight answer," said Hans. "Would you prefer to stay here with Carandini or are you going to come with me?"

Her black eyes shone like embers in her sunburned face.

"I will come with you!"

"Do you have all your papers with you?"

"Here in my handbag."

"Good. From now on, stay close to me. Don't let anybody get you away from my side. Do you understand me?"

"If it were up to me, I would never let go of you again," she said and slipped her hand under his arm.

"Shall we begin then?" asked Carandini.

They walked up to a gaming that was immediately cleared for them and Hans sat down with Monaco to his left and Carandini to his right. Across from him sat the Ghost of Genoa accompanied by a blonde woman wearing a dress of green silk, and a middle aged man with thick dark hair that was just beginning to turn gray at the sides.

"Magdalena Cantone and Marco Bottino," Dordoni said in the way of an introduction. "They enjoy playing here with us and are extremely curious about how our honored guest, Mr. Carandini's Dutch friend will do. We all agree that there will be no limit on the wagers and that I reserve the right to change the croupier or table without warning, correct? . Earlier this evening I gave Carandini the opportunity to inspect all the roulette tables, and he has publicly declared that they are in perfect order. I am a hospitable man and wish everyone as much luck as possible. Andrea is also a hospitable man, who has allowed me to operate a casino in his territory, without ever having been unkind or threatening to me. He has made me a good offer for this house, but it just was not good enough, and now he hopes to influence the hand of fate by inviting his new friend to join in the game. I bid you much success..."

Carandini was brought a small fortune in chips, Magdalena Cantone and Marco Bottino already had theirs. A croupier gave the gathered players a friendly greeting and asked if all were ready to begin. Carandini pulled a stack of chips closer to him, and also gave a small stack to Monaco.

Meanwhile, Hans had been thinking things over and taking stock of the current situation. He had before him two men, Andrea Carandini and Carlo Dordoni, who had their own laws within the legal system, and lived in their own world within normal society. Their peculiar scales were held in balance by pride and honor on one side and ruthless extortion and robbery on the other side. This illegal casino was nothing more than provocation by Dordoni, who waited calmly to see what Carandini was going to do about it. It was strictly against the rules of the underworld to operate on other man's territory, and perhaps that is also why it was so it was inviting.

Hans understood that Dordoni was the more dangerous of the two men at this moment. This was still his house, and his men could produce their weapons at the snap of a finger. He had been searched and he was certain that

Carandini was not armed. Outside however, Duby and Minor were waiting, and it wouldn't surprise him at all if they should try to overpower him when he left with Monaco. It seemed to him like the best idea was to get Dordoni on his side, although that would become more and more difficult as he began to pile up the winnings shortly. Dordoni on the other hand, naturally hoped that he would gamble away much of Carandini's money here...

At the beginning he played calmly and did not wager too high. He watched what the others did, to see if they were playing themselves or following him. After about thirty minutes all he had accomplished was lose a small amount.

If this was making Carandini nervous, he did not show it.

Hans began to become aware of a feeling of power that was growing inside of him. He was happy that Monaco was sitting beside him alive and well. She was very quiet tonight, perhaps she was afraid of disturbing his concentration, but every now and then she gently touched his hand, or gazed at him hard enough until he felt her eyes on him and he turned to look at her.

One time, during a meditation session in the Garden, Flamel had said to him:

"More and more, you are going to be using a larger percentage of your brain capacity. The totality of power lies in the maturing mental faculties."

He knew that as fact now, and it made him feel calm and confident without being reckless.

The stakes got progressively higher and he was certain that he heard Carandini heave a sigh of relief when he finally pulled in some big pots.

"Let's go to another table," decided Dordoni. "And I want another croupier."

He stood up and headed towards another table, followed by the man and the woman. Carandini seized this opportunity to quickly have a word with Winters.

"If we continue this way, everything will go fine," he said. "Eventually he will begin to panic. Listen, Winters, Louise is all yours, but please don't leave as soon as this is over. I want to invite you up to my estate so we can talk."

Hans thought about the hotel in Nice, where Duby had a man with a gun waiting for him. Monaco snorted with disdain and scorn in Carandini's direction when he offered her up like property in a trade, and it made her cling to Hans' arm all the more tightly.

During the game at the roulette table, no one had bothered the small company and now, as they went to another table, the guests who were playing there quickly got up and made room for them. Again Hans played slowly and calmly, winning a lot and then losing a little and his capital was beginning to grow substantially. They changed tables again, and again, and again. The tables had all been used several times each, and the Ghost of Genoa had begun to feel a bit warm and was tugging at his moustache. He talked in whispering tones to Magdalena Cantone and Marco Bottino, and exchanged glances of gloom with the croupiers. He even had the tables where they had previously played examined by his most trusted employees.

The atmosphere began to get hostile, and Hans noticed that most of the guests had disappeared. The remaining tables were empty, but a few people were still hanging out at the bar where they stood and stared at the table where Hans was consistently winning greater amounts all the time. Some men entered the room now and led the last guests towards the exit, then returned and fanned out around the room. Dordoni already knew that he was not going to be able any to pay Hans, and there was nothing he could do about it. No one could figure out how the Dutchman was managing to be so successful. Dordoni's sense of honor was strong though, and he tried to keep a stoic face. He could murder Carandini on the spot and put enough pressure on Hans until he spilled his secrets. For that end he would gladly cast his honor aside, but there were too many people from their underworld who knew that Carandini was here tonight. To kill him in a cowardly way could change powerful mighty friends into terrible enemies. Even the Ghost of Genoa had to live within the rules of this world. He had never considered that a player might be able to get lady luck on his side and keep her there, he had thought from the outset that Carandini would be the big loser this night.

Sitting at a table in the middle of the room, he finally abandoned all hope.

The money he would have to pay out, went far beyond the value of his house. At this moment it was impossible for him to get that much money together. He managed to catch Hans' eye just at the moment all the others were watching the brilliantly shining ball spin around the wheel. He opened his jacket slightly and Hans saw a revolver in a shoulder holster. The man nodded menacingly in his direction and raised a forefinger.

To his surprise, Hans nodded back at him and winked.

"Do you think this is enough yet?" he asked Carandini.

"I would think so, yes," grinned the fat man who was sitting to his left.

"Or maybe my friend Carlo prefers to go on? Well, well, Carlo, we will not make it too difficult for you. You simply hand the house over to me, with everything in it, and then we'll have another glass of that excellent wine that you've been pouring tonight. The only difference will be, of course, that it is now my wine. If you have a problem with that, Hans of course, can continue playing. Maybe he'll lose, but I think it's more likely that he will keep on winning."

Carlo consulted with Magdalena and Marco. They did not seem to be in agreement, and Andrea leaned back in his chair trying to hear what they were saying.

Now Hans leaned forward and said:

"Let's finish this affair once and for all, he is in too deep. Suggest to him that he spin the wheel himself and I will bet only one chip, not on a color, but on a number. That will give him a chance, no? If the ball lands on another number, he will be free of any debt to me. If it lands on my number however, the debt will be doubled. As the Americans say, double or nothing. Imagine if you were he, if you take the chance and lose you will be in real trouble. He will be in your debt for a long, long time if he indeed does lose..."

Magdalena Cantone spoke now for the first time that evening:

"There is no deceit or cheating here," she said with a hint of astonishment in her voice. "Both Marco and I are both well-seasoned in the gambling business and we don't understand a thing that was going on here..."

The Ghost of Genoa remained silent, while behind him another table was checked out.

"A brand new roulette wheel," said Magdalena, pointing a thumb behind her.

"Absolutely nothing can be wrong with it. If you want to go on, we'd better go sit there."

"Who is going to guarantee me that no one messed about with it?" Andrea lashed out. "What are all those men doing there?"

"That will be not a problem at all," said Hans in a soft voice, pronouncing every word slowly and clearly.

"One final game," said Andrea. "Carlo... make the spin yourself and throw the ball. My friend here will put a single chip on a number. Double payment if he wins and you owe me nothing if he loses. So, I give you one last honest chance! Otherwise I want my money now, and quickly."

When the Ghost and Hans looked at each other, they showed no sign of what they were thinking. Andrea rose and took Hans and Monaco with him to the other table. Monaco revealed the fact that she was a bundle of nerves by pinching Hans arm quite hard.

A few moments later they all sat down at the table again as Carlo Dordoni opted for one last game. He stood up and took a practice spin on the wheel to show that it was indeed working correctly.

"Do you want to inspect it?" he asked. "You will see that no one has been messing around with it."

"No need for that," said Carandini. "All I want is for you to say out loud, once more, what is going to happen."

"All right. I will make the spin and let the ball drop. But I want Winters to place his chip on a number within five seconds and his choice will be a final choice. He is not allowed to move the chip, nor even touch it again. If his number falls, I double the winnings. If it is another number, then we are even. That is the way it will be. I will keep my promise."

"It's a deal then," said Carandini.

Dordoni did not wait long. He made the play and watched as the ball dropped and bounced around from side to side. Everyone at the table silently counted out those five long seconds. After the third second, Hans placed his chip on number six as Magdalena stared up at one of the chandeliers, and Marco made an in-depth study of his fingers drumming on the table top. Monaco sat as still as a corpse. Carandini counted on the fact that Hans had come for Monaco and not to cause trouble. He could have stopped after winning a fortune, but now he was about to double it and so ensure himself of Carandini's eternal gratitude.

The ball stopped as the wheel continued spinning.

"Twelve," the Ghost of Genoa almost religiously and then burst out laughing.

"At least he doubled his six..."

Hans stretched out his left hand and grabbed the fat, sweaty neck of Carandini. The Italian screamed in pain and tried to break free as he caught hold of Hans' wrist with both hands. Hans, his arm still outstretched, stood up, dragging Carandini to his feet like a limp puppet. He realized that Hans was strong enough to break his neck, just as he had previously crushed Minor's hand. Without any difficulty, he dragged the fat man along through the room.

"Tell Dordoni that no one better pull a weapon," he warned. "Or else it is over and done for you!"

"No weapons!" whined the man. "Please, no weapons!"

Obviously, there was no one brave, or stupid enough, to draw a revolver. And Dordoni kept his jacket closed. Hans Winters had not only helped him financially, but now he had also given him a reason for not intervening.

There was nobody who could accuse him later of not rushing to Carandini's rescue; it had been him, after all, who had shouted that no weapons should be used. Monaco stayed as close to Hans as possible. He didn't search around for an escape route, but boldly exited exactly as he had entered.

There was no one around to stop him. He glanced behind him and saw, at the end of the corridor, a narrow, weasel-head clearly visible in the light of a glaring bulb..... the Ghost of Genoa. He bowed slightly to Hans and then disappeared behind the door of his clandestine casino.

"Stay right behind me!" Hans warned Monaco.

He pushed the glass doors open and went outside, pushing the heavy, sobbing man out in front of him. Carandini's feet dragged over the gravel path as he held his trembling hands in the air as if he was searching for his way in complete darkness.

Minor, who was standing in the middle of the path with a revolver in his hand, stepped aside. There were cars parked everywhere and Duby popped up from behind a big sedan. Headlights went on and car doors opened all around them. Carandini's men had been all set to take over the casino.

"If anything happens, and I mean anything at all Carandini, I will break your neck and tear your head off," said Hans calmly. "I will be standing here holding only your head and your fat body will be on the gravel. You'd better give clear instructions to your men."

"Let us through!" he yelled, his voice firm and convincing. "Do as I tell you!"

"A bullet may kill me," continued Hans, "but I will stay strong long enough to hear you scream goodbye to life as well,"

Duby stopped a man who was about to draw a weapon. Minor had already put his pistol down. Hans saw the station wagon with the tinted windows and opened the door. He pushed the man inside and made him crawl over the gearshift to the passenger seat. Monaco was already sitting in the back seat slumped low.

"If I see that I'm being followed, Carandini is dead," he said loudly. "Bring me the keys, Duby..."

Duby came running up to him, but stopped a safe distance away, and threw the keys to him. Hans caught them, slid behind the wheel and started the car.

"Do you know the way, Hans?" asked Monaco.

Her voice was clear. He couldn't remember ever having heard a more beautiful voice.

"Blindfolded!" he answered, and that was no lie.

Chapter 6: The Table of the Brotherhood

Hans was feeling quite satisfied with himself. He was satisfied with his awareness that if he had wanted to, he could have used his powers to bring death and destruction to everyone in the casino and, if he had so desired, he have brought the entire building to the ground.

He was also satisfied though with the fact that he had been able to control himself. The man beside him sat deathly still and stared straight in front of him.

He did not even dare slide his hand over his throbbing, bruised neck.

But Hans was most happy with the knowledge that Monaco was sitting in the back seat and that she had left it up to him where to go. He realized that she could have just as well reacted entirely different. If she had actually been working with Carandini, and their intention had only been to bring the Ghost of Genoa to financial ruin, she now had the opportunity to put a revolver to his head and force him to stop.

He no longer had any doubts that she had chosen him.

He drove through San Remo and stopped not far from the coast.

Earlier, he had parked his old car somewhere in the vicinity. He got out, leaving the motor running, and Monaco followed him. Carandini, his face contorted with pain, slid behind the wheel while Hans, still holding the door open, stooped and said:

"I see you have already grasped the situation. You can drive yourself back and I hope we never meet again..."

Carandini looked at him out of the corner of his eye, since he dare not turn his head. His voice was controlled, but full of fear and pain when he spoke.

"But we will meet again, no doubt about that. You were searching for Flamel and that indicates to me that you must have similar backgrounds. We originally began tracking you because you never lost in the casinos. Believe it or not... Flamel once came searching for me. You ask him sometimes about Paolo. Paolo Carandini."

"Your father?" guessed Hans.

"It goes farther back in history than that," said Carandini.

As he drove away he reached for the door and closed it with a bang, all the while staring straight ahead of him, his aching neck too painful to turn. Hans turned to Monaco and pulled her towards him. Just as he was about to kiss her, she began to sob and laid her head against his chest.

"I thought they were going to kill me when I was thrown into the trunk of that car," she said softly. "But Carandini didn't have to send me to hell for to me experience what goes on down there... a life with Carandini is hell on earth itself!"

Hans put his arm around her as they walked to his car. The sea was a deeper black than the starlit sky above it. The old car started with difficulty, and Hans drove along the coast road that led to Genoa. But he did not want to drive directly there. First he wanted to find a dark beach where he could stop and make love to Monaco. After that he would find a place somewhere where they could spend the night. Afterwards, they found that no hotel had any rooms, so they decided to sleep in the car. The next day he would drive on to Austria. Savona was not far away and from there they could drive inland to Milan. From there he could go to Bolzano and then drive to the Austrian Innsbruck. He also considered travelling first through part of Switzerland and then on to Austria. No matter what, he was going to do it slow and easy so that he could be alone with Monaco for as long as possible.

It would be no problem reaching Helgen quickly, but he preferred roaming around for two or three days.

Monaco leaned against him and told him about how Duby and Minor had suddenly appeared in their hotel room the night he went to the theatre. He her shiver every now and then and occasionally a sob ended her sentences. He parked in an inconspicuous spot, where there was an easily accessible beach on the other side of the road. He took out his cell phone, dialled a number, and almost immediately heard the voice of Flamel.

"Hans, how are you? Where are you?"

"Everything is all right," he reassured him.

He told him, short and to the point, how he had gotten Monaco out of the house and then asked:

"What's the story with Paolo Carandini?"

It seemed to him that Flamel answered immediately and with no surprise.

"Did Andrea mention him?"

"Yes. But he did not go into any detail. Apparently you once visited Andrea and I am supposed to assume that you know something about Paolo."

"That's correct. You know that I was interested in the Brotherhood. Paolo Carandini belonged to the Austrian Twentiers, which included people from Germany, Austria, Switzerland, France, Italy and other parts of the world."

"I thought they all vanished into thin air?"

"That was what everyone thought for a long time. I am sorry that I did not bring this up earlier, Hans. Suddenly the names of these men turned up in the news again. He was the only Twentier who was ever found again. Of course, however, that was of great importance. He was living in retirement somewhere in Italy when they discovered him, and everyone wanted to ask him a thousand questions. Unfortunately, he did not seem to be able to remember anything, or perhaps he was simply playing dumb. I read about him in a library in Italy, where I was sifting through some old newspapers, which is something I liked to do wherever I went. I managed to locate Andrea Carandini, his great-grandson and he was willing to sell me some manuscripts that had belonged to the Twentiers. I will tell you more about that later. Up until now it has been a puzzle why this man was found, while the whereabouts of all the other members of the Brotherhood has remained a mystery."

"I'm coming to Helgen," said Hans. "When do you leave?"

"We have decided to leave early tomorrow morning."

"Well, you can expect me in a couple of days. Till then, my friend."

"Till then," answered Flamel's cheerful voice.

"And say hello to Monaco for me!"

On the cool sand of the dark beach, Hans and Monaco again celebrated their reunion. She was impetuous and fierce, finally exhausting herself and asking for a bit of rest.

"This is not the way it's supposed to be at all," she said. "You should be the first one to say that's enough."

They then spent some time telling each other what had happened to them since they split up in Nice. Monaco listened with astonishment to the story of what he saw on the monitor in the van and only then did she understand that she had played a bizarre leading role in a movie that had been shown for Hans' eyes only.

Hans stood up and walked into the sea.

As soon as his feet were no longer touching the ground he began to swim. He turned over on his back and stared up at the sky. With his arms and legs outstretched he floated on the ocean admiring the twinkling stars. A feeling of faith and certainty took possession of his mind and soul. He knew now that he had the power to travel through the immense universe. It was a certainty that was no longer overshadowed by thoughts of impossibility. This knowledge gave him strength, and respite as well. Back on the beach, he dropped down next to Monaco and pushed himself heavily against her lush body and said:

"If it were up to me, we would stay here all night..."

After some time, and some delicious foreplay, they decided to go back to the car. They found a room in a little hotel, where they had been able to park the car out of sight. Monaco told him she hadn't had anything to eat all day and was starving. She had been much too nervous to even consider food. He had seen a coffee machine in the hallway and he offered to get her something hot to drink.

"I'll get you some coffee and then see if I can find someone who can tell me where I can still find something to eat."

She went out with him to the corridor, where he filled two plastic cups with coffee.

"Let's go back to the room," she said, looking up at him. "As long as I can have a big breakfast tomorrow, I'll be fine. I just don't want you to leave me alone now, I'm much too afraid for that."

Suddenly they both began to laugh. After swimming, Hans had put his damp clothes back on and now looked like a hobo. Monaco's dark brown hair was all tangled and her dress was rumpled. The two of them were quite a sight, undoubtedly they would have raised suspicions about their characters wherever they might have gone, looking the way they did. Back in the room Monaco became serious again. She stared at the floor, her long lashes covering her black eyes as she said:

"I understand that you have secrets you cannot share with me. You are a very special man and it is not for any small reason that someone like Carandini begs for a partnership between the two of you. Maybe one day I will find out what Flamel and you are actually chasing. Whatever it may be, I hope that we can stay together..."

"Of course we can," he said. "Why else would I have come for you?"

After about thirty minutes they went to bed. Monaco lay close against him and had soon fallen asleep, while Hans just lay there on his back and stared into the darkness.

He was indeed a special man, more than Monaco could ever suspect.

He felt like a figure from a fable that had come to life and dreamed of helping mankind escape from his terrestrial shackles. The absolute freedom for a man to be able to do exactly as he pleased, whenever he pleased, was a collective desire, a dream stored within everyone's dream. It was a unanimous wish for omnipotence, an aim at perfection. How had Flamel put it when he met him for the first time?

"We look up at the unreachable above our heads and create a world of gods. Like people drowning, we all sit together on a raft knowing that death is waiting for us as soon as we jump off. But you and I can escape, Hans..."

Lost in thought, he only realized that he was crying when he felt the tears trickle down his cheeks. From very far away, from out of a part of his mind where the old instincts still lived and moved, the fright was creeping up on him. He had almost forgotten that he could be afraid, and now these feelings threatened to be known again, and he didn't know how to deal with them.

"But you and I can escape..."

Then he recalled the feeling that he had experienced once before, when Flamel had told him in the car on their way to the sea, about the message scratched in stone that someone left behind a million years or more ago. He forced himself to be calm and tried to believe that the Observator was right when he proclaimed that everything went according to the laws of nature.

"This endless, immense universe is composed of elements which we know most of. What these elements are capable of depends on the circumstances. There is darkness, there is a void, and there is light and life. What has crept inside of you is unique here, but elsewhere in the universe it is undoubtedly something that is very common. Sooner or later we will discover what it is and where it comes from."

He lay there and listened to Monaco's quiet breathing until sleep also came looking for him.

For the next week they took short car trips and long walks through Italy, Switzerland and Austria. On the back seat of the car the new clothes that they bought in each town was piling up and the trunk was full of new books.

Hans had finally parted with his old, worn rucksack, leaving it behind in the vestibule of a restaurant.

On the seventh day, they followed the course of a tributary river of the Danube, which was bordered with pride by soaring mountains on either side of which the snow topped peaks partially disappeared behind the gray veil of low clouds. The river, that could turn into a raging torrent rage when the snow melted and the rains came, was no more than a sleepy little stream now only a few feet wide, and ran through a bed of stones the size of men's fists and heads.

Hans had never been in this part of the Alps before, but he knew the direction to Helgen. To reach the little village, he had to take a road that led high up into the mountains. Grimly he thought that perhaps he would simply drive to Holland, where he and Monaco could live for many years to come on the money he had won in the casinos and had transferred to his bank there.

But he knew that there could be no thought of that; he was very well aware that he would not be able to live a quiet, sedentary life while his future was in Helgen.

He had taken the necessary turn and drove away from the river, following a winding road up into the majestic mountains.

"We're almost there," he sighed heavily. "These are the last few miles..."

He had to downshift gears often to force his old, overloaded car upwards. Thick black smoke poured out of the exhaust pipe as the motor labored greatly. Steep rocks hindered their view most of the way, until a final bend in the road was taken and green meadows spread before their eyes that where edged by pine forests at their highest parts.

Helgen consisted mainly of a little church, a couple of dozen houses, a food shop, a Gasthof with a restaurant, and a few farms scattered around the outskirts of town.

The car climbed on.

"Quite a difference from the bustle of the Riviera," said Hans. "Do you think you can get used to this?"

"Not if I were here alone. With you by my side it will not be a problem though," answered Monaco.

After having driven along for about ten more minutes, Hans brought the car to a halt in front of a high wooden fence. They got out and peering over it, saw a paved path split a grassy hill sloping two. At various spots on the hillock, like islands in the middle of a green sea, large, barren masses of rocks were visible. The path led to a house four stories with a pointed roof, white plaster walls and wooden balconies that ran along the entire length. It was built with its back to the slope and on the right side was a broad stone staircase. Around the house were some outer buildings, a few wooden shacks, and a couple of large barns.

The whole scene gave Hans and Monaco the impression of a small village, but they saw no people, and there were no cars parked anywhere. Behind the buildings the meadow was bordered by a dark pine forest and way above them high were visible the white, serrated tops of the mountains.

"So, this is where Flamel will teach you everything an illusionist needs to know so that you can perform with him next season," remarked Monaco.

"Something like that," thought Hans thought, but only responded with slight nod.

From behind the house a man appeared, who raised his hand as he came down the stairs. It was Augustin Flamel.

He walked down the long path and opened the gate for them.

"Welcome to Helgen," he said.

He looked at Monaco and immediately understood why Hans had gone through all that trouble to take her away from Carandini.

Hans and Monaco moved into a large suite on the second floor and were very soon settled in. Mireille Robin took Monaco along with her to buy furniture and to show her around the area.

Taking a tour of the buildings taught them little more about the Twentiers than they had already known, since very little evidence of their time there was left. Flamel seemed to have had almost everything completely rebuilt. It had cost him a fortune to but the place and he had employed an army of craftsmen to do the renovations. He brought Hans to a stone building that was elevated high up against a slope. From a small square foyer by way of a steep ladder, one could reach a large space under the roof that was divided into five rooms. In one of those rooms they met the Observator who was accompanied by two men whom Hans had never seen before. They were introduced to him as Jack Doyle, a psychologist from New York, and Phil Wayne, a biologist from Boston. Sitting on a low dresser was a square terrarium constructed of thick glass, its bottom covered with a layer of mold in which some plants were growing. Philippe Mundy stood up and pulled Hans over to the tank, which was sealed with a metal cover.

"Look here, Hans, right now it is floating above that orange flower there..."

Hans leaned closer with his hands on his knees and his nose almost touching the glass.

The little creature did indeed bear a remarkable resemblance to a pin. It was a dark little pellet with a needle-shaped back. It had neither wings nor legs, and no noticeable eyes or antennae, but still it made Hans immediately think of an insect.

"I took hold of it without thinking that I might get stung," said the Observator. "It doesn't seem to be able to escape from the terrarium."

Phil Wayne gave an indication that he had been informed about all facts, when he said:

"It is impossible to tell whether or not it has the ability to sting, but it might possibly be more poisonous than a snake. It would be of great importance if we knew for sure if it can spread diseases. After all, something that is not of this earth could be an enormous danger."

Then, turning to Flamel, he said:

"Your trips could cause unimaginable disasters! Who knows what else you might bring back with you from other worlds. At least we are able to see this little creature... something we cannot see is much more dangerous..."

The little creature hung in the air motionless as Mundy handed Hans a magnifying glass.

"Sometimes it whizzes back and forth with incredible speed. Now you have a chance to study it at your leisure. It is a unique specimen! It had nestled itself in Flamel's long hair."

The spherical front was covered with a transparent outer rim that shone like the pupil of an eye.

As the Observator had already told him, there was an amber-colored substance moving beneath it in which black spots were visible. The back part was a shining steel blue color with bits of yellow throughout it that seemed to radiate light. Hans automatically pulled back when the little creature suddenly moved.

First it moved straight forward and then went curved through the air, but without, for example, the vibrating movements such as a dragonfly would make. In the back of the terrarium stood little pots filled with different liquids and solids.

The Observator said that he had never seen the little creature eat or drink.

"It probably doesn't even have a mouth. Maybe it is not able to feed itself, maybe it will be dead tomorrow. Or perhaps it will never die at all."

The room was full of equipment, including a special cover for the glass terrarium on which small, robot-like arms with fine clips were attached that were able to grab hold of the little creature.

After Flamel and Winters had left the room and were standing alone on the landing, Flamel pointed to a door.

"That door will remain locked to you. In there are the drawings that I made after my I returned from my journeys. They are exceptionally well detailed and we will compare them with to the drawings you will be making."

They went down a flight of stairs at the side of the landing, followed by Mundy, Doyle and Wayne. Hans knew that they were very curious about him and had been looking forward to meeting him. Apparently he was now the subject of their studies.

On the ground floor was a gigantic room, in which the only furniture was a table about fifteen feet long and nine feet wide. The top of this table was over one feet thick and stood on four solid legs.

"No one was able to remove this table," said Flamel. "At this table, the Twentiers had all sat together. In order to get this table out of here someone would have had to first pull the front wall down, but then there is yet another obstacle. It seems that the legs are anchored right into the rock floor. It is impossible to move it from where it stands. There are some grooves in the legs that look like handgrips, but when Mundy tried, along with three other men, to lift the table up, it simply could not be moved at all. This room could not have been used for painting or drawing, for not enough sunlight gets in. Come, let me show you what did go on in here..."

In a corner of the house there was a room, set apart from the others, built entirely of brick. There was one window, a door, and the walls had been tiled. There was a steel frame bed and from the ceiling hung monitors and several pieces of scientific looking apparatus that Hans was not familiar with.

He was alone with Flamel now, the others having stayed behind in the big room. Flamel pointed at a circle that was scratched into the stone floor.

"Some believed that strange rituals were held in here. They say the table was a sacrificial altar and the circle had a magical connotation. I had the walls built up here myself. It was from this circle that I began and ended my journey. I believe that the Brotherhood of Helgen also used this spot as a point of departure. Whoever comes and goes from here now must remain in quarantine for some time. We can't be careful enough."

Flamel confided to him in a soft voice:

"Mundy is more or less in charge of all the people you see walking around here. We just have to assume that everyone can be trusted. John Doyle will talk to Monaco.

He discovers quickly whether or not someone is able to keep a secret. When you plan on taking a trip, I think that she should be completely informed about everything."

Hans nodded in agreement.

"I am very glad to hear that."

"It seems that over the course of time, I've become a local celebrity of sorts. If the police ever raid the house, everyone here can explain that we are working on some new tricks for the act. All the equipment can be explained away as things that have to do with my magic shows. Being an illusionist, making things appear to be something which they are not is my business.....I have taken all possible precautions, there is nothing more I can do. Anyone can betray me. Monaco just as easily and quickly as Pirenne, but even my dear friend and confidante Mundy could get into a quarrel with me and decide to sell his stories to the world."

This having been said, they returned to the big room, and Hans looked around. The emptiness impressed him even more now, because he was able to imagine how lively it must have been when the Brotherhood was in residence here. How was the room decorated then? What did they do at that big table? He walked up to it and rapped on it with his knuckles. It responded with a dead sound that echoed throughout all the corners of the vast room.

"It's oak," said the Observator. "It seems that the various parts have been connected to one another without the use of joints and are probably connected on the inside with wooden pins. I would do anything to be able to hear all that was discussed in here. There are pictures from that time, but as far as I know, not a single one exists from this room."

Hans bent down and ran his hand over a groove on one of the table legs. He summoned up all his strength, but Flamel stood there shaking his head.

"Believe me, I've already tried that."

"C'mon Augustin, we are stronger than four ordinary men put together," laughed Hans. "Go stand on the other side."

Flamel went to the other side of the table and grasped one of the indentations in the leg. Both men used all their strength in a coordinated effort, but were unable to budge the table.

"Just give it up," smiled Flamel.

Hans straightened his back and touched the table top. He gently let his hands slide along the surface of this enigmatic piece of furniture until they came to rest underneath it. Bracing himself he gave a tug and much to his surprise, it moved. He had managed to lift the top a little bit, but the legs remained on the floor.

"Did you see that?" he cried. "The grips in the legs are only meant as a distraction. The legs are solid as a rock, but apparently the top can be removed, despite its weight. Help me one more time, Augustin..."

Facing each other from opposite sides of the table, they began to heave. The effort required all of their combined strength, but they finally succeeded in pulling the table top loose from its supports. The moment they put it down on the stone floor, they heard shouts of surprise from the other three men in attendance. For their part, they were glad to be present at what possibly was a very significant moment in their quest for further knowledge into the history of the Twentiers. A few moments later the five of them found themselves staring at a work of art of unequalled beauty.

"The motif of the Brotherhood of Helgen appears yet again," said the Observator in a solemn voice, and laughing nervously, he added:

"If the person who sold the ground and buildings had known about this, Augustin, he would have asked you for double the price....or sawed the legs off and taken this part with him."

What they saw was a wooden tray, approximately forty five square feet, with thick, raised edges. The tray itself was made of dark oak, and was covered with the finest etchings of light brown.

The carvings depicted multitudes of Celts and Germans leaving their homelands and marching on Rome!

There were thousands of miniatures that stood on little square pedestals, and all placed so close to each other that it looked from a distance as if they were all made from the same massive piece of wood. There were gods and goddesses on horseback and on foot, which stood slightly taller than the common folk. Rome was represented as a modest collection of temples and palaces, with a building atop a hill where the advancing hoard was confronting the Romans.

t was the temple of Janus, where Mercury bowed and gestured invitingly to the gate with his hands outstretched and palms upward. Janus was not alone however....he was accompanied by Vulcan, Apollo, Venus, Vesta and Diana. Jupiter, the father of both gods and men alike, stood behind the temple with and his hands reaching skywards.

Belenus, Artio, Lenis, Taranis, Wodan, Tiwaz, Donar and Freyja approached, each with sharply carved details, determined to lead the tribes of Celts and Germans up to the foot of the temple.

Buildings, figures, trees, bushes, animals, gods and goddesses all together formed a puzzle, the pieces of which fit perfectly into one another. The simple German foot soldiers were finished with just as much pride and dignity as the Roman legions. The head of Tiwaz, the war god, displayed a bloodthirsty combativeness. Belenus, the Celtic sun god, radiated a noble pride, as he sat straight up on his charging steed. Armed men waded through a brook, seeming to astonish onlookers as the water splashed. It was Philippe Mundy who was first able to say something.

"Month after month, probably year after year, the members of the Brotherhood sat in this room and discussed the affairs that occupied their minds, and all the while their hands were busy as each one of them carved his part of this work of art."

He stopped talking, raised his black eyebrows, and pulled at the short curls of his beard.

He looked out of the corner of his eye at Hans as he heard him say with a chuckle:

"A theory..."

"Yes. A theory I can't even finish. They sat here, talked, and carved their pieces of art..."

Jack Doyle said softly:

"I have never seen anything as impressive....or as mysterious. Every figure is completely different, and despite the fact that each one is so tiny, they all have their own personalities."

He circled the table, slightly stooped, as the others stepped back to let him pass.

"The Twentier's monument," proclaimed Phil Wayne. "So beautiful, and so valuable, that they hid it from the outside world. When the table top is in place all you see is an oversized table that is not particularly attractive. And when if anyone tries to move it they are quickly discouraged by its immobility."

Flamel had not spoken a word all this time, he just stood there staring, with his hands behind his back and slightly bent forward, as if bowing in admiration to the work of the Brotherhood. He studied the rows of Celts and Germans, the proud heads of the gods. He marvelled at the throngs of Romans who crowded the palaces and temples all the way up to the shrine of Janus, where they met the invaders who had gathered there. Celtic warriors on their knees worshipped Mercury as he invited them inside. Their German brothers stood behind them shoulder to shoulder trying to bring the wild horde to a standstill.

In its entirety, the work was such overwhelming beauty that it was difficult to turn one's head away once they had started looking at it.

"We better cover it again," Flamel said. "It must be quite a long time since this tableau has been exposed to the light."

The Observator and the two Americans tried to lift it several times but their efforts were in vain. Augustin pointed out a score of oddly placed round holes in the back of one of the Roman buildings. He put a finger in one and figured it was to be a few inches deep.

"Probably made with a gimlet, but what do you think they are for?"

"No idea," said Hans. "No idea at all..."

Then the two of them walked over to the table top, lifted it up and replaced with no problem whatsoever.

Flamel decided to express his opinion about the work of art:

"This proves the genius of the Brotherhood of Helgen."

Quietly, and reverently, the five men left the room, as if they had just placed a headstone on the grave of a loved one.

Flamel was on friendly terms with the inhabitants of the town of Helgen. Being world-renowned, he was treated with high regard by the townspeople whenever he did some of his tricks in the restaurant, where he often had dinner with Mireille, the Observator and his wife Simone, Hans and Monaco. He was also a popular figure around town because in his restoration of the buildings of the Brotherhood to all their former glory he had employed as many workmen as possible from the neighborhood.

He and Hans would stop at the restaurant for a drink after they went jogging which was an integral part of the conditioning. The townsfolk understood that Hans was Augustin's new partner who would be performing with him. Monaco was getting along very well with Mireille and Simone, and she loved to drive them around town in the big jeep whenever they went out shopping.

The Observator was an excellent cook who loved to prepare meals for everyone. The people who had gathered around Flamel kept quiet and to themselves for the most part, and even parked their cars in a wooden barn behind the house, avoiding the village. When they wanted to relax, they took long walks through the mountains and in the woods, using a path that ran up at the back of the house.

Augustin instructed Hans for a month until he learned to control the powers that had penetrated his body and mind. It was imperative that he learned how to use them, and master them, so that he could steer them in the right direction. Hours of meditation preceded fierce outbursts of energy. Making objects disappear remained a frightful event for him, for although he was able to do it without too much effort, it seemed so dangerous and unreal all at the same time, that he saw it as something terribly mortifying.

All the Observator would say about it was that he could not fathom how it was accomplished and that it was an unknown phenomenon. Jack Doyle worked with him, and on him, insisting that develop his gifts.

"As long as you don't abuse it, you can continue experimenting without problems," he said. "You serve science, Hans. The exercises are good, for when an action has become a habit, you will have learned to live with it, and then the fear will be gone."

Standing in the riverbed outside of Helgen he made stones disappear, while Mundy, Wayne and others tried to gauge on various equipment, what exactly it was that happened when he utilized his powers.

Everyday Hans concentrated on what the Observator had called the geometric line that was endless and had no substance. Hans called it the "Long Zero", and controlled it more and more until he was able to knit it all into a ball of energy. Every time he got the feeling of floating away from where he was sitting, he allowed the energy to escape by breathing out slow and but strong.

The psychologist, Jack Wayne, proved to be right. By practicing, Hans became reconciled to the fact that he had changed and he was more content with himself and the results he achieved. He was a quick, bright student because he dared to give himself up to the Long Zero.

At the end of one month, Flamel said:

"There is nothing else I can teach you, my friend. You have become my equal."

Now it was time to tell Monaco about everything. Mireille vouched for Monaco's integrity, and Jock Doyle declared that she was an extremely intelligent woman who had decided on a life with Hans Winters and had cut herself loose from Andrea Carandini.

It was decided that Hans Winters would make his first journey alone. The Observator said it as plainly as anyone could have:

"If Flamel goes with you and neither one of you returns, all our experiments are finished..."

That night, Hans took Monaco into Helgen for dinner at the restaurant. As they walked home, they took a detour through the beautiful alpine surroundings, watching the sun sink behind the mountaintops giving a pink glow to the snow. They sat on a wooden bench at the side of a path and watched nature's beauty put itself to sleep for the evening. Hans took her hand and began to tell her about what was going on in his, and their, lives and Monaco listened without interrupting him.

She cried, dried her tears and then cried some more; it never occurring to her that all this might actually be true. She now understood the presence of so many people in Flamel's houses, it also explained the equipment that was everywhere, and it certainly explained the secrecy and the whispered conversations that never included he. It also explained the endless questions she was asked by Mireille and Jack.

It was dark when they finally continued on their way.

"This must be the most beautiful thing that a human being can experience," she said as they went through the gate and were walking up to the house. "But at the moment you disappear before my eyes, it will be a time for me that is full of great sadness.... and mortal fear..."

Chapter 7: The First Journey

There was nobody at home in the big house. And even though the lights outside were burning brightly, it was darkness that ruled behind the windows and in the halls. Hans, who had just come out, closed the door behind him and locked it. He and Monaco then went searching for the others, whom they finally found in the stone building that had its back to the slope. They were all gathered in the big room where the table of the Brotherhood stood.

Monaco was embraced by everyone upon her entrance...she was the last of the company to be initiated. Stefan Weckmann, a doctor who often went along with Hans and Augustin on their strolls through the surrounding area, expressed the feelings of all those present when he said:

"We now form the second Brotherhood of Helgen."

The Observator had deemed fit to involve him in all the events that took place around the compound, but his main task was to keep a watchful eye on the health of Hans and Augustin. He took their blood pressure on a daily basis, subjected them to a battery of tests, checked their hearts and lungs regularly, and used specially designed equipment to measure their brain functions while they were in the depths of their trances.

Right now though, he was helping the Observator and his wife pour wine for everybody. They all raised their glasses and looked at each other for a moment or two before emptying them. Hans and Augustin very carefully removed the table top, and everyone present gathered around the table of the Twentiers to have another look at the fabulous work of art. A lamp hung directly above the table shining like the morning sun on the wooden men and gods.

A silence enveloped the room that lasted for several minutes. During this time, Monaco was the only one who was not totally consumed by the carved images before her. Her eyes wandered around the room, first along the walls, and then finally coming to rest on the window of the smaller room that was adjoining the chamber which they were in. There, behind the door, was the circle scratched into the stone floor that marked the spot from whence Hans would begin his fantastic journey. Gazing at the brick wall, all she could think of was a prison cell.

Meanwhile, Flamel had produced two metallic pieces of artwork that had also been fashioned by the Brotherhood. He showed them to everyone, holding the narrowest part of each one between his thumb and forefinger. They appeared to be human figures which, although very much alike, were also very different from one another. One of the figures was narrow and round, while the other one was broad and more oval shaped.

Holding these two objects, he hovered around the holes that had been bored in the wood at the back of one of the Roman buildings.

"I suspected that these puppet-like objects will fit into these holes," he said.

With this statement he had captured everyone's attention.

"See, I'm right! This one fits in the third hole and the other goes quite nicely into eighteenth. I imagine that at one time there must have been twenty different cylinders standing here, although I cannot be sure what their function was. At any rate, we have apparently taken another small step in the right direction, and I'm asking all of you to think about it, and try to come up with an answer to this problem. It may very well be that there was some symbolic reason for putting the cylinders in this particular place. Here, hidden under this heavy table top, they remained invisible for such a long time, it is impossible to know now if they had perhaps been filled, like batteries with stored electric power, or perhaps with some energy that can be transferred into a human body... the way it has been instilled in Hans and myself."

"I think that this whole sculptured table was in some way a place where they worshipped and paid homage to these powers," said Mireille.

"Twenty cylinders in a row, some inches apart; on one hand they appear to be the pillars of a temple, but on the other hand, it does not seem that they should be a part of a work of art that is made entirely out of wood."

"A long, long time ago, another group of people also stood around this table," sighed Doctor Weckmann. "They were the artisans who created it, and they knew much more than we do. Let us raise our glasses and drink a toast to Ulrich von Drach, Martha Ritter, Wolfram Wikander, and all their companions in misfortune..."

Standing here and staring at the armies, temples and gods gathered on this field, it was more than likely that those former inhabitants also raised their glasses high in respect and admiration. And now, as the present day company drank to the memory of their predecessors, their thoughts were with the Twentiers. They found it strange indeed to think that they were standing on the exact same spot, separated only by time.

"Time is an invisible monster that leaves behind only some obscure tracks," philosophized Jack Doyle out loud. "We can only guess about what the motives of Von Drach and his people might have been."

This statement naturally provoked a discussion about the concept of time. The Observator not wanting to dissect modern thoughts on the subject instead put forth the proposition that it might be possible to step back in time, or perhaps into the future.

"If the monster Doyle refers to bites its own tail, it forms a circle," he said, "and you can step into the future and the past."

Shortly afterwards, Hans and Monaco returned to their own rooms and she went to bed immediately, saying she was very tired. Hans took the time to quickly read a book and then pour over some old manuscripts that Flamel had bought from Carandini that had belonged to his ancestor, Paolo. The bulk of the pages were filled with poems that had been written in ink with flowery lettering, and they described the heroic deeds of the Celtic, Germanic and Roman gods, with emphasis on Belenus, Artio, Tiwaz, Freyja, Jupiter and Juno. Mercury was not portrayed as the god of trade, with his purse and winged shoes, but rather as a friend of the armed throngs, who the caused the doors of the temple of Janus to be opened.

Janus was mentioned numerous times, being referred to as the two-faced god able to look into the future and the past. Another manuscript told a story that was reminiscent of the tale of Astra, although there were some striking differences sprinkled throughout. On many of the pages there were illustrations of enchanting beauty.

It was past midnight when Monaco came to get him. She took away his books and manuscripts, insisting that he get up and come back to bed with her, where she nestled lovingly against his steel body.

"I woke up with a start, frightened," she whispered. "So much has happened, and there is so much to think about. When do you begin your journey?"

"Doctor Weckman says I'm ready, that I'm strong and healthy, although he still cannot explain my exceptional strength. He says Flamel and I have muscles of steel. He had a talk with Philippe Mundy and they have decided that I can start whenever I please. My physical condition is as good as Flamel's, and he was able to leave and return again."

Hans suddenly began laughing and Monaco looked at him as if he were mad.

"What's the matter with you?"

"They say that I must not forget to shave before I go..."

"Why?"

"It's very important to the Observator, because he knows how fast my hair grows. He says that he can tell by the growth of my beard how long I have been away. When I feel as if I have been gone for a month, but his watch indicates only an hour elapsed, the length of the stubble on my face will be the barometer. So my skin may be smooth when I return, or I might have a month old beard, or something in between. Then again I may have a matted, gray, inextricable tangle of hair upon my face..."

Monaco was not laughing with him.

"I'm afraid," she said. "And I know that you are afraid, too. You can still say that you don't want to do this, you know."

He stroked her dark hair lovingly, like a father to a frightened child.

"I am not doing this for Flamel, or for the Observator! This is something I want to do for myself. It is not important whether or not I am afraid. I am obviously destined to solve some major mysteries."

She seemed to accept his answer and then she repeated her question:

"When do you start?"

His answer was short and followed by a sigh.

"Tomorrow..."

Hans sat cross-legged in the garden in front of the house. He had been meditating and was slowly coming back to reality.

Beside him sat the Observator, who waited patiently until Hans was approachable again. Hans leaned back slowly, watching the snow covered hilltops disappear beyond his visual field, and staring at the steel blue sky.

"There are still some things to discuss," said Philippe Mundy. "I will tell you one or two things, and then ask you some questions. It's possible that I might repeat myself, but it is my duty to point out the dangers again. Are you aware of the fact, Hans, that there is the chance that you might disappear for ever?"

"Yes."

"What is the most important thing for you to remember after you have arrived at another place in the universe?"

"I must return to the place where I first appeared."

"Why?"

"It is the safest way. The circle scratched into the rock points to a safe starting point, the one used by the Twentiers. We do not know what would happen if Flamel or I were to depart from another place. Where I appear, must also be from where I leave again."

"Right up until now, this is probably the most important rule. When you begin to experiment, there is a chance that you will arrive in places where you actually wouldn't be at all. Will you materialize in endless space? Do you disappear into the depths of an ocean, or will you end up being no more than a fleeting thought under a thick layer of rock? What will you do, after you have reached your goal? Tell me, step by step, how you must behave."

Hans folded his hands behind his head and the warm sun shone in his face. With his eyes closed, he began to recite what he had learned:

"This is what Flamel has to say about it based upon his own experiences. I have to stay calm and let a wave of thought wash over me. My brain will be filled with unexpected insights, and amazing ideas. When the mirages disappear, the emptiness will turn into panic. I must not resist however, I must wait until the storm in my head has spent itself. Then I must look around and observe my surroundings. I must imprint the land below my feet and the sky above me in my memory. When I look into space, I must remember the position of the stars, so that I can map it later and it can be compared to Flamel's drawings.

Then I must find out more about myself; can I see my hands and feet, am I breathing, can I stand upon my own two feet? It is not certain whether or not a long stay will cause brain damage due to the lack of oxygen, poisonous air, or extremes of temperature. Therefore it is necessary to return as quickly as possible."

The Observator nodded, ran his fingers through the tough curls of his beard, and looked at the fence at the end of the path. A white car had pulled up and stopped there, its motor growling softly. He expected a door to open and someone to step out and open the gate, ring the bell that was above the mailbox on a thick wooden pole.

"No more questions, Philippe?"

With his hands still folded behind his neck, Hans did a few quick sit-ups in the chair...sat the hard muscles of his belly strained. He felt fit and ready for the journey.

"Why is that car just sitting there?" the Observator asked out loud. "It seems like someone is watching us through the fence."

Hans jumped to his feet and ran down the path with Mundy close behind.

"No... don't go, Hans!" he shouted. "Nothing must happen to you!"

But Hans didn't listen to him. He jumped over the fence and saw someone opening the door on the driver's side and made his way there. A man was about to step out, but stopped suddenly, remaining halfway outside the car, leaning on the narrow armrest on the inside of the door.

Hans immediately saw that it was Pierre Pirenne.

Hans knelt down in front of him and pushed him backward until his left shoulder was against the back of the seat. Pirenne looked at him with exhausted eyes that were little more than slits in his face.

The rust colored jacket he wore fell open and Hans saw that his shirt was red with blood. The Observator had caught up to Hans and opening the gate, immediately recognized Pirenne. He ran back to the house as fast as he possibly could to get Doctor Weckmann. Pirenne tried to smile, but it seemed more likely that he was about to cry.

"Andrea Carandini came to see me," he whispered. "I had stayed behind in Nice to take care of some businesses for Flamel. The house he had rented had to be cleaned properly, and..."

"Maybe it's better you don't talk now," said Hans. "Wait for the doctor."

"It's okay, as long as I don't move it doesn't hurt. I was so happy there in that big house, all by myself... Carandini wanted information from me that I simply couldn't give him. I am not an initiate, like Flamel, Mundy and you... When his patience was at an end, he left... but he left Minor behind with me. That stupid giant first beat me half to death before he realized that I really didn't have anything to tell him. Carandini has to give up more and more of his power to Dordoni, the Ghost of Genoa. The fighting between is violent, and escalating, and Carandini says that you have done him a great disservice by taking Dordoni's side in that all or nothing game.

He said that he is coming for you and Flamel! He needs you to restore his honor, to drive away Dordoni and make it clear to everyone that he's running the show again. I... I sent you to Carandini... and now...."

Dr. Weckmann was taking much too long to get to them, so Hans managed to push Pirenne over to the passenger seat, jumped in behind the steering wheel, and drove the car up to the house. The Observator finally re-appeared with the doctor following in his wake.

A few minutes later Pierre was lying on a bed as Dr. Weckmann looked at his wounds and bruises.

"Carandini has been chasing Flamel for so many years," sighed Philippe Mundy. "It would have been better for everyone if those two had never met. But you know the history. Paolo Carandini was a Twentier who once lived here in Helgen with Von Drach and Wikander."

"Only yesterday I was reading some manuscripts Flamel had purchased from Carandini," said Hans.

They stood in the room as the doctor tended to Pirennes's wounds and every so often cast a glance in their direction.

Flamel arrived on the scene and conferred with the doctor and the Observator.

"We must arm ourselves," he said. "We probably should have done so much sooner. The grounds must be guarded day and night. If we let Carandini to catch us off guard, it could mean the end of everything we're trying to accomplish here. Poor Pirenne...this never should have been allowed to happen to him, but we'll take good care of him."

They left the room and headed to the dining room on the ground floor.

There they sat down at a table, and Flamel asked Winters:

"Shall we put off the journey? I can see that you're shocked and have been knocked off balance by all this."

"No, we must go on. Pirenne told me that he had stayed at the house near Nice to make sure that it was left in proper order. He didn't need a whole month for that, did he?"

"Pirenne is very fond of luxury and power. He is also arranges much of my business for me. He remained at the house to receive some important people from show business and television. He met with representatives from a foreign TV network who were vacationing in Cannes and sold some films of my shows to them. They in turn will broadcast them all over the world. What Carandini has done to him, is outrageous. This calls for extreme measures."

"That sadistic giant almost killed him," said the Observator, joining in the conversation. "It is a wonder that Pirenne was able to make his way back here at all. I don't know how he managed to drive a car."

"Who wants something to eat?" asked Flamel. "Is there anything in the kitchen you can whip up for us, Mundy?"

He was trying to remain cheerful, but Hans knew he was worried that Carandini would eventually show up in Helgen. He was also worried about him, now that he was about to start his journey. Hans stood up and said:

"I couldn't eat a thing right now, and besides, I have to go shave. When I come back downstairs, I will go straight to the big annex, Flamel. Make sure that everyone is there who has a task to fulfil, for it is time for me to jump into the darkness..."

The table top was in place covering the work of the Brotherhood, and upon it sat a myriad of equipment. The Observator had taken a chair from one of the rooms on the first floor and sat in front of a monitor on which he could see Hans. Phil Wayne sat next to him and was fiddling around with some knobs trying to get the picture perfectly focused. Simone Mundy and Mireille Robin stood by the window in the brick wall and saw Hans standing inside the circle as naked as the day he was born, his muscular chest going up and down quickly with his breath.

"His heart is beating fiercely," said Mireille. "But it is a strong heart, beating inside a strong body."

Monaco also now joined them.

The small circle in which he stood was lit by neon tubes that lent a sallow tint to Winters' skin. Doctor Weckmann entered. It was imperative that he be present in case of emergency, so he had given Pirenne a sleeping pill and left him. Flamel beckoned to him, and together they went and stood behind the three women so that they could also look through the little window at what was about to transpire.

It was three o'clock in the afternoon.

Hans knelt down with his hands on his thighs. He bowed his head until his chin touched his chest. With eyes closed, he began his ritual of meditation. His will took hold of the Long Zero and rather than letting go of it as he usually did, he began to play with it. He allowed it to curl itself into a flaming knot and then swell up again until it was bigger than he, so that he had the feeling of being completely enveloped by it.

Like a protective eggshell, the force field surrounded him. His mind was taken over by a fantastic blaze of colors that formed a powerful stream that carried him away. Balls of light danced around, burst apart, and then grew again. They continued to become larger and more massive, and were accompanied by flashes of what looked like white lightning that seemed to go right through him.

All in all it was not a terribly fearful experience. He had opened his will to this magical occurrence and allowed himself to be led by the intense speed of the changing colors that now gathered themselves into a new phase that consisted of beams that soared straight up and away to a black point in the distance.

Hans was swallowed.

Monaco, Simone, Mireille, Stephan and Augustin watched as Hans raised his head and opened his mouth. His hands slid along his thighs to his knees and then he disappeared. On the monitor, the only thing the Observator and Phil Wayne saw was an empty room.

"He's gone," said Jack Doyle.

"He's gone..." repeated Monaco, and then hid her face behind her folded arms.

The room was now entered so that measurements could be taken, although nothing appeared to be different there. There was no special odor, and there was no perceptible change in the temperature. The light from the neon tubes made the tiled walls shine brightly and evoked little sparkles in the grooves of the circle of the Brotherhood of Helgen, where Hans Winters had seconds before been kneeling.

The Observator ran the tape for them and showed them how Hans had disappeared. He also showed it several times in slow motion. He looked for the exact moment of the vanishing as they viewed the pictures as slowly as possible. Finding that precise spot on the tape, they were able to see that it had happened in a split second, just as it had shown him on the tapes he had made of Augustin Flamel.

He looked up as someone touched his shoulder. It was Flamel, who handed him a glass of wine.

"To help shorten the waiting..."

He stood up and saw Monaco pacing up and down the room nervously with his wife Simone had put an arm round her to try and comfort her. The glass he had taken from Flamel, trembled in his hand.

"To our young friend, to our Benjamin..."

The only thing Hans Winter could see was a dusky colored glow that beamed towards him from all sides. He had the feeling that he was being transported at great speed, without actually being conscious of his own body. As the speed lessened, he began to think... and think deeply.

He philosophized about the concept of loneliness, but did not wonder at all why he did. He imagined an extensive forest, in which a traveller disappeared every half hour. Every traveller had, at some point, a dejected feeling of desolation that brought him to the verge of panic. On the far side of the forest stood an ice cream vendor wearing man a white coat and hat.

"It is horrible to have to be all alone," said a traveller.

"Still, right here it is busy enough," said the ice cream man. "Every half hour someone new comes by to have a chat."

He handed the traveller an ice cream that burst into sparks of hissing fire.

"You see?" he said triumphantly. "So many stars... How then can it be lonely in the universe?"

A shiver went through him, the origin and end of which he could not locate. It looked as if he had stopped moving, and he tried to see more clearly. He was suddenly seized by panic. Everything around him remained yellow and resin colored, with striations of orange throughout. The iceman laughed from afar with a shrill voice:

"Only eyes can fathom the distances! To see is to fathom! Look around you and be amazed..."

Hans was certain that he had not closed his eyes. The yellowish tint became impregnated with amber colored fragments. He wanted to scream, so that the iceman could hear where he was. He tried to pinpoint the location where he was standing... or sitting. It was as if his body did not exist. He could think about moving his fingers, but he could not feel them. Panic struck even harder when he began to wonder if the situation in which he now found himself might last forever.

In these, the most fearsome moments of his life, he wished that he could cling to one single thought, in order to push all other chimeras into the background.

"To see is to fathom!" echoed the voice of the ice cream man.

Eyes! How had eyes formed themselves, who had made it possible for living creatures to see their surroundings? Had there ever been subcutaneous sensors that could tell the difference between light and dark? And had they now finally emerged in a fold of the skin? The naked eye... Now he considered the fact that the human eye grew worse as they grew older. Had someone ever explored the concept of whether or not shadows, monsters and devils from the past were mainly seen by people with bad eyes? Had an unbalanced diet, alternating with periods of famine, clouded the eye more quickly? What kind of world did people inhabit in bygone ages where the moon looked like a blurred spot in the sky? Where a tree in the twilight was a madman or a monster?

Because he had no sense of time, he could not determine how long he spent thinking about all these things. And then there came a moment when he did not even understand why he found all these questions so fascinating...and that was the moment when his own eyes began to function again and his physical feelings returned.

He saw. He sat. He looked.

The panic had passed and Hans now found himself in a world of magisterial beauty. A landscape comprised of glistening rock stretched before him. On the horizon the last beams of a setting sun were visible, giving everything with any height a long shadow. When he looked to the side he saw high, purple colored rock formations, veined with lilac colored stone. To his right was a plain, as smooth as a mirror, like a golden sea, above which the sunbeams sparkled like rain of the finest grit.

It became dark quickly now. Satellites raced across the black sky that seemed close enough to touch. They were of many different sizes and varied hues. Most of them were round except for one that was nothing more than a giant piece of spinning stone with freakish protuberances. He counted seven of these heavenly bodies. The velocity and rotation of each was different, and Hans realized that he was able to hear again when he could clearly perceive the whizzing sound caused by one of the tumbling moons above him that seemed to be hunting a higher flying fragment.

He smiled and clearly felt his lips curl and his eyes narrow.

Carefully, he stretched his hands out in front of him and looked at them. His relief was immense when he knew that he could actually see them. He then stretched out his legs and looked at his feet, feeling the pleasant sensation caused by the chilly stone on which he was sitting.

He registered two vital facts. He felt. He lived!

The star that had disappeared behind the horizon played a fantastic game with the tumbling moons. The light that was cast upon the satellites was not only reflected down to the surface of the planet, but also flashed in between, so that the sky constantly was impregnated with elongated, transparent, light colored beams. Behind that, the sky became blacker and there appeared gigantic star clusters.

"Only eyes are able to fathom the distances," he repeated silently, echoing the wisdom of the dream figure that sold ice cream, and now, for the first time, got an impression of the extent of the universe.

It was as if he could comprehend the fact that the universe was billions of times larger than the tiny part he could overlook from this place.

He understood. He nodded. He smiled!

A look to his right allowed him a view of the golden plain again, which was reflecting the bright colors of the satellites. His grin even grew wider now. What at first he had compared to a fine rain, now appeared to be the sideway movement of a constantly widening and then narrowing veil of light reflecting multiple dots. He stood up, stretched his arms, and there was a physical reaction to his movements.

A part of the whirling veil became concentrated and came up straight towards him. Soon he was surrounded by thousands of the little creatures like Flamel had brought back to Helgen hidden in his hair. Hans saw colors he could not name, and became aware of a vibration that stroked his skin like a soft breeze. The little creatures pelted the palms of his hands, his cheeks and chest with their round undersides. When he moved his hands though, they withdrew. Their movements were supple and smooth, never jolting or brusque. Man and creatures alike made a game of it. It became a dance of traveller and thousands of spinning, waving and retreating colorful little dots.

Hans sat down again, and the creatures spread themselves out in a wide flight path, back to the golden plain from which they had come.

Hans looked up to the stars again, and knew that he would be able to map out the sky. He opened his mouth, wanting to shout something out that would give expression to his joy. He had the desire to inhale deeply but found, to his horror, that he was unable to do so. His body resisted the extra-terrestrial circumstances, and then, suddenly, there was a melodic singing in his ears. His brain quickly sounded an alarm. He winced and tried to concentrate on the Long Zero, grabbed hold of it and allowed it to knit itself together.

He knew that if he stayed here any longer, he would die.

There was no time to visualize how he would lie there on the stones, on a faraway world where seven moons chased one another, and where tiny creatures played a drumbeat upon his body... he was already slipping off into the force field he had evoked which would protect him on his homeward voyage.

The clock was pointing to five minutes past seven. Monaco had not been more than a few feet away at any time even though the others had come and gone, carrying on their lives as usual. Flamel had always returned from a journey after two or three hours...

Hans had already been gone for more than four hours.

Philippe Mundy had also remained in the room for the entire time, and except for a glass of wine, he had nothing to eat or drink. He had stared at the screen on which the circle on the floor in the other room was constantly displayed...just as Monaco had done.

More than once Mireille had tried to divert Monaco's attention by starting up a conversation with her. At first she got polite answers, but now she got nothing at all. Jack Doyle tried to take her outside for a short walk, but she didn't even look at him. She simply remained standing so close to the window that her nose almost touched the glass.

Then Hans returned.

He did not crash to his knees on the floor as if he had been dropped, but quietly appeared in a kneeling position and did not move. The Observator shouted with joy and slapped his hand on the side of the screen as everyone present gathered around him or pushed closer to the window.

"He's not breathing!" cried Monaco. "Someone must go in and help him!"

She tried to get to the door herself, but Mireille stopped her.

"It's locked!"

"We'll wait a bit," she heard Flamel say, who had come over and stood beside her.

They saw Hans' entire body relax and slide forward. He lay stretched out on the circle with his fingers spread and trembling, and after some time, he sat upright and rubbed his eyes. At the moment he looked up at the window, everyone started to applaud, but he did not seem to see anyone - he showed no reaction at all.

The Observator said something into a microphone and his voice was heard in rooms.

"A hero has returned. Welcome home, Hans Winters!"

Hans remained lying there on the cold floor for over half an hour before he attempted to stand up.

Tottering, he went to the room where Monaco stood looking inside. He tried to smile, but he seemed to have no control over his muscles and the smile was born as an odd grimace. He turned around and stumbled over to the small bathroom that was in the left corner of the room where he took a long, hot shower.

After drying himself off, he put on shorts that had been laid out for him and went back to the room. Exhausted, he sat down on a chair and fastened the sensors to his bare chest and head, which were then connected with wires to a variety of equipment. Heartbeat, breathing, brain waves and other bodily functions were measured as Dr. Weckmann took notes.

"Can you hear me, Hans?" asked the Observator.

Hans looked up at the window and saw Monaco's black eyes staring down at him. He smiled broadly now as his clear, strong voice boomed out:

"I want to get out of here as soon as possible... I want to be with Monaco!"

Flamel spoke little to Winters in the days that followed.

He did not want to influence him with any comments about his own journeys. Hans did however, tell his story to the Observator, Phil Wayne and Jack Doyle, with Monaco always close by. He started to draw passionately. On big, square sheets he reproduced all that he had seen.

One afternoon Dr. Wayne made a decision:

"Hans is well; we have exercised all precautions. If there is anything wrong with him, we have not been able to discover it. As far as I am concerned we can go ahead and open the door..."

The Observator took charge of the kitchen and prepared a banquet for the new Brotherhood. Early that evening, Hans and Monaco retired to their own rooms. Their nights together had always been passionate and wild... and this one was no exception.

Everyone had again gathered in the big room where the table of the Brotherhood stood. The drawings that Flamel and Winters had made, were hung in rows on the walls; those of Flamel were situated above those of Winters. They were works of art ablaze with color, each one telling a fantastic tale. But the beauty of the work was of secondary importance; the men had drawn identical pictures, as if a pupil had been attempting to prove his talent by copying his master!

They had depicted in vivid colors what their minds had seen on their journeys. The surface of a strange planet was shown from varying perspectives. The rock formations, the golden plain with the tumbling satellites above it, all reproduced in exact detail by both artists...and the styles and colors were identical. The Observator pointed to them and said to Wayne:

"Flamel took a journey and saw none of those moons. They had vanished out of sight, but he did see them later on. Hans felt as if he could touch them, but they were in fact, out of his reach, high above the planet. He also believed the rotating spheres had made sounds... and that is something Flamel had absolutely no memory of. It could have been mental suggestion. Look here..."

In one drawing Flamel was standing up, holding his hands next to his head with his palms facing outward. He was surrounded by hundreds of little creatures with globe-like fronts and abdomens, that landed on his hands, shoulders and face. Beneath it hung a similar drawing of Hans standing naked on the rocky ground and looking with delight at a swarm of these little creatures.

"Flamel has never mentioned anything of the sort to Hans. As a matter of fact, things of this nature were purposely withheld from him."

At the end of the long row of drawings hung the star-maps. Here the similarities were also frightfully present.

"Place one on top of the other and hold them up to the light," said the Observator. "You will see that all the white dots are in the exact same place. I have copied them, enlarged them, and then reduced them again, until they matched perfectly. The results were the same every time.

The distances appear to tally and there is, at most, a difference of only twenty stars that have been drawn by one and not the other. Their photographic memory is fabulous! But far more astonishing is the outcome of those comparisons. It's a complete mystery to me as to which part of the universe it is that they have reproduced, but it proves to me nonetheless that they have both actually been there. Even if Flamel had not brought back one of the little creatures by sheer accident, I would still be convinced that he and Winters have been able to bridge these immense distances and still return safe and sound!"

Pierre Pirenne was also present now, and Flamel and the Observator had filled him in about everything. They thought he had the right to know the truth, since Carandini had caused him to be beaten so mercilessly by Minor. He walked past the drawings with his mouth agape.

Earlier in the day he had been allowed to look into the terrarium in which the little creature floated.

"I had all kinds of suspicions about what Flamel was doing," he said. "But I could never, in my wildest flights of fancy imagined anything so fantastic as this...it's all so amazing! It will take me quite a long time to accept all these new ideas. We must all be on our guard to make sure that these wonders are in no way ruined by Carandini's interferences. His passion for money and power could put all of us in danger. Tell Flamel that I will see to it that we are able, when necessary, to defend ourselves."

He was talking to Mireille Robin, who kept him company as he studied the drawings.

"You're right," she said. "Flamel needs time to execute some more experiments. He understands completely how vulnerable we are, that is why he confides in Jack Doyle and Phil Wayne. The Americans are very influential at several universities and have contacts with people from all branches of science. Perhaps we must search for help in those quarters. We need protection, for what we are doing here is of great importance to all mankind. But how shall we arm ourselves? Who among us is adept at handling weapons? You cannot leave, for Flamel has told all of us, especially you, that it is not wise to leave Helgen."

"I have contacts everywhere. One phone call is enough to bring the Ghost of Genoa into action. All I need do is mention the name Carandini, and everything we need will be handed to us on a silver platter..."

Chapter 8: The End of The Second Brotherhood

Just as everyone was about to leave the room, Monaco ran to the door and remained standing there, looking nervously from one face to another until her dark eyes came to rest on Hans.

"I would like to tell you all something," she said. "I don't know how you are going to take this...perhaps it will merely sound ridiculous."

Flame responded even more quickly than Winters did.

"Monaco, my dear, of course we will listen to you... with the greatest of pleasure..."

She walked over to the table of the Brotherhood and the others sauntered along behind her. With one hand she groped the table top for support, and after taking a deep breath, said:

"We all know what the painting of Astra has to tell us. The theme is repeated over and over again, in the stories and poems of the Austrian Twentiers. Hans had given them to me to read. The work of art that lies here, beneath this table, again repeats the story, only this time in wood. I'm also aware of all the theories and discussions that have arisen in connection with those stories. A civilization of Celts and Germans, that was meant to rival the Romans, equally powerful but separate from one another. Or perhaps a German-Celtic dominated world. And the prevailing thought that religion is somehow like a nut without a kernel; so beautiful from the outside, but so empty on the inside..."

She looked up and saw that her words had caught everybody's attention. She drew the courage from this reaction to her words to continue.

"I didn't understand anything about the meaning of these historical falsifications and religious theories until Hans and Augustin removed the top of this table. No one had ever been to get this table out of here, so through all those years it has remained standing in its place, which is undoubtedly exactly what the Twentiers had intended. It is so ugly on the outside, its appearance would never be an incentive for anyone to saw off the legs and attempt to steal it...while the inside is so unbelievably beautiful.

When Augustin first placed the two steel figures into their respective holes, I began to suspect that all the stories and paintings of the Twentiers somehow alluded to the table..."

"That is possible," said the Observator. "But I don't think that theory will take us much further..."

"Maybe not," said Monaco. "But my way of thinking is quite simple. In the fantasy story of the Brotherhood, people from all over are suddenly thrust into motion and march off to the temple of Janus, where Mercury stands ready, and waiting, to open the gate. Why is it he standing there? Is the god Janus, whose shrine this is, nowhere to be found? One must be curious about the two-faced god, who looks into the past just as easily as the future.

It is Mercury however, who is the owner of the winged shoes with the ability to travel to incredible places with such ease...like Hans and Augustin can..."

She fell silent for a moment and made some helpless gestures with her outstretched hands and a shrug of her shoulders.

"Go on," urged Hans. "What is your conclusion?"

"We must take the story literally. Maybe the temple of Janus is not empty... I rather think that the Brotherhood of Helgen has hidden a secret under the wooden roof of the temple..."

"That could very well be possible!" said Flamel. "Monaco! Have you solved the riddle? We will all know soon enough if you have!"

The others stepped back as he and Hans each went to one side of the table. Together, they lifted off the top and put it down on the floor. Suddenly the meaning of this fantastic work of art seemed much clearer to everyone. All those thousands of figures were marching, under the leadership of their assorted gods, towards the very same goal. They flocked to the temple, which was an ingeniously constructed building with pillars all around on, which a broad roof rested. Behind the pillars the most beautiful wooden carvings were to be seen, which created the illusion of gates and windows.

Flamel leaned over the table. There was absolute silence when he touched the roof and then closed his fingers around it. Very carefully he began to pull and pry...and then the roof became loose and separated from its base. He lifted it up high, and all those present came forward and bowed over the table to be able to get a better look at the inside of the temple of Janus.

The interior consisted of walls that were five inches high and made of smooth oak. The gate, in front of which the cordially inviting Mercury stood, could be opened from the inside by lifting a metal hook from out of a small eye. On the floor of the tiny temple lay twenty dark objects that were each only half an inch long and were of an oval shape.

Hans immediately thought of insects, while Flamel's thought was that they were constructed of some synthetic material.

The Observator said:

"Let no one touch them. They must first be studied very carefully."

"You are awesome, Monaco," said Hans. "Who knows where this discovery will now lead us. Whatever it is that we see lying here before us, has been perfectly protected by the Brotherhood... It must have been of incalculable value to them."

Flamel's reaction was short and to the point:

"This could be the great legacy of the Brotherhood."

"...And fate has decided that it has finally fallen into the right hands," said Simone Mundy with a meaningful sigh.

Her husband, the Observator, stood up and went upstairs to the room where the terrarium stood. He came back with a magnifying glass in his hand that everyone was given the opportunity to look through to better observe the contents of the wooden temple.

There were twenty forms, shining dully like tarnished silver, each the size of a coffee bean and gray in color, but all as smooth as polished metal.

"They automatically makes you think of beetles or crustaceans like the Oniscus Asellus," muttered Phil Wayne, the biologist. "But there are no indications that the wing-case can open from the sides to allow the wings to unfold, and I also see no indication of body segmentation either, which would make it possible for them to roll themselves up. If they were living creatures, you might possibly see their tiny legs if you were to turn them upside down..."

He reached out his hand, but stopped directly above the temple, seeming to wait on some objection that might come from either Flamel or the Observator. When the expected response failed to come, he put his hand in the temple and turned one of the little forms with his thumb and forefinger. It momentarily wobbled to and fro and then lay still. The bottom was flat, and was of the same color as the top. With the tip of his middle finger he flipped it back over again.

"No little legs. No antennae. No tiny eyes... I wouldn't dare say if it they are living creatures, or even if they are objects of synthetic material or of natural origin."

Flamel placed the roof back on the temple and beckoned to Winters. They lifted the table top and closed the work of the Brotherhood.

"Tomorrow the research must start in earnest," he said. "I want Philippe to take charge... And after every work period the top will be put back on the table."

Precise maps were made based on the drawings Flamel and Winters had made, and sent out to astronomers who were requested to submit their views on them.

Philippe Mundy did what he did best...he observed. For many hours each day he sat bent over the work of the Brotherhood. When he finally felt sure that the little objects in the temple were harmless, he dared to pick them up with a pair of tweezers. Worktables were set up upon which the little objects could be thoroughly examined. Enlarged greatly on a screen they still looked sound; nowhere could even the smallest scratch could be found on them.

The examination had reached a dead end.

Someone among however, moved a little less cautiously. Nineteen little forms remained behind in the darkness of the sealed temple, but on the twentieth, various tests were performed...and the results were mind-boggling. That heat and cold had no effect on the object surprised no one, but the fact that it was impenetrable caused a good deal of surprise. Clamped in a vice, they tried to scratch its surface it with a diamond tipped drill. That failed. Sweat dripped into the curls of his beard as the Observator worked on it, for he was constantly on the alert expecting something horrible to happen at any moment.

He feared some deadly form of pulsating to begin, or perhaps for the object to begin emitting radiation. He placed 'Number Twenty' into a little melting furnace, took it out with a pair of tongs, set it tight in the vice and then went to work with the diamond drill again. He repeated this procedure after deep-freezing it; but still 'Number Twenty' showed no sign of having been thusly probed.

All around him the others expounded their wildest theories, all of which were scorned by the Observator one after the other.

On one day the object was placed in a cistern. On another it was put inside a vacuum tube and then, at his wits' end, Mundy finally plunged it into a beaker of hydrochloric acid.

The interest of the others was dwindling, and Monaco began to believe that her solution of the riddle had not been so spectacular after all. But Mundy set his teeth into the problem and sent for Flamel and Winters every day to lift the top from the table.

"I refuse to believe that they are stones from another world, as Phil Wayne asserts. He says that they are of great value because they are so hard, and weigh so little at the same time. The specific gravity in this case means nothing at all...you might expect them to be hollow! Wayne is sticking to his assumption that the Brotherhood cherished them like priceless jewels."

Flamel was just as headstrong in his opinions as the Observator was.

"There must be more up with it. All those indications in the manuscripts on the works of art... and then this table... You don't go through so much trouble for twenty little objects that represent a certain value, like diamonds, and then are of no further use at all. What more can you do to get to the truth?"

Mundy's thick black eyebrows furrowed as he looked angrily into the temple and put Number Twenty back in its place between the other nineteen.

"I ponder that question day and night. Even when I sleep I dream about it, and I pity the world if what happens is what I see pass before my mind's eye. A terrible blow puts an end to all life. The next morning I hardly dare touch that thing, and I am overwhelmed by fear when I think about all the unorthodox liberties which I have taken with it..."

The Observator worked with light and laser beams, to see if he could activate the little forms within it. He electrified 'Number Twenty' and then put it on its back, in the idle hope that it would come to life again. He had not cast aside the notion that he might actually be dealing with a form of life, although nothing had happened that pointed in that direction.

Then came the reactions from the astronomers around the world to whom they had sent the star maps. They had studied the pictures but were unable to make sense of them because there was not one single point of recognition to be found. The little creature in the terrarium floated around without eating or drinking, and the Observator remained sitting there, staring into the wooden temple and doing things with Number Twenty that any self-respecting scientist would have rejected as hocus-pocus.

A package from Italy was delivered on the same day that Pirenne had outfitted a barn as a firing range and was teaching everyone how to handle a small revolver. Hans and Augustin continued to train their bodies, and their minds, with their regimen of meditation. They planned to undertake new journeys, but had still not decided whether or not they would go together. Everyone concerned was against that. If something were to happen to both of them, everything was finished. And that was a realistic line of reasoning for which Flamel could show a true understanding.

When it was necessary to go out shopping, Hans went along and Augustin stayed home, or vice versa. They watched over the group, for they were, with their extraordinary powers, the most able to be on the defensive for any attack that might come.

Hans and Monaco were happy. The feeling of mutual attraction seemed to grow and they soon got used to life in Helgen. Monaco was now able to accept the fact that Hans was different from other people, and when she knew he was planning a new journey, she would try to prevent him from it. But she was still so often astonished by him; when she saw how he finished a book in half an hour, she would sometimes picked it up and begin to read randomly.

Halfway through a sentence she would stop and look at Hans questioningly. He would then complete the sentence and drone on until the next section, until she raised her hand as a sign that he could stop.

"What do you need all that information for?" she once asked.

He shrugged his shoulders and answered:

"It is an unquenchable desire for information. I cannot resist it, although I have to admit that I actually never tried to."

On that same day she also asked:

"What's going to happen now?"

"That's difficult to say. Wayne has suggested that we send one of the little objects from the temple to a lab in America. He says he knows a couple of reliable scientists there who will not blab about what they have been told. The Observator is completely against it, and is very firm on the issue. The final decision however, is up to Flamel... he is, and will remain, the boss over everything. But, if he should side with Wayne...well, then he's risking a major quarrel with the Observator."

The telephone rang. It was Flamel calling to tell Hans to get down to the table as quickly as possible. Leaving Monaco behind, Hans ran downstairs, went outside and hurried over to the building as fast as his feet could carry him. He went inside and tried to enter the room where the table stood, but found the door locked. He knocked and Flamel opened for him.

"Come in," he said and quickly locked the door behind him again.

They walked over to the table, where now only the Observator stood. Without looking up he gestured with his hand.

Hans bent over the table and peered into the miniature temple. He counted only twelve of the little objects and was about to ask what had become of the other eight, when he realized that they had moved! No wings or legs were visible, but the small gray beings were an inch higher and were jumping up and down.

"How did you do that?" Hans demanded.

The Observator merely shook his head.

"I have done nothing, Hans. They seem to have come to life all by themselves. Look..."

He put a hand into the temple, opened the hook, and pushed the gate open. One of the little creatures floated straight towards it and then sailed in a sharp curve around Mercury.

"And there!" Mundy shouted, while pointing to one of the steel puppets Flamel had inserted into the holes.

One of the creatures had appeared from out of the steel, making its entrance in an oozing fashion, like liquid mercury. It floated between the gathered armies of wood, and rose up to obtain the obstacle formed by a divine rider. The creature that had gone on its way, now reached one of the metallic objects and was winding itself inside like a screw.

"The roof gets put back on the table, but the gate remains open," decided the Observator. "You must close it right now."

After doing so, Mundy sat down on top of the table as if had been appointed its sole guard and he stared at Flamel.

"We must not part with anything, Augustin. Imagine if we had given any of these little things to Phil Wayne..."

"The researchers would certainly have plunged into their work with extra energy," said Flamel. "I'm still thinking about it..."

"How did Wayne plan to transport them?"

"In his wallet, like they were stones of fortune..."

"There would have been a very great chance that they never would have arrived in America."

"Why not?" Hans wanted to know, still surprised by all that he had just witnessed.

"They penetrate the steel as if it were air! The wood, however, seems to keep them in their place. I'm not saying that they can't get through it, but for one reason or another they remain under this table top..."

He rapped on it with the knuckles of both hands.

"So now we know that they can only be transported in a wooden box or case."

"I understand," said Augustin.

"I need time to think," said the Observator. "For now the table remains closed, and we don't mention a word about this to the others. More and more, people think that we should make things public and hand the research over to someone else. That time will surely come, but first I want to marshal the facts for myself. It's not a problem if you want to discuss it with Mireille or Monaco, they both know how to keep a secret..."

He jumped off the table and opened the door. They heard his footsteps on the staircase. When the Observator wanted to think, he liked to sit in a chair opposite the terrarium and gaze, with his feet upon the table, at the little floating creature.

Augustin looked at Hans.

"Let's have dinner tonight in the Gasthof in Helgen," he proposed. "Just the four of us. Then we can talk safely about this with Mireille and Monaco."

With a smile he added:

"No doubt Monaco will be glad to hear that her discovery has yielded something special after all. And Mireille, being a biologist, I'm sure will find this fascinating! Besides, I know the Observator much too well. He wants to hear her opinion before he draws his own conclusions..."

They were the only guests in the restaurant. They sat down at a long table in a corner by a window. Monaco and Mireille sat on a wooden bench that could easily have held several people. Hans and Augustin sat across from them on chairs. They drank wine and ordered a hearty soup as an appetizer. The main meal of meat and potatoes, was served with salad.

Hans was happy. He was fully aware of his fantastic talents and looked back with satisfaction to the success of his first journey. He was almost overflowing with energy, and would be more than happy to make another journey to that strange, far-away world. He ate voraciously while listening to Flamel fill both women in on all the recent developments concerning the Brotherhood.

Next to the front door of the dining room there was a bar. At this bar stood a man who had come in and ordered a glass of beer. When he noticed the little company of friends sitting near the window, he walked up to them. He appeared to be a journalist from the local newspaper and asked Flamel when he would head out on his next tour of Europe.

"In a few months," answered Flamel. "We are busy now developing new aspects of the act. Everything must be different from the last show, and with Hans by my side we are hoping to give the audience some new thrills. We are satisfied only when the house is full of confused, sweating spectators. We'll only take the stage if we are convinced that we can surpass ourselves."

The man emptied his glass and left again. Less than five minutes later the door opened again.

Hans looked up and quietly warned the others.

"It is Carandini!" he whispered.

Walking quickly, the fat man approached them followed by four men, two of whom Hans immediately recognized. They were Minor, the giant, and Aldo Duby. Carandini sat down at the table on a chair, while Minor and Duby squeezed in beside Monaco and Mireille on the bench. The two unknown men took seats at a table in the middle of the room. Anyone who wanted to leave the restaurant would have to go past them.

"It is beyond the shadow of a doubt that you could, if you wanted to, perform some unexpected tricks," said the fat man with a sigh. "But that doesn't seem advisable...we are all armed and there will certainly be some shooting around here if it appears that I am in any danger whatsoever. I hope, my friends, that we can have a nice, quiet talk together. It was a long trip to Austria..."

Monaco put down her knife and fork, and Mireille stared outside. Hans and Augustin understood that all hell would break loose if they made a move against Carandini. They kept their tempers... and waited.

Beer, wine, and coffee were ordered.

"Put your hand on the table, Minor," said Carandini.

The giant put his right hand on the table with his fingers spread.

"You healed Monaco's face, Winters," said Carandini. "Minor's hand however, which you crushed, is still stiff and numb. He uses it like a blunt axe and cannot even lift a glass with it any more. I think you can do something about it, can't you?"

"Even crippled as he is, he found a way to make Pierre Pirenne talk," said Hans. "We're all glad that Pirenne is well, and almost his usual self again. But I can't imagine that you came all the way to Helgen, with four armed men, just to get Minor's hand examined..."

Minor tapped on the table impatiently with stiff fingers.

"The fingers are numb," he said, "but my arm hurts from the wrist to the elbow. It bothers me night and day."

Flamel responded, saying:

"I'll take care of it...and afterwards, I'll listen to what you have to say to me, Carandini, but you won't have much time. If you had stumbled upon us without Monaco and Mireille being here, I would have already paid you back for the harm done to Pirenne."

Carandini nodded.

"We'll stay together for a while, my friend," he said with a sardonic smile. "We have had a long and extremely journey, and we're very hungry."

Flamel took Minor's hand in his own and closed his eyes. It did not seem as if he was exerting himself at all, and he did not move his own hands. He sat there motionless as a euphoric expression spread across the giant's face. Minor lifted his head and stared at the ceiling with his mouth agape. His body shook as if pulsating vibrations were coursing through it.

Carandini scratched his double chin nervously, looking from one person to the next and stopping on Monaco.

"This is the way I treated Pirenne, too," said Flamel in a calm voice. "I was able to soften his pain, but I couldn't take the fear out of his head. What was done to him is unacceptable...and completely unforgivable."

Minor pulled his hand back and wiggled his fingers. He made a fist and waited for the usual pain that this movement produced since the fight with Hans, but there was no longer any pain. It seemed to have vanished and he was so surprised, that he leaned against the back of his chair, sighed, and shook his head.

Hans considered jumping up and grabbing Carandini, like he had done in the casino, but the risk was too great. He knew that he would be putting both Monaco's and Mireille's lives in danger. Flamel did not seem to have any plan of action either.

"I am so very sorry that we had to be so rough with Pirenne," said Carandini. "We really should abjure violence. I am truly glad that Louise and Hans have found each other, and I would prefer to forget what he did to me at the roulette table in San Remo. I did get some good information from Pirenne though, about my ancestor, Paolo, who left behind a heritage that is due to me. Fate has brought us together and we have the opportunity to make a fortune - which we will share honestly. Flamel and Winters have used something that the Brotherhood of Helgen left behind, and Paolo Carandini was part of that society. I offer you my implicit friendship and expect the same in return from you..."

Minor had picked up a toothpick and manipulated it between the fingers of his right hand. Smiling blissfully, he ascertained that the hand was entirely healed. He softly pricked his fingers and established the fact that the feeling had come back.

Carandini kept on talking. When their meals arrived, he stopped talking long enough to bolt down his food. The two men who sat at the other table hadn't ordered anything to eat, but were watching intently. One of them kept his hand under his jacket, making it perfectly obvious that he had no qualms about drawing his weapon if it should be necessary.

Carandini was rambling on about power and riches, and painted a picture of a future full of heaven sent luck for everyone, while every now and then Duby added some promises of his own. Carandini cleansed his mouth with a sip of wine and put his fork down on his empty plate.

"I don't expect you to make any promises right now. My trip to Austria has been very useful and Minor is his old self again. You will see that I can, and will, achieve my goal without resorting to violence. If I draw first blood, I will only succeed in pissing you off... that is why I have decided to use other methods to convince you that our co-operation is inevitable."

Hans raised his eyebrows.

"What is it exactly you are trying to say?"

Carandini was about to answer him when his cell phone rang. He took the small phone out of his inside pocket and listened without saying a word. Immediately after putting it back inside his jacket pocket he stood up and said:

"Well, we have to go. May I assume then, Hans, that you are willing to pay the bill? It's only a trifle compared to my loss in San Remo, but as far as I am concerned we are even now. You will hear from me soon. Thank you for your kind attention."

He bowed slightly to everyone and winked at Monaco.

"You're looking great, Louise," he said.

Then he calmly left the dining room, followed by Duby, Minor, and the two strangers.

"If this had ended in violence and gunplay, we would certainly worn out our welcome in Helgen," said Flamel with a sigh. "I'm glad you managed to control yourself, too, Hans. But what is the meaning of his sudden arrival? He is not the kind of man who comes all the way from Italy just to make peace."

Hans said nothing. He pushed his chair back with a scraping sound and went to the bar to settle the bill. He gestured at the others impatiently.

Once outside, he said in a hurried voice:

"Come on! We have to get home as soon as possible. I suspect that Carandini has already been in the area for quite some time. He waited until it was safe to approach us in public, Augustin. The restaurant was the ideal place for him to contact us..."

"But why?"

"To be able to extort us with promises...and threats."

Hans picked up his pace and Monaco, who was holding his hand, had to run to keep up with him.

"To give others the chance to break into the compound!" he shouted.

He shook himself free from Monaco.

"Stay together!" he warned. "I'll go on ahead!"

No one could have kept up with him as he sprinted away. He turned down the dimly lit main street of the village and was soon invisible to those he left behind in the dark of the evening. It was about a ten-minute ride by car to the buildings of the Brotherhood, but if he went by foot, taking the steep mountain paths, he could get there even faster. Complete darkness ruled on the slopes, but he didn't stumble once on the roots and stones. He was not even winded when he saw the outside lights of the compound.

Hans jumped over the fence and ran up the path to the front door of the big house, which was wide open. Pierre Pirenne was sitting on the third step, and when he saw Hans he jumped to his feet and came towards him. He looked frightened and his face was wet with perspiration. He took a small revolver out of his pocket and laid it across his palm.

"I'm probably the only one who even considered using his weapon," he said. "Hardly any of the others even made an attempt at defending themselves. Hans, everything is gone! We have nothing left, nothing at all..."

Breathing heavily, as if it had been he who had been running through the dark countryside, he related to Hans what had happened.

A big car had stopped in front of the fence, about fifteen minutes after Hans, Augustin, Monaco and Mireille had left. Ten men, all armed with automatic rifles, climbed over the fence and entered the buildings. They spoke to no one as they forced their way into the house. Jack Doyle, the American psychologist, was the only one who tried to make a stand. He was in the dining room and went after one of the intruders with a chair. He was thrown to the floor and got kicked in the stomach for his efforts. Meanwhile, one of these damn pirates opened the gate, while another drove the car up to the house.

Floor by floor, room by room they searched the house and got anything that seemed to be of any importance was loaded into the car. Then they did the same in the other buildings. The old manuscripts from the Brotherhood of Helgen were taken out in boxes, as was all the expensive equipment that the Observator and his staff use. Photos, films, files with notes, diaries, directories, works of art from the Twentiers, everything found a place in the vehicle. They worked fast and disciplined. Pirenne was locked up in a room and was only freed by Phil Wayne when Carandini's men had all left.

The Observator tried to save the photographic materials by hiding them in a dark corner, but that too was in vain. They had been keeping a close eye on him, and they eventually took all his stuff outside too. He retreated into the little office where the terrarium stood. All the equipment in there was also stolen. One of them looked inside the terrarium but did not notice anything special about it. The table is still on the ground floor...No one even tried to move that.

At least the greatest secret of the Brotherhood was safe and sound.

Augustin, Monaco and Mireille soon reached the house, and were told about the raid by Hans, while Pirenne remained silent along with the other occupants of the compound gathered at the side of the house. Jack Doyle had a pained look upon his face and kept both hands clenched against his stomach. The Observator paced up and down angrily, growling like a wounded bear.

"The fall of the Second Brotherhood," remarked Stefan Weckmann. "So much important material has been stolen...there's nothing left. The next time Carandini comes, it will be to get one of us and be given the same kind of treatment that Pirenne got. It seems to me that the wisest thing to do would be for us to split up and wait."

His remark met with general approval.

"Carandini will have people study the stolen material and their conclusions will undoubtedly surprise him," said Doyle. "If he wants to know more, he will need to force one of us to talk... and that will be accomplished gently, I'm sure."

"I will make a decision tomorrow," said Flamel.

Everyone went inside to see what was missing. Then they proceeded to the other buildings to assess the damage. Carandini's men had not taken any half measures. A treasure trove of information was their prize and it would cost a fortune to replace all the equipment.

The new Brotherhood now began to split up. A Spanish couple, well-to-do freethinkers, both with college educations, decided to leave Helgen that very evening. A German mathematician followed their example and went off to pack his belongings. Tension and confusion ruled in Flamel's camp, but the ones who left promised to keep silent about everything that they had experienced here.

Monaco was furious.

"I am used to dealing with violent people," she said. "I refuse to be intimidated. The next time one of Carandini's men shows up here, I'll blow his head off! I know very well how to handle weapons!"

Hans noticed that the Observator was a nervous wreck...pacing back and forth with strides, his hands in his pockets and his face twisted with sadness and frustration. Later on he caught up to him in the dining room, sitting by the fireplace with a big glass of wine in his hand.

"I hope you are not planning to give up as well" said Hans.

Outraged, the Observator shook his head.

"Of course not! The table of the Brotherhood is still standing there, and inside of it, as you know, is hidden the biggest secret. I think I know what is going on and I will inform you about it soon enough. Again, it is something that we must keep to ourselves. First we must see who remains faithful to us and who deserts us."

It was the middle of the night when the last lights went out in the houses. Hans Winters lay on his back in bed and Monaco had nestled up beside him. She was sleeping, but he was more awake than ever. He could not wait to hear what the Observator had to say and what decisions Flamel had made.

The sun was coming up when he finally dozed off for a while. But one hour later he was back downstairs in the kitchen making coffee, not tired at all. He felt prepared and able to cope with the problems that now confronted them and wanted to discuss some new ideas with everyone. It was a long time though before the other occupants finally all got themselves together and made their way downstairs.

While he waited he read a book, from which of course he would remember every line... forever.

Chapter 9: Changes

Twisted thoughts of Earth dominated Hans' mind as he began a new journey through infinity. He was now a sailing ship from the seventeenth century, built from the finest European wood and storm winds filling his sails. His spice filled holds provided him with a wonderful feeling of satisfaction. His bowsprit loomed out before him like a giant feeler, which he used to help plot his route. Bumping along on a sea of light beams that were accompanied by multi-colored balls that raced alongside him, he felt the pleasant swaying of his wooden timbers. He needed no rudder to help steer his course; the light-stream carried him along to a dark hole in the distance.

His wooden hull was as alive, and as lithe as the body of a fish. He dove into the sea of light and was brought up again by stupendous waves. But then the elements turned against him, and as he was buffeted to and fro, he felt his timbers crack and a tidal wave of fear washed over him.

He reefed his sails and hoped that the area of tension that he had entered would dissipate like passing thunder. Flashes of lightning set his wooden skin ablaze and ignited the powder kegs stored below his decks, causing them to explode. His guns were discharged as the cargo of pepper burned inside of him and bathed him in a flickering yellow light, like bubbling gastric acid. The roaring of a thousand, energy charged hurricanes stifled his cries as he was lifted up... only to be violently smashed down again. He breathed fire and puffed smoke, his deck blazed in the night as he sped forward with charred masts.

Hans Winters was a ship that was about to sink...but still he remained whole, for he drew hope from his fear and refused to perish upon a bottomless sea in which he would continue to sink for all eternity. He closed his eyes to the sight of the horrible walls of light around him and finally came to rest.

It was a long time before he was able to see again, and he found himself seated on a cold patch of stone. Beside him sat Flamel, who had embarked on this journey before him. A small sun sat low in the sky and sent out vivid, piercing beams of heat. He gazed out at the rocky plain and the golden sea. Above him was a saffron-colored sky that contained neither moons nor stars.

Flamel lifted his hand and as Winters placed his fingers against it they exchanged smiles. Then they rose to their feet and held up their arms, which must have seemed to be some sort of invitation, for soon they were visited by countless little creatures that began to push softly against them.

"Can you hear me?" asked Flamel.

"Yes," answered Hans. "I can hear you, and I can see you. I can also feel these little creatures bumping against my hand. It feels like a soft breeze is blowing past my face, but I cannot tell with any certainty if I am actually breathing."

He tried to fill his lungs with air and a feeling of panic coursed through him when he did not succeed.

"We can never stay here too long," said Flamel. "This is not a world fit for humans...after a while we would die here."

They cupped their hands, and scooping them through the air, brought them together catching a number of the little creatures. They sank to their knees and began to concentrate on the journey home. Flamel was once again the first to leave and when he had disappeared, Hans was alone...again...on this far-away world. He grabbed hold of whatever it was that dwelled inside him and curled it up into a knot of energy. And then, with his hands firmly clasped together to protect his precious cargo on the journey, he followed Flamel.

The Observator ignored all of his own precautions and entered the tiny room where Winters and Flamel had reappeared and pulled their hands apart. Both travellers still seemed to be unconscious as they lay on their bellies on the cold stone floor breathing calmly. He gathered all the little creatures into a glass jar and firmly screwed the top on after managing to catch them all.

A few hours later, when Winters and Flamel had substantially recovered from the travails of their marvellous journey, Jack Doyle and Phil Wayne left Helgen. They intended to fly back to the States and have some of their tiny alien creatures sent to them at a later date.

The Observator had figured out what he considered a safe way of handling this. He would put them into slender, unbreakable plastic tubes that he could safely hide between some magazines. Stefan Weckman had also left and taken a bottle containing three of the creatures with him in his medical bag. Everyone who left the Brotherhood, was given at least one of the little creatures to safeguard.

"Everyone is free to have them examined in any way they see fit," said Philippe Mundy. "And we all must decide for ourselves who we can trust...and who we cannot. It is of the utmost importance that you utilize the facilities of well-equipped labs, where you can have access to the latest technology in order to find out what sort of unique life forms these things may be."

Seven people stayed behind in Helgen; Hans and Monaco, Flamel and Mireille, Philippe and Simone Mundy, and Pierre Pirenne.

"We have played a risky game by allowing Hans and Augustin to travel together," said the Observator that evening as they all sat together in the dining room.

"We are also taking quite a risk by presenting our little aliens to the scientific community at large. As soon as the various scientists realize that they are dealing with life forms from another part of the universe, I'm sure that they will contact us immediately...and we will have an awful lot to explain. It is entirely up to Hans and Augustin how far they want to go, as far as their new research is concerned, but before I disappear into the kitchen to prepare dinner, I'll tell you what I think of these little objects from the wooden temple of Janus. I will try to not to be too obtuse, and will confine myself to what I see as the truth."

He began to pace up and down the room, speaking as if he was dictating a letter to someone.

"It is impossible for me to determine what we are dealing with here as far as artificial intelligence is concerned. In either case, it is a curiosity without equal. With these twenty little objects we are probably holding a trump card in our hands, thanks to the people who left them to us. They are indeed objects of great value... extra-terrestrial equivalents of gold nuggets or diamonds. No one, besides Augustin, Hans and myself, has ever seen how they move, float and completely disappear into solid steel.

How this all transpires still remains unclear to me at this time, and I would not dare speculate on it. But that it is in fact happening seems clear enough, and I suspect that Augustin and Hans understand it as well as I."

He stood still and looked at both men for a while, and when he continued his monologue, he directed it mainly at them.

"I have already named that what is nestling inside of you as 'The Long Zero'. And with perfect hindsight, and by comparison to the world as we know it, it is even more beautiful than I could have ever imagined. These things, looking so much like coffee beans or beetles, I have to compare, for convenience' sake, to a caterpillar or spider. They penetrate steel and deposit something there. Like a caterpillar weaves a cocoon, or a spider her web. The difference is, of course, that both cocoon and web are visible objects, while our little objects produce the invisible, and transcendental, Long Zero. They secrete something that is so valuable, that it cannot even be compared to gold or diamonds. They can materialize from out of solid steel and nestle themselves inside living creatures.

Augustin and Hans know all about that. For so long, they felt as if they were out of their element, and forced to roam the earth. They walked so many thousands of miles, until the muscles that rippled through them were as hard as steel. Then, their bodies finally began to accept the intruders within them. The intruder itself appeared to be friendly, and made no ill-tempered assaults on their minds.

Quite often, Augustin and I have sat around until the wee hours of the morning philosophizing about life. I tend to agree with him when he says that man is a creature that knows much but can do little. He refers to space travel as pinpricks in the sky. We are able to form an idea about the size of the universe and we can approximate the number of stars in the night sky.

Billions of stars in billions of galaxies...but those distant stars have always remained unreachable...until now."

"There is divinity in our genes," Flamel said with a smile, interrupting the Observator. "We worship the heavens, which are filled with all the gods that we have placed there. We bestow names on the unattainable, feel familiar with the universe, and eventually realize that we ourselves form a part of it. But something is lacking, something that deprives us of the chance to peer into the vast distances..."

"Yes...this is so!" cried the Observator. "And you have said on more than one occasion that you believe that you have achieved the status of a demigod, because you were given something that you were lacking as a human being. You received what those of the Brotherhood of Helgen had been given, and what Hans is also now carrying inside of him...and this is probably what these little objects are that have fallen from the heavens like manna.

Maybe they were spread across the horizon in thick clouds, like swarms of locusts darkening the sky. Who knows...is there intelligence out there somewhere that has given us this gift? I really don't want to go into that too much now though. I have accepted as fact that these objects, whether living or artificial, whether or not they are here on purpose or by accident, found by the Twentiers and rediscovered by us, do leave something behind in solid steel. For want of a better name, I have dubbed that something the 'Long Zero' and it is able to relocate itself in human beings. My friends...what that old table of the Twentiers hides is, as far as I am concerned, the most valuable possession on the face of the earth!"

Without waiting for a response from the others he walked out of the dining room, and they soon heard him rattling pots and pans in the kitchen.

"We are the only ones who know about all this," said Pirenne, to no one in particular. "The others only have the creatures with them in order to have them examined..."

After dinner, Hans and Augustin went out for a walk. They walked way into the mountains behind the house but the climb did not tire them.

"It is remarkable," said Hans, "how quickly we recover from a journey. I can hardly believe that it was such a short time ago that we stood on the surface of another world."

"Remarkable indeed," agreed Flamel. "But it proves beyond the shadow of a doubt that mentally, we are able to cope with it. I am so happy that the horrible fears that we experience during our journeys disappear so quickly. Although I am now someone who is able to traverse the universe, I could never live with those terrible feelings of fright. Each time I am harassed by those unbearable thoughts that take root in my mind, I long for the rescue of death. And then, just as suddenly as it started, it's all over."

They stood still and looked down on the buildings below them. From this lofty perch it struck Hans that the structure in which the table of the Brotherhood stood, was built in quite an illogical place. If small stones came loose from the mountainside and rolled down onto the sloping roof they would simply bounce off, but bigger stones would go right through it. Where the roof made contact with the rock face, a gutter had been built to drain off water that streamed down from the rocks when it rained.

He drew Flamel's attention to it:

"If a storm were to tear the ground and trees loose, everything could possibly be destroyed. Perhaps only the table would remain standing. Why would they have built it there, on that particular spot?"

"That's clear enough, isn't it?" said Flamel. "The Twentiers performed many experiments and undoubtedly departed on their journeys from many different locations. The best spot lies inside the circle, and they obviously constructed their building around it..."

"I understand. Yes, no doubt they also used other places as jumping off points for their journeys. Would you dare to do that? Do you know of any other places from where the Twentiers began their trips from?"

He looked at Flamel and wondered about his frightened look. Flamel seldom showed surprise, and the evasive answer he gave, was not at all to Hans' liking.

"They have not mentioned it anywhere."

During the descent back down the mountain there was little conversation between them.

Over the next few days, security systems were installed in all the buildings on the property. Pirenne had gone out to buy the equipment and the tools needed for the job, while Monaco proved to be very handy installing cameras and burglar alarms. It was calm and peaceful around the compound...for the moment.

But that soon changed... and many other things began to happen.

First, Flamel ordered Pirenne to make it known to everyone concerned that he had given up his plans for a new tour. He would not be engaging a company to bring a show into the theatres of Europe. He gave as a reason that he did not desire to perform for an audience until he had found something that could surpass the sensations of the last tour. Hans reacted rather laconically and asked him no questions, but he discussed with Monaco what this could mean.

"We can only speculate about it," said Monaco. "We must pay close attention however."

The Observator was very contrite about the entire matter.

"Augustin has to concentrate on what is happening around here. He is devoting all his energy to science, just like you."

One morning Pierre appeared into the dining room with his telephone in hand and sat down at the table with the others.

"I just got a call," he said, as he looked nervously from one to the other. "Andrea Carandini is furious. He has made a threat that I think we should all take very seriously. He says that Hans and Augustin are to come to Italy and join his organization. If they refuse...he will kill them."

He then looked directly at Winters and Flamel, and said:

"If you go, you will be entirely under his control. If you remain here however, I advise you not to step a foot outside the house. I'm sure that he will send snipers to Helgen, who will only be allowed to return home when they can bring him news of your deaths...both of you. He has given you one week to make your decision..."

Flamel stirred his coffee as he searched for words, but Winters spoke first:

"Carandini has had the chance to look at all our material and has thus become much wiser about our doings. He apparently has decided that must be all or nothing for him. If he cannot have Flamel or me, he will put an end to the entire affair...once and for all! That way he can prevent us from making contact with someone else, like the Ghost of Genoa for instance..."

"The matter is a bit more complicated than that," said Pirenne. "I have already told you that Carandini is furious. Hell, I could hold this little phone far away from my ear and still be able to hear every word he shouted. I have heard so many Italian curses that I can't even remember them all. And all this is because he has already lost everything that he had stolen from us...!"

Hans, Augustin, Monaco, Philippe, Mireille and Simone stopped eating their breakfast abruptly to listen more intently to Pirenne.

"Believe it or not...we got everything back! There was a raid ordered by the Italian government. What Carandini did to us, has now been done to him! He has always felt safe in his big house, secure behind his fence and surrounded by his men, all of whom have a disposition like Minor. He always had his affairs fixed and arranged, and the last thing he expected was this raid by the police. Someone made it very clear to him that they knew where all these things came from and that they should be returned to their rightful owners. He asked me, of course, if I knew who was behind this operation. He suspected it to be another of Augustin's little tricks, but I firmly denied that. Carandini is a man who carries out his threats. If

Hans and Augustin haven't made their decision within a week, they will be marked men..."

Monaco nodded and said:

"You can count on that...when he doesn't get his way, he will spring into action without mercy. An alarm system and a few small revolvers won't stop him. You lives are in peril... that is for sure."

"The big question is," said Hans, "who got the Italian government to come down on him? Why would anyone have an interest in undertaking something like that? And has Carandini really said that everything will be returned to us?"

"Yes," said Pirenne firmly.

Nothing further happened for a few days, and then one morning a car stopped in front of the gate and three men stepped out. One of them pushed the button of the intercom. The Observator, who was sitting in the dining room drinking coffee, looked at the monitor and immediately recognized the American biologist Phil Wayne. He had never seen the other two before.

"Phil!" cried Mundy. "I didn't expect you at all! I'll come right down and open the gate for you."

"Hello, Philippe," replied Wayne through the speaker. "I'm here with Colonel Patrick Kelly from America, and Mr. Rudolph Brendel of the Austrian police... and lots of good news..."

The Observator went outside and as he began to walk down the path to the road, Monaco caught up to him, walking quickly. She had also seen the car, and had gone on the alert immediately.

"I'll stay right behind you," she said. "If something appears to be wrong, I'll use my revolver."

"It's Wayne!" said the Observator.

"That means nothing. Who are the others?"

"An American colonel and an Austrian cop."

"We'll soon see. Hans and Pirenne are keeping an eye on us and have also armed themselves. Be very careful, Philippe."

He opened the gate and the men all stood there facing each other. Monaco stood a bit to the side and kept her hand in her jacket pocket clutching her gun as the biologist introduced everyone to each other. Patrick Kelly was a tall man with broad shoulders. He had white hair and bristly sideburns, a square face and steely blue eyes. He wore a striped, custom-made suit and shiny black shoes. Rudolph Brendel was also in plain clothes. He wore corduroy trousers and a checked jacket. He was smaller than the American and balding, but where he still had hair, it was cut so short that his scalp was clearly visible. Monaco was now standing next to the Observator, and asked them if they could show her some kind of identification. The American produced his passport, the Austrian a laminated card from the police with his photo attached. He spoke to her in a friendly voice, as he nodded at the hand that had remained inside her pocket. He said:

"Possession of firearms is forbidden, madam, and you don't need weapons any longer so I will not mention it."

"What happens here is of great importance to the whole world," said the colonel. "You could even get the President of the United States out of bed to vouch for me..."

He walked back to the car, saying to the Austrian:

"We'll park the car wherever these people want us to."

The Observator pointed to a low wooden barn.

"There is enough room in there, and the back doors are open."

Ten minutes later they were all sitting in Flamel's living room on the second floor of the house. Wayne explained why he had come back; the little creatures he had taken with him in a sealed cylinder had been examined closely and it was established beyond the shadow of a doubt that they were not of earthly origin. All of the scientists he had allowed to be involved in it were convinced of the gravity of this conclusion. The director of the laboratory in Boston, where Wayne was from, had had a serious talk with the biologist and made it clear to him that he must inform somebody associated with the government. If the stories about the Brotherhood, about the talents of Winters and Flamel, the journeys, the table, and the contents of the temple of Janus were in fact true, he was on to something which was much too important to remain silent about. So, along with Wayne, he had made some contacts that resulted in a meeting with Colonel Patrick Kelly.

Now the colonel, in an unmistakably military fashion, began to speak. He explained that there was an invisible government network in existence, like a subcutaneous nerve system, which could be activated as soon as something happened that could pose a threat to the people of the world, or seemed so fantastic that an inquiry was justified.

"It is an American initiative that has international branches," he said. "Those who never have to deal with it, will never even know of its existence...but we are everywhere. For example; if one of the enormous radio telescopes that are mounted all around the world and aimed at the cosmos should perhaps receive a decodable message, we would get to hear the recordings immediately. Anything that can be possibly connected to extra-terrestrial infiltration is taken very seriously by us and will be examined. In most cases, it turns out to be a false alarm, but every now and then we are confronted by a riddle that we are unable to solve, and that frightens us. We have always been prepared for anything that might arise, and we knew that someday something would come up that would be of the greatest importance. What it would look like and where it might happen was, of course, impossible for us to say. Now we know though, that it is in Helgen and that we are fortunate enough to be dealing with wise men that know how to guard, and keep a secret. I am all for a tightly knit co-operation between us. Various funds are available and I can pay everyone a more than adequate salary. Anything amount needed for research can be paid...we have the money, and the people for everything. It is my fondest wish that my proposals fall on fertile ground..."

"We have waited for this moment," Flamel responded quickly. "It is necessary, of course, that we work together. Everyone in our group has always recognized the importance of these events. Our support and cooperation will be unconditional. The only thing that I insist on is that Philippe Mundy remains the key figure, who pulls the strings and makes the final decisions."

The colonel heaved a sigh of relief.

"Is it really that easy to embark on such an ambitious project research with you?"

"It most certainly is!" said Flamel resolutely.

Patrick Kelly stood up to shake hands with Augustin Flamel, and the men looked at each other and smiled. After the colonel sat back down, Rudolph Brendel began to speak.

"I have been assigned to make the work as pleasant as possible for you," he said. "We are on Austrian ground and it is my job to protect you. If no one has any objections, I will have some temporary barracks built around the fence as soon as possible to house some of my men in."

Hans then told them about Carandini's threats.

"The week is almost over..."

"In that case, I will begin guarding you myself immediately. Would you be willing to turn your weapons over to me?"

He looked out of the corner of his eye to Monaco, who nodded in agreement.

"Jack Doyle will be returning soon," said Wayne. "And Doctor Weckmann is waiting for a call and will arrive as soon as possible, once he hears from me. Our little friends, that everyone has been caring for, will be brought back to Helgen, with the exception of the two I left behind at the lab in Boston. But every one there knows the importance of keeping this a secret as well."

"This takes a heavy weight off my shoulders," sighed Flamel. "Together we can move mountains!"

"To the outside world it will appear that we are establishing an institute for paranormal research," said the colonel. "This will especially require the empathy of Flamel, who the press will see as the inspired psychic leading a team of researchers in the quest for the hidden powers of the human mind. With Winters seemingly his assistant and student, the plan will certainly succeed...and it will allow us to work in peace."

"Perfect," said Hans. "I see that you have thought of everything."

By the following, morning huge cranes had delivered prefabricated barracks that were lifted over the fences and set down in place. Rudolph Brendel introduced his men to all the residents so that everybody knew and recognized each other. The Observator showed the Colonel the circle and the table. The table top was removed by Winters and Flamel, and the roof was lifted off of the temple so that the Colonel could have a good look at the twenty little objects.

"Even this secret is now revealed, Mundy," Flamel thought to himself.

The Observator told the new arrivals everything he knew.

"The Brotherhood of Helgen has done some amazingly fine work," he declared. "They conducted their experiments here, behind these walls, and kept their sensational discoveries to themselves. That is how they found out that the objects were able to penetrate steel and leave a deposit of sorts there...something that I began to refer to as the 'Long Zero'. The steel works much like a battery, storing the energy imparted by the creatures, but not everyone is sensitive to the powers stored within. Maybe we will discover a way to permit the 'Long Zero' to creep into the body of any human being. The Brotherhood of Helgen never described how far along they were towards their goal at the beginning of the twentieth century. We only know that it works... but not how it works. Hans Winters and Augustin Flamel took mammoth walking tours that were obviously necessary for them to get used to what they were carrying around inside themselves. The contents of the temple of Janus belongs to science now!"

The Colonel replaced the roof of the building that stood on the table beside a pillar constructed of reinforced concrete. He had more...and bigger... plans, and needed to have more barracks built to house additional scientists. He had long phone conversations everyday with people whom he was attempting to entice into coming to Helgen.

"We will be busy with all the preparations," he said to the Observator. "And when everything is in place...when we have living quarters, a kitchen, a lab and a strong roof protecting the table of the Brotherhood...this place will have become like a small world unto itself, an impregnable fortress that no man will be able to breach."

Jack Doyle, the psychologist, and Stefan Weckman, the doctor, soon returned.

Everything Carandini had stolen taken was delivered right to the front door, thanks to the intervention of the Colonel, and the excellent co-operation between the Italian and Austrian police.

Hans sat and read a book, which he finished in half an hour, barely glancing at the accompanying photos, but remembering every detail. He was unable to sleep and spent the entire night pouring over a new and very special book that he had recently obtained.

The week of Carandini's threat had expired without anybody attempting to make good on it. Meanwhile, Brendel and his men kept the entrance to the compound securely sealed to any unauthorized persons.

Among the things that were returned was an item that actually belonged to Carandini, and that Hans never even knew existed. It was a scrapbook full of old photos that had no doubt belonged to Paolo Carandini.

Commenting on the elder Carandini, Flamel said:

"He was a stay-behind...the members of the Brotherhood of Helgen had all disappeared... except for him. He would not, or could not, go with them...and the only possible explanation I can come up with is that he was not susceptible to the 'Long Zero'. So Andrea's ancestor went into hiding and remained silent. When someone finally stumbled across him after many years, he was old and senile. Not that it mattered, for even when he was of sound mind he would never have divulged any of the Brotherhood's secrets. I bought Paolo's manuscripts from Andrea...but he never even showed me this unique scrapbook, never mind offer to sell it."

Hans looked at the photographs taken between 1920 and 1930 over and over. He recognized the house, the table, the annexes, the garden...filled with rocks, and the snow covered mountaintops.

He found himself deeply affected by the portraits and group photos.

Ulrich von Drach was a slender man with a curly beard and moustache, between which thin lips formed a firm line. Wolfram Wikander seemed to be more frivolous and full of life. He had a moustache that pointed up, sparkling eyes and in most of the photographs he wore a shirt adorned with a flamboyant bowtie. Martha Ritter, an architect and Von Drach's wife, sported high, tightly closed blouses and wore her hair up. She stood behind a high wooden drawing table with a pencil and a ruler in her hands, and a grave look on her face. She was somewhere in the garden, on the path which led to the house. Her name was inscribed below the photo. The photographs had all remained bright and clear, because they had seldom been exposed to the daylight. They allowed Hans to have a look into the past and he saw people there to whom he felt a strong feeling of solidarity.

There was a photograph of Ulrich von Drach and Wolfram Wikander standing together in a dry riverbed and laughing. They wore long coats with broad lapels and high leather shoes. It looked like the black and white formal wear of a merry holiday, but Hans knew that what they had actually been busy doing there was making stones disappear into thin air, just as he had done himself.

Around the table of the Brotherhood sat twelve men and women on tall wooden chairs.

He would have loved to been able to hear their voices...to hear what they were talking about!

Had they also been wandering, year after year, driven by the change in their bodies and minds, and caused by the Long Zero? How had they come to meet each other? Wolfram Wikander had been a long-distance runner, an athlete. Von Drach was a physicist, a colleague from the past for the Observator.

As soon as Hans got to the last page of the scrapbook, he started from the beginning again.

There was a picture of Paolo Carandini, the only one in the book that had faded. Perhaps some member of the family had framed it and put it on a sideboard, and later placed it back in the thick album. Paolo was slightly built and had deep lines in his face for such a young man. His black moustache had been heavily greased in order to keep it in curls, and his smile showed a mouth full of healthy, white teeth. He was leaning on a rough- hewn walking stick that he probably used when he went hiking in the mountains.

Wolfram Wikander stood with an axe beside a big pile of wood that was used for the fire in the hearths.

He was wearing a flannel shirt, and his trousers, which were held up by suspenders that crossed a powerfully built chest and broad shoulders, fit snugly.

Hans would have given anything to know what these people were thinking about at the moment the picture was taken. Wikander looked out at him from the old paper with impudent eyes, Von Drach seemed thoughtful and philosophical, his wife self-confident but nonetheless fragile and full of doubt. Safe behind her drawing table she radiated energy, but standing amongst the others at the big table she looked almost shy, with half closed eyes and her hands resting on the table top.

The photographs revealed none of the Twentier's secrets. The carvings that depicted the march on the Roman temple were not visible in any of the photos, nor were any of the rituals that might have taken place there. He saw pictures of them working in a studio on drawings and paintings, and a man and woman who's names appeared to be Charlotte Schimanski and Janko Ventura, cutting ten inch high sculptures from wood.

Finally he put the thick album down turned off the light under which he had been sitting all evening.

Monaco didn't wake up when he slid in to the bed beside her. He carried the feeling of the photographs into his dream world with him, but the following day could remember none of it.

While Colonel Kelly directed the rebuilding of the houses and barns, and the Observator, and Wayne initiated newcomers and placed gave new equipment, Winters and Flamel undertook new journeys. They wanted to bring back as many of the little creatures as possible in the shortest amount of time. Sometimes they made two trips a day, but it never became routine...or predictable.

On each trip, they were surprised and overcome by horrible fears that would enter their mind's eye and wreak havoc there. They had never dared to imagine that fear could materialize in so many disguises. Hans would get the feeling of falling and have no doubt that he was about to smash into the hard ground. Or he would think that he was being squeezed and that the air was being pressed out of his lungs. But the worst was when he became afraid of apparitions that he would have found very normal under other circumstances. He cried out, longing for death, when he saw a vividly colored bird with long legs passim. He tumbled through a field full of luminous marbles and hoped that soon he would be able to close his eyes forever. He imagined himself in a loft where the sunlight filtered in through an oblique window and the dust motes he saw whirling were so terrifying that he thought his heart would burst. He was a rat on the run, a ponderous locomotive without wheels, a bullet smashing into a wall.

He felt strong and happy though, when he returned to the circle in the small room, his hands full of little creatures that bumped softly against his skin.

Flamel seemed be worse off however. He complained about headaches and said he was exhausted.

"Then stop toying it," proposed Hans. "Let me go alone."

After a good, solid meal, they walked back to the building to start on a new journey.

Flamel suddenly stopped and put a hand on Winters' shoulder.

"I can stick it out. It is not our journeys I'm worrying about."

"Are all the changes around here happening too fast for you? It had never been your intention to have people like Colonel Kelly get involved, had it? I mean, you never invited him... Why, you don't even know him."

"No, that has nothing to do with it. I'm just as happy that things are working out this way. Thorough research must be done. It is in the interest of all of mankind, and we can believe with confidence that everything is in good hands now. How different it would have been if someone like Carandini had been able to take control of this project."

"What's up then? What are you trying to tell me?"

Flamel remained silent for a bit, searching for words, and then cleared his throat. He avoided Hans' glance, and said:

"You know how happy I am that you have joined us. You must also know that I care a lot about you...you are young and intelligent and together with Monaco you have a wonderful future ahead of you."

Hans looked at him in surprise.

"What exactly is it you want me to understand, my friend?"

Without responding, Flamel started to run to the building.

"Come on!" he cried. "Let's see how a full stomach reacts to a journey!"

Hans ran along behind him, confused by Flamel's words.

He had complete confidence in Flamel's good intentions, but he also knew that he was holding back something important from him.

Chapter 10: The Hellish Road To Paradise

Colonel Kelly had no problem with the stipulation that the most important decisions concerning this unique gathering were to be left up to the Observator...but he insisted that it be he that personally oversaw any plans that involved rebuilding the compound in a secure manner...and it was beginning to look very much as if this quiet country estate would indeed be turned into an impregnable fortress.

"I am your guest," he said to Mundy. "But I represent an incredibly powerful force, and have at my disposal any amount of manpower or money that I may deem necessary, but everything depends on Winters and Flamel, and any discoveries that are made here. As a military man, I have assumed the responsibility of protecting your secrets. Keep in mind...I am not here to train recruits how to use steel cylinders to pick up the 'Long Zero', so that they may swarm off to conquer other worlds. Imagine the chaos that would ensue, Phillipe, if anyone who so desired, from any random spot on Earth, were able to leave the planet at will."

"Still, I suppose that it is the ultimate intention of the project to give others the ability to participate in this brave new method of travel," remarked the Observator.

"Of course...and the sooner the better...but I'm only talking about a very select company, who we are sure will be entirely dedicated to science."

Winters and Flamel had reached a point where even they needed rest. They had brought many of the little creatures back to Helgen, and would only embark on another journey after the reconstruction of the compound had been completed, and all of the rooms had been properly outfitted. Doctor Stefan Weckman had taken samples of their blood and hair, and sent them off to the lab in Boston.

"Eventually we will succeed in finding out exactly what this thing is that has changed you so," he said.

Hans continued to meditate and train his body with Flamel, with whom he went running every morning; but, because there was still the threat of an attempt by Carandini, they preferred to train indoors now, where a varied assortment of exercise equipment had been installed. Carandini had made it known, through Pirenne, that he was aware of everything that transpired in Helgen, which obviously meant that he had some of his men in the area, who were keeping an eye on the compound from somewhere up in the surrounding mountains.

Hans worked out with weights every day and was now able to lie on his back and bench-press one hundred kilos. He needed to do these exercises to get rid of his excess energy and there were times that he lifted the barbell so often, that it actually began to feel lighter. Instead of running, he skipped rope...and this he was able to do with such speed and vigor, that the rope emitted a whizzing noise as it spun past his body. He would fall into a trance at the sound of the rope speeding past his dancing feet and be able to keep this pace up for an hour or more.

The door to the makeshift gymnasium opened and Mireille came in. Hans put the barbell down and sat up. She stroked her thick hair and looked at him nervously.

"Do you know where Augustin is, Hans?"

"I have no idea. He was not in the dining room this morning for breakfast but I thought he would show up here with you to work out with me."

"I woke up in the middle of the night and he was lying beside me. When I woke up again early in the morning, just as the sun was coming up, he was no longer there. I have searched for him everywhere."

"That's very strange. Have you talked to the Observator?"

"Not yet."

"Wait a minute, we'll go see him together."

He was hardly sweating as he put on a shirt, buttoned it and walked outside with her. They saw Mundy standing near the building by the rock wall, from which the roof had been removed. Only a few people knew what was under the table top... twenty cylinders, which the Observator had ordered from an Austrian factory, had been placed in the holes. The gate in the temple was open and the little objects floated around in the darkness over the heads of the wooden figures. Mundy hung around the table like a watchdog and Rudolph Brendel saw to it that his men were always there throughout the night.

The walls of the building had to be supported and braced before the new roof of reinforced concrete could be set on top of the building. It would protect the table against any boulders that might happen to become loose high up on the slopes and roll down.

The Observator bid Mireille and Hans good morning and began telling them about the other activities available to them, besides the gym, such as the firing range that

Pirenne had set up. Of the seven occupants in the house, she was the one who could handle a revolver the best.

Hans thought about the Twentiers all the time now, ever since he realized that they must also have performed these same experiments, and he was troubled by fearful visions when he considered what the consequences might be if something went wrong. In his mind he saw a bearded man, dressed in the fashion of the early twentieth century, crossing the galaxy with his eyes wide open...a lifeless traveller on his way to the frontiers of the universe.

He told them that he had been discussing Flamel with Monaco.

"I told her that it seems as if he is concealing something."

"My eyes and ears are wide open," she had assured him. "I am watching everything and everyone."

The Observator placed the twenty little objects back into the temple.

The little gate was closed, the roof was put on, and the artwork was once again covered with the heavy wooden top. He spent most of his time in the garden, where he would sit in the sun, or pace up and down with his hands behind his back. At night he disappeared into the kitchen and prepared the evening meal.

Mireille said quickly, so as to keep him from going on:

"I'm looking for Augustin. I'm sure you know where he is!"

"There's not too much for him to do at the moment, and that, of course, also applies to Hans. As everything around here is constantly changing, he searches for some respite in isolation and separation...Flamel wants to be alone to think, meditate and make plans."

"Why didn't he say anything to anybody then?" asked Mireille in desperation. "He left... just like that. Don't you find that a bit odd? He should have discussed his plans with me first..."

The Observator simply shrugged his shoulders.

"You know how Augustin is...he goes his own way, and some decisions he makes on his own."

Hans left Mireille with the Observator...he had heard enough. Perhaps Mireille thought Augustin was visiting another woman. She knew, as did everyone, that he had many girlfriends. After all, he was a celebrity throughout Europe and there were many wild stories around about his incredible prowess in the bedroom. But Hans knew that there was more to what was going on. Augustin had fallen in love with Mireille and would not be sneaking away from her to spend his days in the company of other women.

He asked Monaco what she thought about it and received an evasive answer.

But that night, when they made love, she was more passionate and fierce than ever. And when they finally went to sleep, she held her arms tightly around him, as if she were afraid that he might run away too.

Hans trained intensively for days at a time. A new period had begun for him in which he could go his own way. He kept his eyes wide open, spoke often with the Observator and the Colonel, and watched the progress of the ongoing reconstruction. He would remain in a trance state for hours and hours and read at least three or four books every day. Monaco made it a point to always stay close to him and made love to him every night, lying sleeplessly beside him until she was sure that he was sleeping.

The days passed without anything out of the ordinary happening, and with no news about Flamel.

One morning, a group of journalists from different countries showed up, who wanted to talk to Flamel about the cancellation of his tour and about all the changes taking place in Helgen. They were all frisked by Brendel and his men, and were required to leave their ID's with him before they were allowed to go on up to the house.

There were two Frenchmen, two Italians, a Dane and a German. One of the Italians was a woman with raven black hair and dark eyes like Monaco's. Hans did not trust her, and suspected that she worked for Carandini. He spent the entire day with the six reporters... introducing them to the Observator and Patrick Kelly, and explaining what the new institute for parapsychology would eventually look like. This chore came easy to him and he held them in his grip them with stories about the special workings of the human mind and the hidden powers of mankind.

He gave some demonstrations, making stones disappear and performing some tricks that he had learned from Flamel. Monaco was with him all the time keeping an eye on the journalists, as well as him. She talked with the Italian woman during lunch, but she could find nothing wrong with her...she seemed to actually work for a big daily newspaper. She was the first one to depart that afternoon, along with the other Italian reporter. The French also left together, and the Dane, who was interested in psychology, stayed a bit later to interview Jack Doyle.

The only one who remained behind with Hans was the German, Friedrich Klinger. He was a pleasant man in his early forties with many interests, and was a specialist in paranormal affairs who was able to keep his audience spellbound with one remarkable story after another. He made Hans laugh with tales of poltergeists and levitation, and at the same time demonstrated his exceptional knowledge in all of these matters. He had studied much about everything...and knew as much about recent research in the paranormal psychology field as he did about occult events from the distant past.

They found themselves out on the field and Klinger picked up a stone the size of a billiard ball and handed it to Hans.

"No," he smiled, "I'm not asking you to make it disappear again. I'm still completely amazed from seeing it at all, so I think I want to take some to think about it before I see it again. You know... I have really seen, and learned a lot in my life, and I too have mastered something that looks, at first glance, unexplainable."

He pointed to the staircase at the right of the house.

"Come with me... And bring that stone with you."

Hans followed him, a bit of surprised. They climbed the stairs that swept around to the back of the house. From here they could see the other buildings and behind them the steep slopes that he had climbed with Flamel were visible.

"It's really a very simple trick, when you know how it's done," grinned Klinger. "If you promise not to tell anyone, I'll show it to you. It could be something that might be used in Flamel's act, if he ever goes out on the road again. Now, give me that stone..."

As Hans handed the stone to him, he already knew what was going to happen.

The Italian journalist had apparently been sent to Helgen as a diversionary tactic. She was undoubtedly a genuine reporter, who had been dispatched by her editor, but it was Carandini who had pulled the strings to arrange it. The plan was obviously to have her be suspected of being two-faced, just like her Italian colleague, a little man with clever eyes and a bright mind. But in fact it was this likable German who actually had been hired to attack Augustin or Hans. He could not have smuggled a weapon in with him, for Rudolph Brendel would certainly have found it. But here, behind the house, a big stone was enough to bash his head in which would certainly wound him seriously, if not kill him. And the proximity to the slopes would do very nicely as an escape route, leading him high up into the mountains where he might have a good chance of getting away.

Klinger held the stone in his hand and closed his fingers tightly around it. Staring at Hans he tossed the rock up and down softly in his hand, while Hans remained standing there looking at him, emotionless. Hans was waiting for the man to act first...he had to be absolutely certain that the man intended to attack him.

Klinger suddenly threw the stone higher than he previously had, and as it came down, he caught it and brought his hand swinging forward in one fluid motion. The stone shot out of his hand...and towards Hans' head. Before it had reached Hans however, it disappeared into thin air. Klinger, who was now frightened and amazed, was given no time to recover his composure. An infuriated Hans flew at him, frustrated and annoyed with himself because it had taken him so long to realize that this man was here to carry out Carandini's orders. Hans was not a fighter, and even during his long hikes he had seldom been forced to use his fists. When violence threatened, he preferred turning around...but he was so furious now, that he lost all self-control. He beat Klinger violently with his fists as the man tried to defend himself. He had represented himself as a journalist who could offer interesting anecdotes regarding the same fields of research that Hans and Augustin were involved in, but in fact, he was a trained fighter who was dispatched to assassinate people. But he was no match for Hans. Blow after blow rained down on him hitting him about the face and chest. He fell to the ground as Hans kept up his attack.

Hans had complete control over himself when he meditated or embarked on one of his insane journeys, but he had never trained to be a fighter and now he simply beat on in a blind rage. A rattling noise escaped from Klinger's throat as he lay on the ground, his head twisted to the side. The part of his head that was visible was a bloody mess and he had five broken ribs. Blood streamed out of his mouth...his chin seemed to be crushed and his jaw was broken. Hans fell to his knees beside him and buried his face in his hands.

"I have killed him," he thought.

Someone put a hand on his shoulder and he looked up in fright. It was Monaco.

"Klinger..." she hissed softly. "I knew I should have followed you from the beginning."

She did not seem too worried about the man lying there lifelessly. During the time she had been associated with Andrea Carandini she had seen more than her share of violence and bloodshed.

"I'll get Brendel," she said. "You are not to blame for this...It was self-defence. This man had every intention of splitting your head open."

Hans realized that a murder committed at the compound could mean the end of the project. He also knew that Friedrich Klinger would be reported missing by Carandini when he did not reappear in Italy soon. But he did not think about these things at that moment. Staring at the person lying on the ground, he put his fingers against his temples and began to stammer:

"It was as if I were suddenly having an out of body experience. Look at what I have done...what my mind and body have executed. I never wanted to do anything like this..."

A shiver ran through Klinger's body as his head moved slightly and his arms and legs twitched. His heels kicked with staccato bursts upon the ground where he lay.

Then he was lying still again.

"Stay put, Monaco," said Hans. "Let's keep Brendel out of it for a bit..."

Still sitting on his knees, he leaned forward. Carefully, he compressed Klinger's chest and slid a hand under his head and concentrated. Klinger opened his eyes. His troubled eyes grew bright and he began to smile.

"How did you do that?" he asked.

Then he clenched his teeth and moaned.

"I think some of your ribs are broken. You need a doctor. I will ask Dr. Weckmann to take a look at you. If I had not helped you, if I had not given you some of my own strength, you would have died here," said Hans.

The face of the man was still quite damaged, but not the bloody mess it had so recently been. Klinger tried to get up, but the pain in his chest was too great and he sank back down again.

"You didn't have to help me," he said. "I had every intention of killing you... and Flamel, if he had been around."

"By order of Carandini?"

"Yes."

Hans stood up, took Monaco by the hand and went down the stairs along the house. He informed Weckmann about what had happened, and it was decided that Klinger would remain in Helgen under the guard of Brendel until he had recovered, and Pirenne would make contact with Carandini and tell him that his plans had failed.

The Observator only listened with half an ear as Hans told him what had happened, and closed the topic with a short remark:

"So everything is all right again, isn't it?"

He had something to tell Hans which he thought was much more important.

"We have made some progress with our little creatures...Phil Wayne and I have become quite experienced in handling them. We now know now that they take moisture from out of the air and give it back by leaving it on the leaf of the stinging nettle. We used different types of terrariums and put plants, minerals, stones, a variety of metals and small amounts of soil in them. But only with the stinging nettle did they feel compelled to act. It looks like the moisture is pressed out of the front, like sweat through pores. We have collected some droplets and we can now analyze what is in it."

"That is interesting," said Hans. "Keep me posted, Philippe, and please don't forget, each time you handle them, that I did not risk my life for nothing to get those creatures here..."

When he asked if Flamel had sent any news of himself, the Observator did not answer him, he simply shrugged his shoulders and turned away.

That night Monaco surpassed her usual sexual appetite. Hans was tireless, as usual, but she simply would not surrender in their game of love. Even when Hans was sure that she was physically exhausted her lust remained unquenched, and when she put her arms around him and attempted to set out on a new expedition of discovery into erotic delights, he took her by the shoulders and pushed her away, looking deeply into her dark eyes.

Before he could ask, she tried to explain her behavior...crying all the while, but never trying to hide her tears from him.

"This maybe our last night together," she said. "That is why I want to enjoy it as long as possible...at least until I am done..."

Hans released her and sat up. Monaco panted heavily and kept her eyes tightly shut for a while.

"Our last night together...what do you mean? You're not planning on leaving, are you?"

"Of course not...but I have kept something from you. After I have told you what I probably should have said sooner, you will probably leave and I'm not sure if you will ever come back again."

"You're speaking in riddles, Monaco. Can't you be more clear?"

"Flamel has stayed away so long," she said. "Too long..."

She sat up also now. She stroked his face and looked at him intently as she began to speak.

Hans listened without interrupting her.

"I have learned to be constantly on my guard...I can sleep and keep watch all at the same time. The softest sound puts me on the alert."

She wiped the beads of sweat from her face. As she spoke, she tried to get her breathing under control and pointed at the window. The living room of their apartment was at the front of the house and their bedroom at the rear.

"So often, I hear the sounds the other people in the house are making. Someone going to the kitchen to get a drink, someone walking down the stairs... all are familiar to me. The other night though, I heard something outside. I got out of bed and walked over to the window. It was very early in the morning and was still dark out. Not far from the window I could see Flamel and the Observator. They went carefully along the side of the house and disappeared from sight. I remained standing there for a bit longer and then suddenly saw a beam of light flashing up and down between the trees. Silently, I went outside. The light continued to move, and every now and then it disappeared.

As it became visible again, it was higher up the slope than it had previously been.

Flamel and Mundy had gone up into the mountains, towards the right flank until they had reached a high point. Once there, the light continued burning for another fifteen minutes or so. Then it came down again and finally disappeared completely after the daylight had made use of a lantern unnecessary. I went back to the bedroom and peeked from between the curtains. The Observator had returned...but Flamel was no longer with him."

They continued to look at each other.

"I remembered where the light had been shining longest, and as soon as I saw my chance, I scurried up and began to investigate until I found something..."

"Was it a circle?" asked Hans.

She pulled back so astonished, that she landed with her back on the pillows, her eyes wide in amazement.

"How on earth did you know that?"

"I have the feeling that Flamel has set out on a journey. He told me that he cared for me, but said it as if he were bidding me farewell. He's definitely kept something from me. He has gone...the way the Brotherhood went, so long ago. Tell me...was it a circle, Monaco?"

"Yes, on a flat, slightly inclined rock hidden behind pine trees and other stones. If you weren't looking for that particular spot, you would never stumble across it. Not far from there, hidden in a deep hole, I found a sports bag full of synthetic material. Inside of it were Flamel's clothes, so I closed the bag and put it back again. The Observator is the apparently the only one who knows about this and will never suspect that I have gone out investigating."

"Why have you kept this from me for so long? Were you afraid that I would follow Flamel's?"

"That should be clear...no?"

"But then why tell me now?"

"I just thought you should know. Within a few days the fence that the Colonel is building to protect everything within the compound will be completed. There will be state of the art electronic monitoring equipment and bright lights all over the place. He is very apprehensive about an attack from the rear by Carandini's men and soon it will be virtually impossible to get up there inconspicuously...do you understand? If you decide to go the same way Flamel did, you must do it by tomorrow. I will bring you up there at the crack of dawn. I don't know the route well enough to find my way back up there in the dark using only a lantern, it's that complicated...which also proves, by the way, that Flamel and the Observator must have been there more than once."

"If I do decide to go... shouldn't I inform the Observator first?"

"I really don't think that he could provide you with any more information that you would find useful."

"No, I don't think so, either. And he will try to talk me out of it, that's for sure. But why hasn't Flamel returned yet? Am I going to my death by following him? Or is he lost somewhere...screaming for my help?"

"You must make this decision yourself," said Monaco. "If you go, I will tell the Observator about it afterwards and it will remain our secret until that time."

She stopped talking, but fell he knew what she was thinking.

"You mustn't say anything to him until you're one hundred percent sure that we will not be returning again." he said, supplying the words for her thoughts.

"Flamel has decided that this is the appropriate time to take this risk. Later on, the Observator and the Colonel will want to involve the entire research team. Flamel is convinced that the members of the Brotherhood disappeared of their own free will and did not commit suicide, as some people have suggested. He has probably never mentioned a second circle to me because he was unsure of all the facts."

"I'm not going to give you any advice," said Monaco in a sombre and determined tone. "But I'm sure you will understand that I would much prefer keeping you here, with me, rather than see you disappear before my very eyes. I know you are determined to find out the truth. No...I don't think I'll give you any advice...and I also think that there's no time left for you to make love to me...again."

They both burst out in laughing and Hans said:

"I must think...Flamel didn't know what to expect when he left from the second circle, just as I don't know."

"This is true, and as long as there are all these people around here, busy with the reconstruction project, it isn't safe for you here. We know that from Klinger's attack on you... perhaps Flamel was a lot more sure of himself than we think."

"What do you mean?"

"His clothes, neatly put away, protected from the elements...you would only do something like that if you were sure that you would be needing them again...someday."

They left the house early the following morning at first light.

By the time they were halfway up the mountain it was light enough for Monaco to find the way. There was a small path that led upwards, but at some points it was so steep that they were forced to make their way on all fours, like mountain goats. Monaco ran out of steam quickly, lagging behind Hans but clutching his hand the whole time, and every now and then telling him where to go. She allowed herself to be dragged along and finally, when her feet began to hurt, she asked him to please stop so that she might take a breather. From an outcropping that ran along above the path, they were able to look down at the buildings far below them. Hans saw someone walking down there, and squeezed himself back along the rock wall and beckoned to Monaco.

"We must take care that no one sees us. Brendel's men use field glasses to observe the area."

"Come, we can go on now," said Monaco. "But please, don't walk too fast. No one can overtake us anymore, now. I'm beginning to get a whole new respect for the determination and stamina of the Observator, who must have done this climb several times..."

Hans had made his decision the night before.

He would make the journey, even though he knew he was undertaking a great risk. He could not sit still and do nothing now that Flamel had proceeded with the plan. They finally reached the rock that Monaco had told him about. The circle, scratched in the stone, was clearly visible and was much the same as the one in the small room next to the table of the Brotherhood. There was a pile of pebbles beside it and Hans suspected that the circle had been hidden from view until Flamel and the Observator had swept them away to reveal it. Monaco showed him the bag with Flamels's clothes.

Hans entered the circle and stood in the centre of it. It was quite cold at this height so early in the morning, and a stiff breeze blew through his hair. Suddenly overcome with doubt he sank to his knees. He was still able to see the buildings below and he tried to visualize the members of the Brotherhood gathering here and readying themselves for their departure.

He screwed up his courage and decided once and for all that he would also depart from this place, but now Monaco was seized with doubt and she began to work on him.

"Maybe I'd better keep silent about this permanently," she said. If you never come back, I will always feel guilty. I love you too much to let you go...come, let's go down and first ask Philippe Mundy what has happened to Flamel."

"It's obvious what has happened to Flamel, you know that just as well as I."

"I love you, Hans...you...you mean so much to me..."

She kept on talking and pleading, and finally she began to cry, making gestures of despair with her hands as if to beg him not to go. In the meantime Hans had taken off his clothes and put them in the bag with Flamel's. He did not know how to bid her farewell, so he didn't. He knelt in the centre of the circle and began to concentrate. He could no longer hear Monaco's voice any more, but could still see her as she shook her head fiercely and the tears were thrown from her beautiful black eyes.

A cry of horror produced a triple echo across the alpine valleys as she wiped her face with her sleeve. When she looked up again, Hans had disappeared.

At the beginning of the journey Hans was still able to think clearly. He was swept rushed along on a river of exploding colors, and was surrounded by brilliantly fluorescent spheres. They were above and below him, to his left and to his right. They shot past him and crossed each other's paths. He was convinced that he too was now a colored orb. His body had become so tightly knit unto itself that it felt like a lead bullet, and he wondered if all these quickly whizzing balls were not travellers crossing the universe, just as he was.

Then the fear took hold of him, in all its horrible manifestations.

There was a rending pain that hit him in the very core of his system, and he felt as if he were suffocating. He was drowning...and his spirit could find nothing to hang on to. His battle was a mighty one...he was hoping for the moment that his life would end while remaining conscious of the thousands of fears that were crushing him all at once. The pain threw him forwards, but he could not escape from it no matter how fast he allowed himself to speed along on the streams of light. He was susceptible to all possible feelings of misery and too vulnerable to resist. The elusive, transient fears were not as bad as the visions that were born from human, more or less earthly, origin.

Mercury appeared beside him and presented him with ankle-high shoes complete with wings.

Able to see himself as a human again, Hans put on the boots and increased his speed. The boots seemed to clamp themselves around his feet and now a scorching pain in his lower extremities sang along in the choir of all the other pains that harassed him. Celtic and Germanic warriors materialized turned who thrust swords and spears at him attempting to drive him upwards towards the temple of Janus, the two-faced god.

The gods had exchanged their horses for multi-headed dragons. Hellish flames cascaded down his body. He tumbled and bounced on his journey through hell.

His flesh was gnawed upon and torn apart. He could not take a breath and began to burn from the inside out. He was a fiery comet that burned and fed upon itself until only a kernel of consciousness remained, and that kernel was tormented by fear and pain...and a desire to obtain eternal oblivion.

There seemed to be no end to the torture. He was sucked through open jaws, grabbed by razor-sharp claws, torn to pieces over and over again, pulled apart, spit out...and thrown away like yesterday's trash.

The death wish transformed itself into contempt of death - he began to draw fatalistic courage from his misery. He sunk imaginary teeth into the phantoms that attacked him. He ate his way through the body of a screaming god of thunder, spitting out his flesh and bones as he went.

Myriad shapes of pain were concentrated into a feeling that lay beyond the human reach, vibrating at a frequency to which he was not susceptible, and he was finally able to dispel the evils.

Mercury returned to his side and blew cool air on his burning feet. The wings upon his boots increased his already dizzying speed. His flight was now parallel to the beams of light.

It was as if Pandora's box had reclaimed all its vile wretchedness and slammed the lid shut.

Janus bowed and turning a key, opened a door for Hans.

Hans was thrust down onto a soft patch of ground. He lay on his belly, turned his head and opened his mouth, sucking cool air into his lungs. The scent of a hundred thousand flowers filled his nostrils...and he smiled.

Mercury bent over him.

"Mors janua vitae," he whispered softly. "Death is the gateway of life."

"But I am not dead!" thought Hans. "Let me lie here, let me rest, let me sleep... but I am not dead!"

He did not dare open his eyes, too afraid of what he might see. The recent visions of horror still haunted his brain. His battered body shivered. Carefully, and with eyes still closed, he moved his fingers. Then he rubbed his feet together in an effort to rid himself of Mercury's winged shoes.

It slowly dawned on him that he was wearing no clothing at all...including shoes. The air was rich in oxygen and made him sleepy. He was exhausted, hungry, thirsty, and all his muscles and bones ached.

His mind sunk into a quiet darkness.

He awoke to the sensation of raindrops on his skin. Carefully, he tried to get up. He did not succeed at this and once again fell into a deep sleep. Bright, pleasant dreams washed through his badgered mind.

Waking up again, he felt the warmth of the sun and knew he now had the strength to stand up. But before he attempted that feat, he wanted to think. He thought about the climb up to the rock, Monaco, the circle, Flamel's clothes in the bag, the insane journey, the pains, the fears, and his torn soul. His thoughts became clearer. He understood now why Flamel hadn't returned to tell him that everything was all right. At least he understood it if the reason was that Flamel had found himself on this world! In that case he had neither courage nor strength to return immediately. Hans managed to get to his feet and take a deep breath. He opened his eyes and saw a world of great beauty around him.

He stood on a gently sloping plain that was overgrown with wildflowers of all possible colors and as big as dinner plates. Shades of pastel dominated the array of colors and here and there were flowers of deep purple, vivid yellow or black. The sky was light blue and the line just above the horizon milky white. The sun, standing above him aslant, was huge and radiated dim light. To his right was a lake, between two hills, with waves gently fanned by the cool breeze. The surface of the water was multi-colored, and the movement of the waves combined with the sunlight had the effect of making all the colors run together.

"Water," muttered Hans, surprised at the sound of his own voice.

He gave himself a quick self-analysis after this remark and knew that he was reacting to his environs in a fairly logical way...so far. But he was still behaving differently than when he had been a bearer of the Long Zero, his longing for water was certainly a human need. After everything he had been through, it might almost be expected that he would be prone to panic attacks, hysteria, or fear of aggressive behavior.

Instead he felt like a traveller who had finally reached his goal and now wanted to quench his thirst and hunger. When he looked down he noticed that he was standing inside of a circle of stones. They seemed to be the only sort of rocks or stones in the entire area and this made him chuckle with delight...for this had to mean that he was not the first person to have stood in this spot and surveyed this world.

Hans ran his hands over his arms, legs, and stomach and realized that he had lost quite a bit of weight on his journey. He had always been lean, but now his muscles, tough and as hard as steel could be seen under his skin. His fingers were bony, and his breastbone and ribs protruded. His neck too, was pencil thin. Certainly, if he was in the shape as Hans, a quick return journey would have meant the death of Flamel. Hans realized that it was impossible for him too to let Monaco know that he was fine, and that he had reached his goal...alive.

He started to walk in the direction of the water.

The flowers he stepped on as he proceeded slowly bounced up again and he stooped to feel the leaves. They were thick and felt like rubber. When he reached the shore he stood and gazed out upon the water and realized that the lake was not even two feet deep. Amazingly, the flowers also grew under the surface of the water and their pale colors seemed to be of a deeper hue.

Hans sank to his knees and filled his hand with water. It felt cool and good. He washed his face and tentatively sipped the water from his cupped hand. It was sweet tasting. He leaned forward now and drank straight from the lake. Just behind him a salamander-like animal shot away from under a flower and disappeared in the water. It had a shiny, bright red coloring with black stripes running from head to tail.

Hans remained sitting silently by the waterside as toads and frogs of all sizes scooted about. The little amphibians did not seem to be afraid of him and were not at all startled when he moved. He didn't notice any insects and could not help wondering how the frogs managed to feed themselves. The lake didn't seem to contain any fish and he saw no birds in the pale blue sky. Except for the soft rustling of the wind through the flowers it was absolutely quiet. He stood up again and turned around. The circle of stones was visible in the carpeted landscape of flowers.

Hans saw what appeared to be a path on the far side of the circle, an impression created by a long strip of orange flowers about three feet wide. They were smaller than the other multi-colored flowers that dominated the landscape.

A few moments later he walked across the tough little orange flowers, went around a hill, and through a valley which was a few feet deep and then around another hill. The path ended near a square plot of vegetation that was overgrown with vines growing along stakes that were heavy with fruit-bearing plants. In the middle of the little garden stakes and parasitic plants formed a natural hiding place, with three sides closed to the vagaries of the wind and a closed roof...only the side where Hans stood was open.

The path of flowers, the garden and the solid roof were, as far as he was concerned, proof of the presence of human beings.

At the moment he decided to take a look under the roof of leaves and flowers, he heard a humming sound behind him which began to get louder, then softer, and then rose again. He turned around and ran up the hill.

Above the lake, swarms of little creatures had appeared that looked just like the life forms that he and Flamel had brought back to Helgen with them. But there were also bigger ones, the front of which was as big as a clenched fist. The amphibious inhabitants of the lake jumped up through the clouds of creatures, fell back into the water and then disappeared beneath the surface. Hans could not see if the frogs were using their tongues to catch the creatures. He saw a salamander as long as his arm leap out of the water with a powerful beat of its tail and also snap at the creatures. The humming gradually became softer and the swarms vanished, floating low above the flowery sea until they were out of sight...

He went back to the square of vegetation, walked between the fruit-laden stakes and stopped in front of the open side of the plant house.

Inside, the ground was bare and covered with a friable, black and brown of soil. There was a metal plate about eighteen feet long and six feet wide in the centre. It was just about dusk, but Hans could clearly read three names engraved beside one another in the metal.

He read aloud:

"Ulrich von Drach, Martha Ritter, Wolfram Wikander..."

The leaders of the Brotherhood of Helgen were buried here! Ulrich von Drach, his wife Martha Ritter, and the mysterious Wolfram Wikander had spent the remainder of their lives on this world and their grave was not far from the spot on which they had originally arrived. Hans bowed deeply and remained standing there, lost in thought, for a long time and then left this peaceful place where big, ripe clusters of fruit hung heavy above the metal plate. The fruits of the parasitic plant looked like grapes, but out of respect for the resting place of the founding members of the Brotherhood he did not reach for them.

Back at the lake he drank more water, picked the rubbery leafs of several pale colored flowers and tasted them to see if they were at all fit for human consumption. A lilac leaf he put in his mouth tasted like almonds. He went on the assumption that his body would eliminate any poisons and ate the leaves until he was full. Small amphibians were crawling around him again, and it struck him that the adult ones still had external gills leading him to believe that they were still able to breath under water. A salamander, more than three feet and a half long stuck its head above the surface and gazed up at the sky with brown-veined yellowish eyes. Its open mouth revealed a sharply pointed tongue and sharp, oval teeth in the upper and lower jaws.

Hans clapped his hands loudly and the animal plunged under the water, wriggling away and losing itself in the riot of colors of the flower sea.

The pale sun was setting. Hans had seen a clump of tall flowers whose stalks bent under their weight. He went over to it and slid under the sweet smelling flowers. He had eaten and drunk, and was sleepy again. He was asleep the second he closed his eyes and his mind was immediately filled with marvellous dreams. He smiled insensibly in the dark night, pleased with the visions that were just as new and wonderful to him as this world of flowers.

Chapter 11: A New World

Visions, filled with clarity and revelation, drove the fear from the dark recesses of his mind.

Just as the mighty Hercules had diverted eternally flowing rivers from their prehistoric courses to wash the stables of King Ageas, Hans' dreams cleansed his troubled brain. Heaven-sent dreams delivered to him a respite filled with serenity, and his tawny body was able to finally relax. With a smile upon his face, Hans welcomed the blessings of the night.

It was the warmth of yet another sunrise that woke him...woke him to the surprise of another human body pressed against his flesh as he lay upon his side and his body shook with excitement. Still half asleep, the thought entered his mind that perhaps this was the place where the gods allowed mortals to share their happiness...perhaps this was heaven, nirvana, Valhalla.

He turned around and opened his eyes.

The woman who now lay beneath him had bright blue eyes and long blond hair. She breathed deeply through slightly parted lips, her arms and long, muscular legs wrapped around him. Her hips pushed upwards to meet each of his downwards thrusts, as he slid in and out of her tight body. Whenever his erotic assault upon her genitals ceased for a moment, she encouraged him to continue by holding him even tighter and gyrating the lower half of her body.

His thoughts wandered to Monaco, whom he felt must be countless light years away from him. Wherever it was that he now found himself, his thoughts remained those of a mere mortal, which was also true for his animal instincts, and he continued his lovemaking with renewed desire.

When his passions were finally released, his orgasm was so wild that he would not have even noticed if he had hurt her, yet nothing in her demeanor or behavior gave him any indication that she was not enjoying it as much as he.

With his steely muscles still tensed, he rolled off of her and came to a squatting position beside her, sitting on his heels like a small animal that had suddenly been frightened. He slithered away from under the long-stemmed flowers where she had found him sleeping.

Her clothing lay crumpled on the ground not far from where they lay.

Hans basked in the unreal pallor of the sun sitting low in the sky, the pastel colored landscape of flowers surrounding him, and the naked beauty sitting before him smiling. His astonishment grew even greater, when she said:

"Hans Winters..."

He shook his head in disbelief and wiped the sweat from his brow. It was a few moments before he was able to utter a sound in response, since the entire ethereal situation seemed to have cut off his stream of thoughts and almost completely eliminated his ability to speak. Anything he might have wanted to ask or say seemed unreal, and inconsequential, until finally he said:

"How... did I...did you..."

She pointed at the big flowers.

"A dreamcreeper," she said. "You were easy prey for me. We put them by our bedsides when we cannot fall asleep easily. While you sleep the flowers feed your unconscious with the most beautiful dreams."

"You speak French..."

She nodded, laughed, and closed her pretty blue eyes for a second.

"I don't speak Dutch, Hans...but my German is perfect and so is my English."

She moved closer to him, put her arms around him and pushed his head down against her shoulder.

"I am young and fruitful... and you are new here. We knew that there was a better than average chance that you would arrive at this location, so we took turns waiting here...and it was I who happened to be the lucky one."

After she let go of him again she stood up and walked over to her bundle of clothes. With each garment she put on, she began to look more and more like someone from the early twentieth century...on earth. Her skirt was long and stiff, and her white blouse had a circular collar that she closed with a dark knot of ribbons. The sleeves were decorated with lace frills. With quick skilful movements she put her long hair up and fastened it with little combs. Some clothing remained on the carpet of flowers near her that she picked up and handed to him. They consisted of a tightly cut jacket with broad lapels and long trousers, made from a material that looked like cotton.

"I hope they fit you well, Hans," she said. "Augustin described your physical appearance, but we had to guess at your actual sizes."

He looked up in surprise.

"Flamel!"

"Yes. And you... you really are Hans Winters, aren't you?"

"That's right...but what is your name?"

"Eleonora...Eleonora Ventura."

Hearing her name gave him a shock. In an old photograph of the Brotherhood he had seen a man by the name of Janko Ventura. He pulled on the trousers, which were a bit too wide for him. The legs of the pants and the jacket sleeves were too short, and the effect of the entire outfit was to make him look like a scarecrow. He plopped down on the thick petals and rubbed his temples with his fingertips.

He was having a good deal of trouble trying to process all these recent events at the same time, so it seemed to him that the wisest course of action would be to not even try, and simply let matters take their own course.

She had met Flamel...that, at least explained why she spoke to him in French.

Eleonora picked up two cleverly entwined straps from the place where her clothes had been lying. They were made from some sort of a leathery material, and their ends formed loops and the middle formed a long oval. With rapid movements she tied the belts around her waist.

"We call our world Drach," she said. "In honor of Ulrich von Drach, the first to arrive."

She looked at him proudly.

"My surname is Von Drach also. I am a direct descendant of the great adventurer. When I married Stefan Ventura, I took his name."

"You are married..." said Hans, a bit abashed considering their recent sexual acrobatics.

"Not to worry...it is simply one of the many old traditions we have chosen to maintain," she laughed.

She helped him to his feet up and together they walked along the lakeside where the amphibians dwelt. Hand in hand they walked along the shore and Eleonora told him all about life on Drach. He found it curiously pleasing to listen to her. Her dialect was kind of odd, and every now and then she used phrases he did not quite understand,

and words that belonged to the language of people from Earth's past.

She continued talking in a manner that echoed old earth in texture but interspersed with words such as he had never heard before. Words such as dreamcreepers, flydolls, toothapparatus, hangstrings, purplefields, ringlaws, songstrings, flowmetal, steambread and the goldwine of Drach. In addition to the new vocabulary he was learning, there were words no longer generally used in modern conversation, except by those people intelligent enough to know when, and how, to use them. Interspersed in her sentences were words like nevertheless, adorable, heraldic, continuance, draught-screen, wrath, suffused, herborize, eager beaver, anxiety and sorcery...and while they were not all passé, they simply did not occur in normal speaking. Using her more than adequate knowledge of language she was able to paint a portrait of the environment in which her race lived side-by-side with the pastel flowers that dominated the landscape.

Sitting by the waterside they watched the varied species of amphibians scampering about their watery home.

"These are only found in this area," explained Eleonora. "It is said that these species did not originate on Drach, but were brought here. You know better than most how my ancestors got here, for you came the same way. The others that came before you...well, no one has a clue as to where they came from."

A swarm of little creatures flew low above the surface of the water. Eleonora pointed at it and said:

"It is a known and established fact, that those earliest visitors, wherever they came, released these flies. They are very useful, in fact, they are essential to our existence. They are edible and produce a liquid that is not only tasty, but extremely therapeutic as well. They have the uncanny ability to spontaneously regenerate themselves and therefore be able to maintain a large, and viable population. But we have also learned from Wikander's documents that they are not actually living animals...and that they react to one's thoughts!"

She stared in front of her, concentrated, and the swarm rose in a flowing motion and approached them. They flew in a wide circle around them before flitting out to the middle of the lake again, where the salamanders stuck their heads out of the water attempting to catch them.

Hans recalled how the little creatures had approached him when he and Flamel had travelled together and found themselves on that strange rocky surface.

"You called them flies, but what kind of flies are they?" Hans asked.

"They are simply called flies. There are countless species of them, and I'm sure that with your unquenchable thirst for knowledge you will learn and understand much more about them later."

Eleonora edged closer to him and put her hand on his shoulder.

"If you had not been sleeping under the dreamcreepers, and had woken up naturally to my touch...would you have made love to me anyway?"

Her blue eyes sparkled and she smiled. She looked shy but self-confident.

"I think so," said Hans.

"Prove it to me."

Still sitting by the lakeside, they got undressed again. The pale sun had risen higher in the sky, warming their bodies as the day aged. In this sweet smelling paradise, surrounded by and reclining on the soft, springy flowers, they took some time and made love once more.

After they were both spent, they cooled their hot bodies down in the lake. They drank from the clear water as Eleonora searched for tasty flowers and dug up little carrots that were as sweet as honey. After they got dressed, again, she gave him one of her plaited straps.

"You must always carry a hangstring with you," she said. "We will go to the manhouses now, where you can be reunited with Flamel... and all the others, of course. Pay attention now..."

With arms akimbo, she raised her head, pursed her lips and made a shrill, whistling sound. From behind a hill rose a swarm of large flies. As they came closer he noticed that the balls of their bodies were as big as a human's head, and that their stingers were about twelve inches long.

"See the big flies?" said Eleonora. "Follow my lead and catch two of them."

She grabbed two of the black veined bulbs, which made him think of grotesque eyes, and they immediately took on a subservient attitude, hanging motionless in the still air and allowing themselves to be pulled down. Hans did likewise with two others as the rest of the swarm sped away again. Eleonora attached the loops of her hangstring over the stingers and sat down on the long oval piece in the middle piece of it. She then placed her hands around the fat part of the creature again.

Slowly, elegantly, she ascended.

Feeling ill at ease, Hans mimicked her and sat down on his own hangstring. The two flies remained horizontal to each other and rose into the air. Hanging ten feet above the world of flowers, Hans began to take a fancy to this mode of travel, until he began to float higher and higher, and became quite uncomfortable. He thought that it would be wiser to get closer to the ground, and immediately the flies began to gently lower themselves. It was not even necessary to think in words about what he wanted to happen; the action of these creatures was a direct reaction to his impulse to descend. Eleonora allowed him the time he needed to acclimate himself to his new situation and remained wheeling above him while he got the hang of it. After a period of trial and error he finally dared to go up again. The world of flowers appeared to be less vast than he had earlier thought. The soft pastel shades formed an abstract painting enclosed in a frame of green vegetation. It made him wonder if this unique field had come into existence when he made his appearance on Drach. He saw the lake with its flower covered bottom and its amphibious denizens, the stone-edged circle, and the path of orange flowers which led to the graves where the bodies of Ulrich von Drach, Martha Ritter, and Wolfram Wikander rested.

He felt himself getting weaker as he sank forward, becoming dizzy. He had to fight the emotions of melancholy and sadness that swept over him. He looked up to Eleonora Ventura. After their fervent lovemaking she had let her remain free and loose, and now, as she floated through the sky, it fanned out wildly behind her. Hans followed her, his unbuttoned coat flapping like the beating wings of an insect.

Eleonora looked back at him.

"Would you rather fly a bit lower?" she shouted.

"No!" he shouted back. He had regained his composure enough to say: "I feel safe."

They then flew off at an incredible rate of speed. Their steeds felt cold and smooth. Even when he let go of them they continued to fly in the desired direction. High above the ground, he carefully crossed his arms and legs, as if he were sitting in an easy chair. But his back was unsupported and it was a struggle for him to maintain his balance. He rested his forearms on the front of the body of his transport and looked at the changing world beneath him.

At first glance, the landscape below him looked very much as it must have on earth several hundred million years ago, during the Carboniferous period, within the Palaeozoic age. High ferns, palm-like plants, scaly trees and horsetails in all shades of green and brown formed an almost endless forest occasionally dotted with shallow lakes in which vegetation alternately grew and rotted. Wolf's claws, covered with small tapered leaves stood upright, the stems of the horsetails were adorned with broad crowns of much smaller side-stems, and the palms spread out majestically above a ground of copper and mint green colored moss. But unlike the earthly Carboniferous, here were also cup and funnel shaped flowers that were purple, bright red and yellow.

Hans allowed the creature he was riding to slow down and sink until it almost touched the tops of the highest conifers. The hairy leaves waved softly to and fro under his bare feet. All around him, everything grew in a land that was eerily silent. The scents that reached his olfactory senses were pleasant, although sometimes strong...almost musk-like...while at other times reaching his nose as fresh and stimulating aromas.

Eleonora had seen him descend and stayed near him. She watched him, amused, and left him in peace, understanding that everything here was new to him and full of surprises.

He saw so much all at once that he didn't even have the time to be surprised by the strength of the things that were keeping him air-born and the great wonder that made them able to do so. The origin of these balls of energy that responded to thought and the genius behind them was a riddle unto itself.

The pale sun had completely risen now and caused an almost tropical heat. Increasing dampness made the land seem hazy where the stiff grasses and succulent plants formed dark green meadows.

Hans went still lower...flying over the meadows and between trunks and stalks. He stopped abruptly when he saw, directly above a number of ferns, a miraculous creature. It was a fist-sized, insect-like form of life with long legs hanging beneath it. It had spread a thin, circular, multi-colored transparent membrane around itself that seemed to be the source of its ability to float. The membrane vibrated at immense speed in order to move itself forward.

Elsewhere, he saw more little, hairy things, with black and bright orange stripes, hanging from transparent balls that he compared to soap bubbles. They floated through the warm air, rising and descending by making the bubbles bigger or smaller. Directly above his head skimmed an insect-like creature under a transparent circle that measured more than three feet across. As it passed over his head a soft vibrating sound reached his ears. As soon as it had passed him, Hans was aloft again, sitting comfortably now on the hangstring, and waving to Eleonora.

In the distance he saw thickly wooded hills, and as Eleonora's speed increased, he followed her and managed to come up alongside her.

"Do you dare go higher?" she shouted to him. "Just beyond those hills is Mantown, where we live. It is such a beautiful sight from up here!"

"Don't worry about me, I'll keep up with you," he shouted back.

The far side of the approaching hills was overgrown with the same kinds of flowers that grew by the lakeside, and Hans realized that they were cultivated as a source of nutrition by the people of this world. The different varieties of pastel flowers had been planted in long, broad fields separated by narrow paths. Elsewhere, there were fields overgrown with vegetation of a mousy gray color surrounded by herb gardens and bare ground.

Then he saw Mantown, and he knew immediately why it had been given that name. The houses were constructed of a dark, almost black wood, and the roofs all had a metal shine to them...and all the buildings were shaped like humans! Some of the figures lay outstretched on their sides or backs, while some were in sitting positions with legs of wood that seemed to disappear below their knees into the ground. Some even stood erect on enormous wooden boots. The centre of town was a formation of eight buildings... eight wooden giants that stood upright, holding their arms out to their sides and touching the shoulders of the ones standing beside them, thus forming a circle, in the centre of which was a square of brilliantly shining black stones. Mantown was a work of art without equal.

There were gates, doors and windows built into the feet of structures, and the torsos and heads of all the figures were surrounded by gardens. The roads were wide affairs but there seemed to be no logic whatsoever in the planning of them. Broad balconies were adorned with flowerboxes from which hanging plants and multi-colored flowers grew.

Behind Mantown, there flowed a river spanned by a wooden bridge that led to a green and hilly countryside.

Hans remained floating above the town for a long time. He saw people gathering in the streets below and one of them was waving to him. He and Eleonora prepared to descend to the square where the eight giants stood. He could not help but smile as he got a better look at the inhabitants of the town.

The men wore flamboyant suits and outlandish hats. Their faces were all clean-shaven. The women, for the most part, had short, curly hair and wore dresses that made him think of the period on Earth known as "The Roaring Twenties". They all wore hats decorated with flowers and ribbons, long chains around their necks and ingeniously plaited hangstrings around their waists.

Several people had used their hangstrings to capture two of the flies and came up to meet them. They swarmed around him, handling their aerial antics as if they were birds.

"Hans Winters?" they asked and he nodded enthusiastically, actually daring to reach out and shake hands with them even though he was still having some difficulty keeping his balance.

He landed bare footed in the centre of the square, and the black stones felt chilly against his naked flesh. Eleonore undid her hangstring and the flies disappeared like gas-filled balloons into the air. Hans loosened his hangstring and handed it over to her as he received a hearty welcome from the assembled crowd, hearing names he recalled from the photo album that had belonged to Paolo Carandini.

Plukfelder, Schimanski, Wikander, Ritter, Stubbendorf, Lemming, Hape, Friman, Olrik, Ventura, Frederiksson, Mitropoulus, Von Drach...all names which rang a distant bell in his mind.

A dignified looking man, who introduced himself as Jeremias Plukfelder, took off his hat and bowed to Hans.

"Everyone will be given the opportunity to get better acquainted with you later, Hans," he said speaking in German.

"We shall be delighted to listen to you tell us, over a good glass of goldwine, all about the world our ancestors came from. But first, come with me, and I'll take you to your friend...Augustin Flamel."

With one hand on his shoulder, Jeremias Plukfelder escorted Hans as they walked up to one of the wooden giants that stood around the square. He looked back at Eleonora, who was whispering to some other young women, but stopped long enough to glance in his direction.

Hans felt clumsy in his ill-fitting clothes and bare feet, and was glad when a door opened and he was led inside through the left foot of the wooden giant.

There was a strong scent of resin in the room where he now found himself.

The pale sunlight was shining in through green tinted windows. Thick carpeting covered the floor. There were chairs and sofas, and near a door there was a wooden counter, which they walked alongside of and climbed up inside the leg of the giant via a seemingly endless winding staircase.

Hans walked behind the man, being able to see only see his legs, swathed in brown trousers and ending in shining black shoes.

Finally they reached the top and Plukfelder swung open two large doors. He led Hans to a platform that looked out on an enormous hall, the walls of which were hidden from view by many bookcases. On the floor were wooden writing tables where men and women sat at typewriters. Behind a desk, sitting in a chair with a high, round back, sat Flamel.

He was quoting passages from memory from some philosophical work.

"Augustin!" cried Hans.

Flamel stopped abruptly and looked up at the balcony.

He wore a black suit that seemed to have been made especially for him, for it fit him like a glove. Quickly, he jumped to his feet and ran up the staircase that led to the platform where Hans and Jeremias Plukfelder were standing. By the time he had gotten halfway up the stairs, Hans was standing in front of him. At first they shook hands, and then gave each other a hearty embrace.

"I am not going to say that I did not expect you," said Flamel. "You can tell me later how you figured out what point I left from. But what is important is that you have arrived, you have made it... Lean, yes, as lean as a rake and totally exhausted...but welcome to Drach! Welcome to Mantown! The journey must have been worse than the horrors of hell for you. Who knows that you have left Helgen? Does Colonel Kelly know about it? Is..."

Hans grabbed him by the shoulders and shook him, laughing and saying as he did so:

"How can I answer any of your questions if you ask me another one before I have a chance to answer the first? Don't worry...the Colonel knows nothing. No one will ever know where the starting point is for a journey to Drach..."

Jeremias Plukfelder nodded with satisfaction, took off his high hat, and remained leaning over the balcony looking at the men on the staircase. Then he turned around and walked away, his brilliantly shining shoes reflecting the sunlight pouring in.

Augustin took Hans down to the hall, where the people who had been sitting behind their typewriters all introduced themselves before leaving the room, understanding without having to be told that these men would like to have some time to talk quietly and in private.

One of them, Tanja Lemming, a middle-aged woman who had her hair wrapped around her head in a long braid, returned shortly, bringing with her a jar, two stone mugs and a plate filled with food. She put everything on the desk where Flamel had been sitting and said, with a nod in Hans' direction:

"He must eat and drink well, Augustin, so that he may regain the weight he lost just as quickly as you did. We will spoil him tremendously in the coming days."

Augustin sat down, and Hans pulled a chair up to the table across from him and looked around the room in silence.

From down on the floor, the hall seemed even larger than it did from the balcony. Then he took notice of the typewriters again. At the moment, he did not feel like talking about his horrifying experiences during his journey and therefore all he said was:

"Metal! Those machines are made out of metal."

Augustin understood that Hans would rather talk about such mundane matters as this for the time being...to learn and understand more about Drach, and to have time to acclimate himself to his new surroundings. Between the lofty wooden walls with green windows, one could imagine that the hall was part of an earthly building, and Hans was happy just to sit here with Flamel.

Flamel filled the mugs from the jar.

"They make use of flowmetal here. It comes from the hills. Shortly after it has come in contact with the air it becomes hard and it is very easy to process. The Drachians can make anything and have a striking penchant for machinery that is full of gearwheels. They build clocks and other pieces of equipment, and their typewriters...well, those are truly sublime."

With a mug of goldwine in his hand, Flamel rose from his chair and began walking around the hall.

"Erich von Drach and his people put everything they knew down on paper. Paper here, by the way, is manufactured from the stalk of a special horsetail and the bindings are made from specially tooled scaly trees. You can find any scientific book here, even novels. But so much has happened since 1920, and that is why I am so busy trying to quote from all the books I ever read. And I can tell you right now that you too will be in here tomorrow, and the typewriters will be clacking away. All your knowledge and book learning is what is needed here, and you will expound on it until your tongue begs for goldwine and your voice begins to crack."

Hans ate sweet cookies, pretzels and tasty little fruits. He listened to Flamel's voice, but what he was saying did not actually penetrate Hans' mind. Halfway through an explanation about the arable farming on Drach, Winters interrupted him with a sigh:

"We are here... we are actually here! I can hardly believe it. We have followed Von Drach, Ritter and Wikander..."

Flamel sunk back down in his chair again. Hans Winters was with him now, and he too was finally overcome by his emotions.

Both men were greatly relieved because they had survived the journey. They had conquered their fear of the unknown, and were totally surprised by everything that had happened to them. They also both knew how confused they were. Now that Flamel had stopped talking, the silence of the hall was more terrifying than calming. They both stared at the floor and shivered as if it had become icy cold. For an hour, measured in earth time, they were lost in thought trying to recover their composure.

A feeling of resignation washed over them that seemed to finally release them and allow them to look at each other again.

Flamel had Hans fill him in about the state of affairs in Helgen, and asked him how he had found the circle on the rock. He felt reassured when he heard that only Monaco was in possession of the facts.

"Drach is a paradise. It is a place where feelings rule above laws, and freedom is never disturbed by outside aggression. Everyone does the things that he or she can do best and there is plenty of everything to meet everyone's needs. Their hunger for knowledge is great though...you must dare not skip a single passage when you have them copying books. Earthly religions, for instance, are studied here thoroughly without passing any kind of judgment over them. Just from seeing how Mantown is constructed, you can easily come to the conclusion that everyone here is very trusting of one another."

"You mean the enormous wooden human shapes," said Hans with a sigh as he continued: "A paradise which they want to keep as peaceful as it is right now for as long as possible. Do you think that they will allow us to return home?"

"And take the chance that we will reveal our starting point, so that Colonel Kelly can send people up here who have absorbed the Long Zero?"

"That's exactly what I mean..."

"Jeremias Pluckfelder is a trusted representative of the people here. He and I have discussed this, and he knows that I can keep my mouth shut where that is concerned. Your arrival will not change the situation much. It would be much different however if everyone in Helgen found out about the starting point. You would have then betrayed a special world...you would have destroyed their paradise."

Hans looked at him searchingly and then burst out laughing.

"What's the matter?" Hans wanted to know.

"I was just wondering who picked out the clothes you're wearing. If you wish to preserve your sense of self-esteem, I advise you not to look in any mirrors for the time being..."

That night there was a celebration in Hans' honor in the black square between the wooden giants. Lights burned brightly behind the green windows and there were lanterns hung all around the square. Still barefooted and dressed in his ridiculously fitting clothes, Hans walked from one group of people to another, a mug of goldwine in his left hand, his right hand kept free to wave at anyone who might catch his eye. Jeremias Plukfelder was never far away so he could answer any questions Hans might have.

Eleonora introduced him to her husband Stefan, a tall stout man with a red face and light brown eyes. He was one of the few men who sported a colossal moustache. Stefan took him to the side and said:

"Of course, you are welcome to stay with us, but I know that Charlotte von Drach would be very pleased to have you in her home tonight. When it is time, I will bring you to her."

Later, Hans asked Augustin where he stayed and he received a short, but cryptic answer.

"That changes."

Hans was standing near a table filled with delicacies watching a woman whose name he had learned was Rita Friman. She had brought her little daughter with her, a girl of about six years of age, who was wearing a chequered dress, white socks and golden shoes. The little girl hugged a small pale doll under her arm. Hans waved to her, and when she waved back he saw, much to his surprise that the doll had no eyes or mouth, and that it made odd movements with its blunt arms and legs...not to mention the fact that it was floating beside the child in thin air. He came a few steps closer and asked Rita Friman how it was possible that the doll was doing this.

"It is a flydoll," she said. "You have to go to Boris Stubbendorf to obtain one, for he is our maker of dolls. He makes all the children so happy with them. You have come to us with two flies and a hangstring, haven't you? Well, Boris removes the stinger from a fly and then peels off the outer shell. It is completely transparent and can also be used for windows in the houses, for the colors of the fly soon turn pale. Boris knows how to model the shell-less flies using clamps and threads. He pinches and kneads them, taking great patience with each one. He can give them a wide assortment of shapes and forms. Sonja's doll follows everywhere...always. She guides her toy with the power of her will."

The little girl smiled at Hans and then had the doll fly out above the heads of the people and around a lantern at the edge of the square before it returned to her and she tucked it firmly beneath her arm again.

All around the square there was merry-making. Some made music on songstrings, which were instruments made from nutshells and stems and strung with spun hairs taken from plants that grew wild out in the woods. As Hans danced with Eleonora he looked up and noticed that the dark sky was studded with stars. He asked her if Drach had a moon and much to his surprise he had to explain to her what a moon was. She had never heard of such a heavenly body.

Augustin saw to it that Hans ate and drank constantly.

"You look just as bad as I did when I arrived here, you old beanpole! Steambread is very healthy, but it doesn't fatten you up at all, therefore I advise you to eat a lot of the syrupy cakes and little pies. Don't ask me what they are made of, but they are very tasty and definitely add on weight."

Jeremiah Plukfelder turned out to be, besides a number of other skills he possessed, a very capable tailor and promised Hans he would make him a new suit first thing in the morning.

Another extraordinary duo Hans encountered, was comprised of descendants from Twentiers from Greece and Sweden...Aeneas Mitropoulos and Nicolai Frederiksson. They both wore pocket watches that they had made themselves. Aeneas' watch-chain stretched tight around his belly, while the one belonging to the leaner of the two, Nicolai, swung to and fro with every move he made. Aeneas' moustache was even more imposing than Stefan Ventura's, and hardly moved when the lips that were hidden behind it smiled... and Aeneas laughed loud and often. These two men, immaculately dressed in the fashion of twentieth century Earth, were the most stubborn researchers on Drach as far as technique was concerned. They had designed clockworks and had developed major improvements for the typewriter. But they had also built a steam-driven vehicle that was strong enough to drag wood from out of the forests to Mantown. They were also working on an internal-combustion engine, were able to generate electricity and had thrown themselves into discovering the secrets of the telephone.

"We are forced to start here with nothing at all," said Aeneas in his deep voice. "What we draw on paper, we must make a reality. Once we are able to understand the principle of steam power, we still do not have a big enough kettle so that it will not explode when the pressure is beginning to build. Once we know how to wind a coil, we still have not been able to find a suitable substitute for copper wire. We have to make everything ourselves...from the biggest flywheel down to the smallest screw."

"There are hundreds...no...thousands of questions I have to ask you," said Nicolai.

"And I'm sure that you could help us construct things! Please come to our workrooms, then you can see for yourself what we have already achieved."

Hans had become very curious, and now he became enthusiastic.

"Of course! I will come visit you as soon as I can."

"You must dictate everything you know to us. Talk as fast as you wish...we can write as fast as you can speak."

The men took him along with them, their arms around his shoulders, and led him along the table on which all of the delicacies of Drach were displayed. Aeneas Mitropoulos never allowed their mugs to empty of goldwine. His moustache was shiny with the wine, his eyes aglow from its effects, and his voice sounded even deeper.

"Once we build an airship we will explore all of Drach, he asserted. "But it must be a ship whose engines have four, six or perhaps even eight propellers. This is a miraculous world, Hans, but we need tools to make other tools. Only then can we work properly, what do you say to that?"

They walked along, Hans shaking hands with all the people who greeted him and slapped him on the back.

"I would take a large number of flies, as you call them, tie them up in a canvas the size of a ship's sail, hang a gondola underneath it and set out on a journey," said Hans. "Then you have would have a good airship."

Aeneas made a shrill sound as he produced his hangstring from under his waistcoat. Flies immediately came down and he selected two, shoved the loops of the string over the backs of them and sunk down heavily upon it.

"When I drink too much goldwine, my legs soon let me down," he said and floated along next to Hans and Nicolai.

"Such an airship would not bring you too far," said Nicolai. "The flies can only be steered as long as they are allowed to swarm around freely. Sure, you can use two of them to float along the way Aeneas is doing now, but pressed together under your sail they would all prefer to go in different directions and perhaps even burst right through it."

"The flies originate in another part of the universe," remarked Aeneas. "No one understands anything about flies, but we make use of their abilities. You can float in the air with them, eat them, you can even make dolls out of them. But we have to widen our knowledge of them as far as techniques are involved for that is what we understand best and can improve on. That is our task on Drach. And we enjoy ourselves immensely..."

"In the same way that you sit comfortably here now," said Hans, "you should be able to explore Drach."

"That might be possible, for they never run out of energy...but no one has ever undertaken a journey like that. Not us... and not our ancestors either..."

"Why not?"

"Well, for one thing, there is more than enough to do right here. Maybe we don't really want to know what is hidden elsewhere, because we are afraid of discovering things we should not know at all. Once we have an airship however, we can travel with a larger group of people."

"That would also be possible if everyone used his own hangstring and flies," continued Hans, but he understood that the inhabitants of Mantown felt safe here and were not of a particularly adventurous nature. "I would like to go out on a voyage of discovery myself..."

"You would stay away too long if you were to do that," thought Nicolai. "And that would be a waste of time. If you stay here with us, we could make excellent use of your knowledge. You and Flamel are men of great value."

The people had all gathered in the middle of the square, where Jeremias Plukfelder was now giving a speech.

Hans and his two new friends went over to listen and met Flamel, who was accompanied by Boris Stubbendorf, the doll-maker, and Ernst Olrik, a man who constantly studied medicine in the library. Jeremias Plukfelder waved his hat in the air and pointed in the direction of Augustin and Hans.

"I can assure all of you," he said loudly, "that we can trust our visitors. I have seen for myself how they have guaranteed one another that one no one will ever know how they arranged to journey to Drach. Augustin Flamel and Hans Winters are free to leave Drach whenever they wish, although we will bemoan their departure. We can only hope that they will wish to return to us and live here forever. Friends, they have at their disposal so much knowledge that it staggers me! I have listened to what Flamel was quoting and know that much has changed on the world of our ancestors."

He put his hat back on and folded his hands across his chest.

"Is not this a beautiful and perfect moment to give careful thought to the discoveries of the great Ulrich von Drach and his people? The world was on fire, when the physicist, Von Drach, made his astounding discovery high in the Austrian Alps. The horrors of a world war planted the seeds of desire for a different, better world. But what would remain a dream to others would become reality for Von Drach. He found twenty strange little objects and scornfully called them coffee beans! He began to experiment with them and noticed how they reacted to the impulses of his thoughts..."

Hans and Augustin exchanged a swift glance of understanding. They had proceeded on the theory that the little creatures had begun to move on their own and could be kept imprisoned in wood. They had lay in the temple of Janus until someone - Flamel, Winters or the Observer - had transmitted a stream of thoughts that woke them up, as it were, from their deep sleep.

"Their power was absorbed by steel and passed on to Ulrich von Drach, his wife Martha Ritter, and their associate, Wikander and all those others. I bring this subject up, my friends, because we must understand that the Brotherhood of Helgen travelled off to Drach and left the twenty little objects behind...hidden inside a table!

They also left behind the steel in which the power was stored. Based on this fact I must conclude that it was their intention to pass their knowledge on, and make it possible for others to make the same journey and bring news, others who can tell us about new developments in every field of scientific endeavor. That is why I pause now to remember our ancestors...and emphatically declare that our two esteemed visitors cannot, must not, be denied the right to go back.

Do not misunderstand this...we are not naïve, and should not be very shocked if evil spirits were to penetrate our society. We will trust Augustin Flamel and Hans Winters, and together with them we will toast to the Brotherhood of Helgen..."

The stone mugs were filled with goldwine, and everyone drank in silence, until Jeremias Plukfelder said:

"Everyone must do their part to make sure that Hans Winters gains weight every day. He must be fit and strong when he returns..."

A few minutes later the gentle sound of the songstrings sounded again. Hans felt a strong feeling of friendship all around him. He drank and thought of Ulrich von Drach and his people and suddenly he understood why none of the Drachians had ever started out on a long journey of discovery, and why it would be a long time before Nicolai Frederiksson and Aeneas Mitropoulos would build their airship. Mantown and its surroundings were, as Flamel had already said, a true paradise. It was a horn of plenty and everyone was happy here.

In Mantown they made tools...not weapons.

It was already very late when Stefan Ventura approached him.

"I will bring you to Charlotte von Drach," he said. "She was not here at the square tonight. She is a painter and was working late."

Hans walked with him through streets lined with wooden manhouses.

He had passed the stage of astonishment and wonder...what he felt now was deep admiration...

Chapter 12: Behind The Façades

Early the next morning Hans made a few quick sketches on some sheets of a material that were paper-like, but were not as he knew paper to be on Earth. He was also supplied with writing implements that seemed to be made from compressed charcoal. The photographs from Paolo Carandini's book were still succinctly clear in his mind, and he made a drawing of the Austrian Twentiers, with the physical surroundings of Helgen in the background.

Charlotte von Drach wanted to use his work as models for the paintings she did on huge wall hangings. The previous night, after she had showed him where he could sleep, Hans had fallen asleep immediately and in the morning, at her insistence, he had a hearty breakfast and began to work.

Charlotte von Drach was in her early thirties, slender and pretty with greenish-gray eyes and light brown hair. She had two children, Ulrich and Diana, twins, who were eight years old. Their father, her man, had died of a disease called flamefever. The house she lived in was in the shape of a reclining man and thus had no upper floors. Its thick wooden walls were decorated with various tapestries that she had designed. Some of these beautiful tapestries were painted with scenes of life in Mantown, while others depicted the rolling countryside and thick woodlands that lay beyond the town.

She wore a long skirt and blouse, and her hangstring...ever-present as it was with everyone in town...was pulled tightly around her waist. Her long hair flowed luxuriously down her back. She smiled as she looked at a portrait of Ulrich von Drach.

"The only pictures we have of him are the ones that he agreed to pose for while he was here," she said. "I will transfer these sketches on to one of my most beautiful tapestries, and then, when you have some free time, I would like to get some drawings from you that represent the present situation on earth...the towns, the villages, the landscapes. You're coming back tonight, aren't you? I was lying beside you last night and I watched you as you slept. Your sleep seemed disturbed however and you were probably troubled by some dream."

And then with a coy smile she added:

"I certainly hope you will be able to stay awake for a little while longer tonight."

Someone arrived to pick up the twins, who attended classes in another part of town. Hans put his paper and sketching tools aside and allowed her to lead him through the house. He counted twenty rooms, all of which were excessively decorated with heavy wooden furniture. The manhouses were all very solid affairs and all the furniture within them showed great craftsmanship. It gave him the feeling of walking around an art museum and even included utensils from the first decades of the early twentieth century on Earth.

"Does everyone here have so much room?" he asked.

"This is not even considered a big house in Mantown," answered Charlotte. "There are houses with twice as many rooms, where no more than four or six people live. We all helped build each other's houses in similar fashion because we simply love to have lots of room. When we desire solitude or privacy, we have it right in our own homes.

Almost everyone here is able to make their own furniture in their own workshop."

For the second time that morning the doorbell, which was connected by a cord to a slide outside, was ringing. A man by the name of Albrecht Happe had come looking for Hans.

They left together and walked through Mantown towards the giants standing around the square. In the library, Flamel was already busy reciting whatever he could recall from any of the books he had ever read, and the typewriters were rattling incessantly. Nicolai Frederiksson and Aeneas Mitropoulos were present and immediately began to question Hans.

For the next three days, without interruption, Hans could be found quoting chapter and verse from his own warehouse of knowledge.

He paced up and down the hall or sat behind a desk, and in between recitations he ate and drank as much as he could...and then spent his nights with Charlotte von Drach. On the fourth morning, he entered the library reluctantly, fearing he would lose his voice if he had to continue speaking again for hours and hours at a stretch. But this time, only Nicolai was there, who said with a friendly smile:

"You have rendered us a service of incalculable value. Flamel, for his part, has made Ernst Olrik especially happy with his wonderful lectures about medical procedures, and he has completely thrilled Rita Friman with his treatises of natural science and philosophy. She is a woman with a sharp mind and has catalogued all the books here...not to mention having read them all as well! Maja Wikander is a specialist in the field of arable farming and the science of nutrition, but also does in depth studies on the water economy, and Flamel has given her all the information on these topics that he possesses. Allow me now to invite you to come with me and take a look at mine and Aeneas' workshops, which we have built down by the river. From the location where we constructed our shop, Mantown had the natural tendency to grown inland. We are working on the same spot where Von Drach and Wikander had built their sheds, and we even have the tools that they made from flowmetal and still use them occasionally..."

Hans felt greatly relieved when he was allowed to depart with them, and Augustin sighed:

"It's about time...I was not looking forward to spending another whole day quoting. Slowly, but surely, I'm beginning to feel like an automaton, a robot that does not have the faintest notion what information he is passing along...he simply spits it out for others to digest."

When they reached the square, Nicolai summoned up a swarm of flies and the men all floated away on their hangstrings. They climbed to a great altitude from where they could see the town surrounded by purplefields, which produced the main ingredient for steambread. They gazed down upon the farmlands, the fields of flowers, the river, and the hills...finally alighting near some long sheds that followed the naturally winding course of the river. Once on the ground, they set the flies free and tied the hangstrings tightly around their waists. Aeneas Mitropoulos slid open a tall door and nodded to the others.

"Welcome, friends! Come inside! Come in!"

Nicolai, Hans, and Augustin entered a great hall in which the pride of the inventors was proudly displayed... a colossal, shining, steam powered vehicle made out of metal.

Aeneas, knowing that they were expecting guests, had stoked up the fire immensely and the steam boiler had a terrific head of pressure up. The monster stood on four wheels with spokes, had overstuffed leather chairs in the front, a sofa in the back, and there was a steering wheel and an odd assortment of levers on the dashboard. They heard a hissing sound and Aeneas pulled a lever that caused the machine to blow off steam in an ear-splitting, shrill whistle.

"First, we make tools, and with those tools we make other tools," he said cheerily. "Remember how it's done? We deal with one problem after another, which invariably, leads us to create a whole new set of problems for ourselves! The concept is really quite simple...we want to transmit the raw power of the steam to a wheel. But after several steam boilers exploded, and after about ten attempts at building a suitable piston, we began to realize that we were working on something that is quite impossible. And we cannot, of course, order components from anywhere so we must make everything from scratch...and we have no one to consult but each other."

He climbed into the vehicle and began pulling the levers as Nicolai climbed up beside him and gestured to Hans and Augustin that they should take a seat on the sofa. Coughing and jolting along, the vehicle came to life and rolled out of the shed. The proud driver navigated a short trip around the small track. Hans thought it a true work of art, and knew that they had taken great pains building it. He was thoroughly impressed by the stubbornness of the inhabitants of Mantown, who did not know the meaning of defeat and felt compelled to complete every task they set their minds to.

Back in the shed, Aeneas left all the valves open, allowing the remainder of the steam to escape.

"The fire will burn itself out soon enough...come, let me show you around."

There were men and women were working on various projects in different sheds. Clocks were being constructed here and furniture was being made there. Everything needed for prefabricated manhouses was available at a sawmill in one area, while in another spot people were working on the development of an internal-combustion engine. Others were working on transmitting and receiving equipment, telephones, recorders, cameras and ventilation systems. Electricity was generated by dynamos and huge batteries, which gathered their energy through the use of waterwheels built alongside the river. Fossil fuel was obtained from a muddy, stinking black mass from the swamps, and Nicolai told them that their first internal-combustion engine had run for over an hour before it broke down, ceasing up beyond repair.

The last shed was built with its back against a hill, and from out of one of its walls stuck pipes and taps.

"The proximity to the river is not the only reason that we built the workshops here," Aeneas explained. "It is also because that it is on this exact spot that Ulrich von Drach once worked on a dream he called Mantown. There, on the wall, hang his hammers and saws. In his documents he mentions that his world had been on fire...that there had been a war that had cost so many lives that we cannot even begin to grasp the horror of it. He left the bloodlust and aggression behind, and came here to work in peace with his intellect and hands. Sometimes, when I use a chisel that I know he used... held in his own two hands...I become so overwhelmed with emotion that the tears burn my eyes..."

At a workbench stood a woman surrounded by flies who had all sorts of little tools hanging from them. She looked over at the men and Hans noticed that she was wearing glasses.

"This is Ursula Olrik," said Nicolai. "Her husband, Ernst, is an acquaintance of Augustin, and a devoted medical student. Ursula is one of our most gifted women. She has the ability to work on both large and small projects...She is an expert glazier, and she is a sorceress where the flowmetal is concerned. Would you be kind enough to show us some of your skills, Ursula? These gentlemen have heard about flowmetal, but still do not know what it is."

Ursula walked over to one of the taps, followed by the flies with their tools softly jingling as they moved. She rolled a table under one of the taps and placed a mold on it that was made of baked clay.

"Never touch the metal while it is still in its liquid state," she warned. "It dries quickly and you will have a hell of a time getting it off your fingers."

Carefully, she opened the tap a bit. Several silver drops fell into the mold and she immediately closed the tap again. The metal instantly began to congeal. Ursula waited a moment or two and then tapped the sides of the mold gently with a hammer. A gearwheel plopped out on to the table.

"We are all fond of working with gears," she explained. "We can construct the most complex machines with them. By using a flywheel, which we can construct using a series of gears, we are able to lift over four tons of weight. The flowmetal lies in thick lodes beneath the surface of Drach, and there are different varieties. It is easy to process, and is hard... but flexible... all at the same time. The most important component of the steam-boiler consists of a bent plate made from the same metal as this," and she pointed at the gearwheel she had just made.

In another shed, the workers had gathered for lunch, which was comprised of a warm drink that tasted very much like coffee, dewcooks, hard and soft nuts, fruits, and a sweet, syrupy, substance that everyone dipped their steambread in. During the course of the meal the inevitable questions arose about the home of Von Drach, Ritter and Wikander.

It was Augustin who supplied most of the answers, while Hans stuffed himself and drank to overflowing.

Afterwards, Augustin suggested that he and Hans take a flight around the city, to which Hans eagerly agreed. They bid farewell to the workers in the sheds and down by the river, and asked Nicolai to summon a swarm of flies. After they had both selected two of the creatures, they sat down upon their hangstrings, became airborne once again, and crossed the river.

Floating beside each other they looked at the explosion of nature below them.

Hairy conifers, wolf's claw, and horsetails fought for the light of the pale sun and climbed up from the ferns and low palm trees that overgrew the land. Hans saw living creatures sailing on air and floating around in front of him. He watched as a big, amber colored fly split in half, and suddenly there were two of them, floating side by side through the hot air.

"It's good to be able to be alone together for a while," said Augustin. "Now you can concentrate better on what you see, and actually appreciate the feeling of just how far away from home you really are. How are you doing, my friend? Have you gotten over the horrors of your journey yet?"

"Yes," answered Hans. "I'm getting better every day."

He was, in fact, looking extremely well and gaining weight. It also improved his appearance to be wearing clothes that fit him...for a full day now he had been wearing a suit custom-made for him by Jeremias Plukfelder that was accessorized by a shirt, bowtie, and soft leather boots with sturdy soles.

The men talked for some time, but as they left the city far behind them, and looked at the green world beneath their dangling feet, they fell silent. They breathed deeply through their noses as they floated over dense, multi-colored flowers, watching strange species of life forms materialize beneath the palm branches or moving through the air on gossamer wings. Hans commanded his fly to rise and turn, so that he could orientate himself. He could still see the town in the distance, the wooden human shapes now becoming tiny and lost in the distance. Where he figured the river must be, he saw the long caterpillar formed by the sheds of Nicolai Frederiksson and Aeneas Mitropoulos. He saw Agustin landing in the middle of a thickly wooded area and directed his flies there too.

Augustin jumped to the ground and began caressing tree trunks and plants with his fingertips.

He stroked the leaves and flowers.

"We have found a special place indeed, my friend," he said as Hans joined him. "Is it not strange that I stand here touching vegetation which is growing an unfathomable number of light-years away from my own world? I bought the buildings and the ground in Helgen and took long walks through the Alps, discovering the circle on the rock quite by accident. Does anything in particular strike you, Hans, when you think about the photo album of Paolo, or about the people here on Drach?"

Hans nodded.

"There seem to be a number of family names missing. Keneko, for one, was a Japanese scientist who had joined the Twentiers... And I can clearly recall two photographs that he was in. I also remember a Belgian couple by the name of Roelants... and Yrjöla, a Finn... These are names I have not heard on Drach..."

"Maybe they jumped into the void...and ended up somewhere from where they cannot leave, or are still whizzing through the endless universe. It is a bitter thought to imagine that they were probably sacrificed to find the route that ultimately led to this glorious world."

"Then again, perhaps they simply left Helgen and returned to Japan, Belgium and Finland, just like Paolo Carandini returned to Italy. It could even very well be possible that they were not susceptible to the penetrating power of the Long Zero, therefore not even being able to make the journey."

Returning to their hangstrings, they took off again, and at that moment saw someone approaching them from the direction of the town. It was Jeremias Plukfelder floating towards them. The two men burst laughing and had to hold on tightly to their flies to prevent themselves from falling. For the first time since they had come to Drach, they felt at ease enough to laugh out loud...the man looked absolutely grotesque with his big hat, flapping coat, old-fashioned suit and stiff collar.

Jeremias greeted them and took off his hat. With his head tilted, he looked at them and asked:

"I hope you gentlemen have not held any crazy-calyx under your noses? They are the black and purple flowers that creep up the sides of the scale trees. It starts with laughter, but the mood can quickly turn into a chronic melancholy! There are people who suffer from it for the remainders of their lives once they are affected."

Hans wiped the tears from his eyes with the sleeve of his jacket and tried to get control over himself. As soon as he looked Augustin's eyes however, he roared with laughter again. It was good to be able to laugh so freely again...and fortunately Jeremias did not realize that it was he that they found so amusing. The man put on his hat, smiled, and remained floating there patiently until they were approachable again.

"Would you gentlemen be so kind as to follow me?" he asked them in a serious voice. "I would like to share something with you of the utmost importance."

They turned their flies and followed him back towards Mantown.

They flew over the town and landed on the far side in a circular pit surrounded by wooden walls that looked from the outside like the walls of just another manhouse. Inside, benches lined the walls like an amphitheatre and in the middle the floor was made of black, three sided stones. Jeremias stood up and left the loops of his hangstrings hanging from the flies. The flies remained floating low above the stone floor as Plukfelder made a wide gesture.

"We find ourselves here behind these façades...where our ringlaws are enforced. All points of contention and differences of opinion are resolved here. We also call this place The Truth, for within these walls no lies are tolerated. You can say anything that is on your mind within the facades without fear of reprisals or repercussions on the outside. This place has proven its worth countless times over the years. I have asked you to join me in this place because I have something to tell you."

He sat down wearily on a bench with Hans and Augustin sitting on either side of him. Plukfelder then produced a little book from out of the inner pocket of his coat. Its cover was leathery and its pages fibrous, thick and coarse.

"Ulrich von Drach's notebook...from which I would like to read a certain passage for you."

After quickly flipping through the books pages, he handed it to Hans and pointed to a series of lines that appeared to be written in black ink with a broad tipped pen.

Hans read aloud:

"Visitors... again. A shining vehicle has appeared in front of our houses. No contact was possible however. I approached the craft myself, frightened and curious, but when I was within fifty feet of it, it disappeared at an incredible speed."

Plukfelder took the little book back from him and turned to another page.

"Read here now."

Hans read once more:

"Four strange creatures walked our streets surveying the town with dark, eerie eyes. Everyone stayed inside...strange visitors departed leaving all who saw them quaking in terror...Meeting to be held to decide who will confront them should they return... No volunteers...loud frightful discussions taking place behind the façades."

Plukfelder took the little book back from Hans and placed it back in his pocket.

"There are numerous accounts of other sightings...and we still them occasionally. It is perfectly understandable that von Drach, Ritter, Wikander and all the others opted for this world when they had the chance. The atrocities of a world engulfed in global warfare did not fulfil their vision of mankind's existence so they left. We are psychological descendants of the Brotherhood of Helgen...but different from people such as yourselves.

This new generation learned from the Brotherhood what the origin of man was; the following generations had to read about it in books. Our frail little community threw all of its willpower into science and discovery... we are hard workers and passionate researchers, people who concentrate on projects that promise to yield tangible results such as home construction, city planning, transportation, glassworks, farming, and machinery full of gearwheels. We hold our heads up high and proud...but good heavens, my friends... we still feel so lonely!"

He sighed deeply, took off his hat and stared into it as if hoping to find the words he needed there.

"Somewhere far away, was that ambiguous world of war and peace...where billions of people lived...and died... and now we read the books about them that the Brotherhood has transcribed. We learned its history, from Australopitecus to Homo erectus, from Neanderthal to Cro-Magnon. We read all about Mesoptamians, Egyptians, Greeks, and Romans - fairy tales with horrible endings! Their heavens were populated with thousands of gods...of whom the Brotherhood did not take a single one along. We learned about the untold masses of people who stayed behind, as we became a small isolated community with higher standards, and new goals. The Brotherhood had found a way out...but there was, and is, no way back for us...just as there is none for you."

He stood up and fidgeted with his hat, turning it over and over between nervous, shaking fingers.

"We have our mysterious visitors who, we suspect, are responsible for our nutritional flowers, the amphibians, and the swarms of flies. The answers to all your questions about universal travel are right here!

Oh how we hoped for a sign from someone, anyone, who was from our world of origin! And then when you two appeared on Drach, although so lean and naked as you were, our hearts leaped and shouted with joy.

You and Hans proved to us that the Brotherhood was speaking the truth and not telling us some fantastic story.

And yes, Hans was right... A vast number of the flies are able to carry a gondola with passengers around Drach. An airship with propellers can be built. Someone could go on a voyage of discovery equipped with only two flies and a hangstring. Unfortunately however, there is no one who would dare to do so...we are so afraid, so very afraid. But we do not cry out from our fear - that is not in our nature. We simply wait in silence until the unavoidable happens. And while we wait we keep ourselves busy with our little problems, work on our machines full of gearwheels, build our wooden manhouses, and make so much furniture that our rooms are bursting with it..."

"What exactly is this "unavoidable" fate that you are talking about?" Hans asked, knowing all the while that he could probably guess what it was.

"The confrontation with the creatures... with whom we obviously share Drach. We have built ourselves a city where we can live in peace, but we all know that there will come a time when everything will change. As long as the community remains small, we can focus on our projects, solve our problems behind these façades, and apply our ringlaws to our little society. The day will come however, that quarrels will erupt and the first murder will be committed, and that all that we have achieved will go wrong. We feel like we are mentally locked in. Oh yes, the possibilities are understood all too well...

All you have to do is leave town and start walking or floating, and you will eventually arrive in other lands. There are probably mountains, deserts, rivers and seas out there just waiting for us to find them. It must be so difficult for you to understand us."

"It is not difficult at all," said Augustin. "I understand you."

Jeremias Plukfelder donned his hat resolutely, bent over, with his hands resting on his knees so that he was face-to-face with Hans and Augustin and said:

"I know you both have things to do in Helgen...so far, far away. But on behalf of all the inhabitants of Drach, I am asking you to please come back to us as soon as you can. You, Augustin, could help us improve our techniques and together we could explore new scientific theories; while you, Hans, could explore Drach for us, and go where we are afraid to go. And, it would also be in your own best interest, for you want to find the source of the Long Zero. Perhaps you will be able to convince others as well, to come along with you...just so long as they are reliable people... What do you say?"

Flamel shook his head slowly.

"I don't want to make a snap decision Jeremias. After all, this is quite a large request that you are making."

Jeremias looked at Hans hopefully.

"Hans," he said softly, "Don't forget that it is very possible that your children may be born here."

Hans jumped to his feet, scaring Plukfelder with the rapidity of his movement.

"Are you telling me that is the reason you people had me sleep with Eleonora and Charlotte? To increase the chances of my staying on Drach and sway my decision?"

"You see, this is the benefit of having a conversation behind the façades," said Jeremias with a wry smile. "It allows you to say exactly what you want to. You can throw anything at another's feet and be sure that the answer you get is the truth and nothing but the truth. We are a small, isolated community that hungers for new blood. That's the reason.... there are no other plans or ulterior motives."

Hans sat down again and Augustin put his hands on his shoulders.

"Well it certainly gives us something to think about in the meantime," he said. "Our children could be born here and to be quite honest with you I have been thinking about spending the rest of my life on Drach. Yes, we must go back, but the route remains open to us, even though it is a path lined with all the horrors of hell!"

Hans was looking at Jeremias and said:

"Have you personally seen the creatures Erich von Drach mentioned in his notebook?"

"I have...but please forgive me, for besides telling you about dark eyes, slowly moving figures and silver vehicles, I cannot give you any more details, because they kept my eyes shut each time visited us. Our little community is held together by fear, Hans! We stay close to one another...afraid of becoming lost...afraid of losing our identities. We feel desperate and stranded. We would gladly erect a statue in your honor to show how happy we are with your presence. All I ask is that you consider our proposal. Augustin calls Drach a paradise, and with your help it could remain a paradise for a long, long time.

I will leave you two alone now, so that you can talk together in peace and quiet. Float back over the woods and look at the beauty of Mantown and its surroundings from high in the sky. We will not ask of you to work in the library today. Enjoy the day as best as you are able...and think about us."

He sunk down heavily on his hangstring and the flies lifted off silently as they carried Jeremias Plukfelder back to Mantown.

"What would happen if someone behind the façades told a lie?" Hans asked himself aloud.

"That will never happen," said Augustin. "It is a matter of simple decency. And besides...if and when that does ever happen, it will mean that very different, very bad times have arrived."

After they were also sitting on their hangstrings, they flew high into the sky and looked down at the town but they saw it through changed eyes now. The houses revealed the fact that intelligent, creative people lived here. The lack of ramparts, canals, gates and towers told them that this was a free town that feared nothing. The wide-open spacious farmlands made it clear that the harvest was there for everyone. But it was also clear that this was a particularly vulnerable place, not defended by anyone. The fear however was well concealed and everyone had a task to carry out that helped keep their minds off of their troubles. It was a paradise without walls that no one dared to leave. There was no one willing to venture outside to search for the truth about the visitors Ulrich von Drach had mentioned. Mantown was a desolate place, the most remote corner of mankind...but a place where the status quo would be maintained on a daily basis.

Suddenly...Hans knew how to put into words what he had been thinking.

"Mantown is like an abandoned child in the wilderness," he said sadly.

"And when the child cries, there is no one to hear it and come to comfort it," added Flamel. "You're right. Mantown is an orphan..."

That day they probably flew further away from Mantown than anyone had ever been. They enjoyed the views, the forests and the hills and felt the strange sensation of the presence of creatures that watched them without showing themselves.

Augustin Flamel was the first to undertake the return journey.

Having totally regained his strength he dared to go through hell again...but first he had to quote for several days in the library, answering questions and telling stories. He also paid a visit to the doll maker, Boris Stubbendorff, from whom he had learned how to break the prickle from the ball of the flies and press it together into a flat disc.

Flamel knew how to get the flies to react to his thoughts, and could have them split or force them into a single existence. What he had not figured out was exactly what purpose the hard, back piece of the flies served. He had taken the flat disc that he had formed with him on his return voyage.

"If I succeed in endlessly splitting the balls when I return to Helgen, we will have an unlimited food supply," he had said to Hans. "I have been thinking about this for quite some time. They are certainly edible and hopefully someone in the lab will be able to figure out just what they are comprised of."

Followed by a great number of inhabitants of Mantown, Flamel had gone to the spot where the stones lay encircled by the field of flowers. There he had gotten undressed, sat down on his knees to concentrate, and had pressed the disc against his chest. Then he disappeared.

It was difficult for Hans to remain behind, especially while everyone was now looking at him. He could read the despair in the eyes of the people, but they never spoke about their fears, and none begged him to stay. Everyone knew about his conversation with Jeremias Plukfelder behind the façades.

He would stay for another week and just like Augustin, he would quote what he had read and could recall, answer all possible questions, draw and tell them about far-away earth.

What he enjoyed most though, were his lonely flights far outside the town. He did not have much time for this however, so when he was able to get away, he let the flies go at full speed. He was also alone when he visited the graves of Ulrich von Drach, Martha Ritter and Wolfram Wikander, and hoped he would find the inspiration there to help him decide whether or not to make Drach his home.

He floated over the lake where the amphibians lived and dragged his feet through the water. He did not succeed in reaching his decision and was saddened by his lack of resolve. On his way back he saw the beauty of the virgin forest, followed a number of little creatures that dangled under transparent air bubbles and he experienced the wonderful silence all around him. He had put on weight and was looking healthy again. He thought as little as possible about the hellish fears that awaited him when he followed Flamel to Earth.

On his last day on Drach, he went flying with Aeneas Mitropoulos, who wanted to show him a place in the mountains where flowmetal streamed that was very much like gold. The roofs of the wooden men around the town square were decorated with it, and it was also used to make ornaments, trinkets and cups.

The stout man with the big moustache sat on his hangstring with his feet still on the ground. Proudly, he took his pocket watch out and held it out to Hans as far as the chain permitted.

"You see? This is made out of golden flowmetal, while the clockwork itself is silver-colored. The riches of Drach are so enormous, so abundant...that everyone here considers himself rich without really having much. What you see around you belongs to all of us. Come, let's go..."

They went up near the sheds along the river. They floated quietly over the hills and looked at ferns in shades of green and yellow, the palm trees and wolf's claws.

Aeneas talked about the power of steamboats and locomotives, the use of clockworks that could be wound, and the wonder of electricity. He did not understand much yet of the refined technology that Hans was talking about, but he was eager to learn everything he could about it.

The pale sun shone behind a thin veil of white clouds and it had become unbearably hot.

"We are almost at the flowsources," he said, after they had covered a considerable distance. "Come, let's go up, so that we can see the lay of the land better. Then I'll show you the spot where we have tapped into the stone."

They climbed almost vertically.

Again Hans was struck by the silence...he was used to the sound of birds when he was in the country. In the forest beneath him he saw a narrow brook that flowed into a muddy lake where ashen plants with thorny tops rose above the surface. The spur of freakishly formed hills, covered with scaly, low vegetation, penetrated into the wood.

It was there, at the end of the spur, that Hans saw something moving. He had to concentrate hard to be sure that his eyes were not deceiving him. He was convinced that he had seen a figure moving among the ferns. The form was hazy but he thought he saw black eyes set in a pale face.

Aeneas Mitropoulos had seen it also, and had immediately turned his flies in the opposite at direction and fled at a dizzying speed. Instead of following him however, Hans descended and kicked the ferns he had seen moving just a moment ago with both feet. He discovered nothing though and went up again looking for Aeneas. Still a bit afraid of falling to the ground, he did not dare go fast enough to catch up with him. Aeneas flew over Mantown and landed inside the circle of the façades. Surprised at his choice of landing spot, Hans remained hanging above it and watched as the man jumped from his hangstring and began to pace up and down passionately. The man clenched his fists and beat the air, ranting and raving.

It was impossible for Hans to hear what he was saying. After a while Aeneas returned to his hangstring and ascended again...finding himself eye to eye with Hans. He smiled blandly and said:

"Tanja Lemming has invited me for over for a meal and would greatly appreciate it if you came along. I am sure you will enjoy it very much, for there is no better cook than she. We will all drink goldwine and then she will spoil us with a solid dish of crownfiber with ripe fruits and fresh wolf's stalks."

Neither of them said a word about what they had seen... or thought they had seen.

Outwardly, the big man seemed calm enough. He guided his flies directly straight to the home of Tanja Lemming. Hans watched him closely and noticed how greedily he drank, refilling his stone cup again and again.

That last night Hans slept alone in a room in the home of Charlotte von Drach, beside him a vase full of dreamcreepers. That way he was assured of a good night's rest and sweet, peaceful dreams. The Long Zero inside of him had guaranteed him a complete and speedy recovery and he was feeling like his old self again. Without the influence of the dreamcreepers, he would undoubtedly have stayed awake for a much longer time... dreading the terrors of the impending return journey.

He was a small astonished boy who floated above fields of flowers finding joy in the simple act of looking around and taking in every detail.

He did not want anyone to accompany him to the stone circle and said farewell to everyone in the town square. Charlotte had seen to it that he had eaten a solid breakfast and he was now ready for the voyage. He looked around, seeing only cheerful faces, and wondered how many of these people would go behind the façades after his departure to unburden their souls.

He shook hands with the men and kissed Eleonora and Charlotte. Aeneas clapped him firmly on both shoulders and Plukfelder attempted to deliver a speech but got choked up with emotion halfway into the opening line and hid behind the others.

"Thanks for the clothes," Hans called out to him. "You will find them back at the circle."

Jeremias pushed two men aside and looked at Hans with sad eyes.

"We all hope that you will put them on again someday," he said, putting everyone's hopes into words.

Eleonora summoned a swarm of flies come and Hans selected two of them, threw the loops of his hangstring over the back pieces and sat down. He ascended, waved one more time and never looked back again. He was very adept at keeping his emotions in check, and mentally he now started to prepare for hell. He floated over the green forest quickly, without looking down. The pale sun stood high in a clear sky.

It promised to be a hot day on Drach.

When he reached the circle he released the flies and threw the hangstring in the flowers. He undressed and knelt within the circle. His body relaxed, his mind searched for and found the Long Zero and wound it tightly into a ball.

And he was gone.

Chapter 13: The Decision

"Mors janua vitae," whispered Mercury.

Hans Winters' naked body lay stretched out across the rocky surface of the Austrian Alps. He was merely a sack of skin and bones, and his steel muscles were no more than thin cords. Slowly, he rolled over onto his back and stared at the sky with frightened eyes. The horrors of his journey had made a physical and emotional wreck of him, but as the benevolent Mercury floated slowly away on his winged shoes, he took with him everything that had badgered, stung, or bit him.

A warm sound reached his ears and a vague smile passed over his face as he once more heard the chirping of birds. He sat up, and leaning on his bony elbows on the hard rocky ground, carefully rolled himself to the spot where he had previously hidden his clothes. He managed to grab hold of it, but his fingers were too stiff and painful to open it.

Now he lay on his side with his head resting on his outstretched arm and he sunk into a deep, dreamless sleep from which he would not awake for many hours.

He felt the sun burning his skin and figured it must be afternoon by now as he watched puffs of white clouds slowly passing by.

This time he was able to open his bag, and to his great relief found a water bottle inside. There was also food packed in the bag, but he knew he was not yet able to eat anything. He drank and thought of Monaco...she must have been the one who had taken care of this. The water refreshed him. He sat there with his back against the rocks for more than an hour breathing slowly and deeply, but he could not ward off the panic that took possession of him, and in his mind he saw himself creep up to the edge of the rock and fall into the abyss so that eternal rest would be his salvation.

He scanned his surroundings, looking desperately for something to focus on besides his fear. He saw that the circle of stones that the Brotherhood had left behind had disappeared. Now no one who was not previously privy to the secret of its location would be able to find the point of departure. Hans suspected that Flamel had done this. He carefully took a few bites from the food in the bag and managed to dress himself. To his surprise, the clothes fit perfectly - dear sweet Monaco had even taken into account the fact that he would have lost a few pounds on his journey.

Hans stood, taking the food and water with him. He found it quite difficult to walk. He had not gone more than a couple of hundred feet when he felt the need to seek out a safe place behind some trees and lay down again.

It was pitch-black out when he awoke from a deep, deep sleep. He found his life-sustaining bag by touch in the darkness and ate, drank, and then slept some more.

Early the next morning he felt strong enough to continue on his way down. The pain in his mind was worse than the pain in his bruised body and thought with melancholy of the beautiful sleep that the dreamcreepers had provided him on Drach.

He came to the spot from where he could look down on the buildings of the compound of the Brotherhood.

The new concrete roof was in place and protected the table. Behind the house was now a high fence that made it impossible for him to return to the house in the same way he had left. That was a disappointment, for now he would have to go further around, along the mountain path, in order to reach the road that led to the gate that was now guarded by the Austrian police.

He continued along with short, measured paces.

He followed a path that gradually sloped downwards and after an hour's walk he reached a green meadow with a ramshackle wooden barn in the middle that had been used as a storage facility for lumber and other building materials. He decided to rest there for a while and take a bite to eat again. With a heavy sigh he leaned against a wall and slowly lowered himself down to the floor.

At that moment the door flew open and there were suddenly three men standing before him. He looked up, and although he gazed through weary eyes he immediately recognized Andrea Carandini, Aldo Duby, and Minor. The obese Carandini bent forward and raised his eyebrows.

"Just when I was thinking about giving up and admitting that the fortress is impregnable; just when I had decided to go back to Italy...the man I have been seeking is right in front of me," he said without smiling. And with amazement added: "What on Earth have they done to you, Winters? To look at you one would think that you have looked death in the eyes and then found joy in the fact that it obviously wasn't your time. Bring him inside, Minor."

Carandini had a sudden thought and stood up to have a quick look around to convince himself that Hans was alone. Minor put his hands under Hans' armpits and lifted him up high off the ground.

"He weighs almost nothing," he said and carried him inside the barn like an old rag doll.

The barn was empty except for a dark red Peugeot that was standing in the middle of the room. The giant tossed Hans on the cold clay floor and it felt cold against his skin. The building had no windows and Carandini left the door open to be able to see.

"We just had a short meeting," he said, looking at Hans carefully. "We had actually decided to leave here, but now our waiting has been rewarded after all. Can't you talk, Winters? Open your mouth, will you? No doubt there is much you have to tell. I want to know all about what is happening down there..."

Hans jumped to his feet and bolted, being much too quick and agile for the clumsy Minor to catch. He had not expected Hans to be able to undertake such an escape attempt. Duby jumped to the doorway in an effort to block it and pulled out a revolver. Just as Hans was about to slide past Andrea, the latter reached out with his fist and hit him right on the cheek. Hans tumbled backwards, landing with his head against the wall. A second blow caught him in the gut, which was followed by two hard kicks to his legs.

"That's what I've wanted to do to you ever since you made me look like a fool in front of the Ghost of Genoa!" Carandini cried out. "If I did not want to hear so much from you, I would put an end to your life right now... which, by the way, is hanging by a thread."

But he was on the alert now and he also took a revolver from his inside pocket. The kicks and blows he had dealt out had left him panting. With his free hand he opened the car door and sank onto the front seat, keeping his feet outside firmly on the ground.

"There is a small, rough road that runs along the mountainside which leads away from here," he said. "After about a mile it becomes much more traversable and a couple of miles beyond that it is quite usable and we can use it to drive all the way to Italy. We don't even have to go through town...we can drive around Helgen without anyone seeing us. And trust me...you will be taking a ride with us to Italy very soon. But first I want to ask you a few questions, and each time you refuse to answer me, or I catch you in a lie, I will ask Minor to kick the crap out of you! And trust me Hans, you won't enjoy it. Do we understand each other?"

"Is that your first question?" asked Hans.

He knew that his situation was hopeless. There were two guns pointed at his head and a homicidal giant towering over him. Carandini had hit him hard and he feared for a while that his legs might have been broken. He very gingerly tried, and succeeded, in stretching his legs, but the pain was almost unbearable.

"As you very well know, everything I took from you has been returned," said Carandini, who was a bit calmer now. "But I had plenty of time to take a good look at everything and I consulted people to help me understand it all...but I'll come back to that later. What interests me the most right now is how you managed to end up in the mountains, outside the fences...and what the hell happened to you!"

Hans looked at him dully. He felt sick and exhausted, and at that particular moment logical thought seemed to elude him entirely.

"My question is this," said Carandini, leaning forward with his elbows resting on his knees. "Did you disappear, as I have seen it done in films? Did you just come back? Where have you been?"

Receiving no answer, he shot a glance at Minor, but as the giant clenched his fist and prepared to strike, Carandini quickly shook his head.

"You know that I wanted Flamel by my side so that he could help me make a fortune in the casinos. And then later, my men, especially Duby, tracked you down. And you seemed to have at your disposal the same talents, my friend. Slowly but surely I discovered that there is more to these gifts of yours than meets the eye. I seem to have stumbled across something that is more powerful than all the money the casinos could ever offer...and now I want some answers. So you'd better just start talking. First, I want to know to where you've been, and how you ended up here in the mountains looking like a worn-out bum!"

Again Hans said nothing, and Minor shot Carandini an asking glance.

This time though he gave a nod of affirmation and Minor reacted immediately. He grabbed hold of Hans' bony shoulders, lifted him up and pulled back one of his enormous hands. He dangled Hans as if he weighed nothing at all and began to beat him in the face. Hans' nose and lips began to bleed.

"Okay, put him down," said Carandini.

The giant relaxed his grip and Hans crumpled to the ground, where he remained sitting motionless.

"It doesn't matter," said Carandini. We have all the time in the world now. You will be sitting in the back next to Minor on the trip back to Italy and I'm quite sure that by the time we arrive there you will have told him everything we want to know. We have been in the area watching you continuously. When I realized how well protected and fortified you were, I called my men off a bit and began my own personal surveillance of the compound and finally found you...and now that you're mine, Winters, I'll never let you go again.

Of course there can no longer be any discussion about friendly co-operation; our roles are simple...I give the orders; you carry them out. You will have all the time you need to describe in detail what you and Flamel have been doing and why all those other people joined you here. And in between we will visit some casinos and make some real money. From now on you can consider Minor your big brother...he will always be at your side and will be very happy to punish you if you piss him off."

He stood up and closed the door softly.

"We must be as quiet as possible," he said to Minor and Duby. "It's possible that there are others in the area. Fortunately, the path is not too steep. Push the car outside without starting the engine then we'll jump in and coast down silently. As soon as we are far enough away we can start her up and get out of here. Come on, let's go..."

He put away his revolver and walked to the back of the car. Now it was Duby who pointed his weapon at Hans, while Minor released the handbrake and slowly pushed the car through the door.

"Get in," said Carandini. "Aldo, you drive and I'll sit beside you. Minor and Hans go in the back."

Hans got up. He was staggering on his bruised and unsteady legs, but at least he had control over his mind again. He followed Duby, blinking his eyes against the glaring sunlight. Minor stood with his arms crossed on the other side of the car as Carandini opened the rear door.

"You first, Winters," he said.

Hans walked past him looking as if he would lose consciousness at any moment. When he almost collapsed he put his hands on the roof of the car for support. As quickly as he could, he tried to gather the strength he needed to make the car disappear as he had seen Flamel do so many times.

"Get in!" sounded Carandini's voice.

Hans raised his hands and the car vanished almost immediately and even he could not be sure where it had actually gone. The Observator had a theory that the metallic particles were flung through space in billions of pieces, sending the car on a dizzying journey that would last forever.

Carandini, Duby and Minor jumped back in astonishment and Hans grabbed the opportunity to attack the giant, hitting him on the jaw. There was a sound of bone breaking and the man fell backwards onto the grass. Duby had pulled himself together and was pointing his revolver at Hans.

A shot rang out, but it was not Aldo Duby who had fired.

"Stay right where you are!" boomed a voice. "It's the police! And we've got you covered!"

Two of Rudolph Brendel's men, who were part of the Austrian police contingent charged with the responsibility of guarding the compound, had stumbled upon this violent and confusing scene.

As they approached, Duby dropped his weapon and raised his hands, deeming it wiser simply to remain silent, since the unconscious Minor could provide nothing in the way of protection. Andrea Carandini thought differently though and with lightning speed, he pulled his gun and fired four times in rapid succession. Three bullets missed their mark, but the fourth struck one of the policemen in the chest.

Before he had a chance to fire again and finish the job, Hans knocked the weapon out of his hand with such force that it sent Duby to his knees moaning in pain, where he sat on the ground and watched Hans pick up the weapon.

"Take care of your colleague and send for reinforcements," he shouted to the policeman who did not know what to do first. "I'll make sure these gentlemen do not move a muscle."

He took the weapons from Minor and Carandini and sat down on the grass a short distance away from them. Behind him he heard the injured policeman softly moaning.

And it was at that moment he made a decision...

Just as Ulrich von Drach had made a decision such a very long time ago.

Hans needed to know the origin of the Long Zero and therefore must return to Drach. Colonel Kelly and his men could stay here in Helgen and continue their own research, but he had to return. He knew that a second journey to Drach would be his last one, because he would never be strong enough to go through that hell again. His poor worn out body told him that. And if he ever managed to find what he was searching for, he would be able to travel as far, and as often, as he cared.

He considered all these things as he stared at Carandini, Duby and Minor through glazed eyes.

An ambulance and two police cars appeared and stopped in front of the little wooden barn. The badly wounded officer was laid carefully on a stretcher and carried into the ambulance, while the other three felons were taken away in one of the police cars.

Someone leaned over him and said softly:

"Hans... Are you awake?"...

It was Monaco.

He raised his head and fell back as someone caught him. He thought he heard Flamel's voice as he was lifted up. Once again he heard people talking, but he could make no sense of what they were saying.

He felt his body begin to shake and was certain that he was being driven over a bumpy road. Cold fingers grazed his face and he thought to himself: "Mors janua vitae," as he saw Mercury's divine face loom up before him.

"I'm not dead," he told himself. "The gods must know that I need more time."

He woke up in his own bed not knowing what day or time it was.

Monaco had pulled a chair close and sat beside him reading a book. She had not noticed that he was awake...lying there silently...watching her. She held the book loosely and her dark eyes moved from left to right as she read. She was wearing jeans and a sweater. Every now and then her lips formed words without sound. There was so much he wanted to tell her, but he knew he must start with a single word:

"Hello..."

She put the book down on the floor and flew to his side, giving him a big wet kiss and a smile.

"Welcome home," she said.

Once again, Hans Winters had proved to be no ordinary mortal, but had attained, as Flamel once put it, the status of a demigod. He felt alive and strong and did not want to stay in bed a moment longer. He was hungry and thirsty, and wanted to take a long, hot shower.

Monaco tried to prevent him from getting up, but she was no match for him as he grabbed her by the wrists and pulled her down to his side with a smile.

After he was washed and dressed, he went to the refrigerator, took out a half a gallon of milk and drank the whole thing directly from the plastic container. Monaco told him to sit down so she could take care of him.

"I'll make you something to eat," she said. "You tell me what you want."

"Is it time for breakfast, lunch or supper?"

"Breakfast. It's five-thirty in the morning. Everyone else is still asleep."

Monaco wanted to embrace him, but she controlled herself and went to work on his meal, watching him closely to see if he was really as good as he seemed. After he had consumed an enormous breakfast, accompanied by five cups of coffee, she was convinced that he would soon be his old self again, and that his miraculous journey had not left him with any long-lasting injuries.

After having established that, she finally gave in to her pent up emotions, bursting out in tears and collapsing on the bench beside her, shaking like a leaf. She lay on her stomach with her face buried in her arms.

She had heard nothing of Hans until Flamel's return, and he looked so exhausted, and so emaciated, that she feared for Hans' life. She had blamed herself for allowing him to leave in the first place, and now that he was back, she planned on nursing him back to health and never leaving his side again.

Hans stroked her dark brown hair as it moved softly on her shoulders with each sob.

He recalled clearly the decision he had made during his violent confrontation with Carandini.

At the moment he had sworn to himself that he would be returning to Drach though, he had not been thinking about Monaco.

He definitely could not go without her...

Monaco sat up and nestled in his arms. He continued to caress her hair as she asked him to tell her about his adventures. But first, she had something important that she needed to tell him.

"Of course, the Observator, Simone, and myself have already heard much from Augustin," she said. "...About the beauty of Drach, about the people there... He has brought a ball of something with him that can split itself like a cell and everyone is busy analyzing it. It seems that the thing can also fly...and is edible too! But listen carefully, Hans... he has only told this to us. By showing the ball to Colonel Kelly he has virtually admitted to having taken and returned from an incredible journey, but the place of departure remains a secret and he hasn't told him a thing about Drach and its population. It's good that you woke up when you did so that I could bring you up to speed."

"How did Kelly react?"

"He said he wouldn't ask any questions, because he just knows that he wouldn't get a straight answer anyway. He has told Augustin and the Observator over and over that he is their guest in Helgen and cannot impose his will on anyone. And now I want to hear about you trip..."

Hans told about the horrors of the journey... About death lying in wait on all sides, about waking up near the graves of Ulrich von Drach, Martha Ritter and Wolfram Wikander, about his mystical sleep beneath the dreamcreepers and his awaking with Eleonora Ventura. He described Drach and its inhabitants...laughing when he told her about Jeremias Plukfelder, and becoming respectful when he discussed Nicolai Frederiksson and Aeneas Mitropoulos.

He told her about his nights with Charlotte von Drach, his work in the library and his flights over the breathtaking landscape on his hangstring. Monaco listened intently and became calm again. She wiped her tears away with the sleeves of her sweater, and nodded thoughtfully when he told her about the decision he had made.

"But now I am not so sure...without you, I would not want to leave this world."

She looked at him searchingly with her black eyes.

"So...there is the possibility that. Somewhere far, far away from here...so far that we cannot even fathom it...children will be born who will know you as their father..."

"Yes...it is very possible indeed," said Hans. "I imagine that you blame me for...well, that I..."

She put her fingers on his lips to silence him, and at the same time she tapped his belly with her other hand.

"Flamel and I have already discussed this in great detail. I have also talked it over with Mireille Robin, who of course, also knows all about Flamel's journey and the events on Drach. If I understand it correctly, Drach is a small, friendly society where all newcomers are welcome. Well, I am expecting..."

He caught hold of her hand and placed it, together with his own, on her belly.

"What are you trying to tell me? Are you pregnant?" he asked.

Monaco began to laugh, pushed his hand away and stood up. She paced the room nervously.

"It's more than that... there's something else. I need to move. I want to go out hiking, just like you did. Just start walking and hope that the Long Zero will begin to grow inside of me too..."

She unfastened the leather belt on her jeans and showed him a hidden pouch with a silver zipper sewn inside her pants. She opened it and took out a little steel figure.

"I am under its influence," she said. "It has taken hold of me. The Observator insisted that I be given priority and reserved one of the steel cylinders for me that had been standing on the table and into which those little objects had flitted in and out of."

He jumped up and embraced her.

"Is this true? This is terrific... Tell me more!"

The Observator has placed as many cylinders into the holes as is possible. Colonel Kelly has selected recruits who are brave enough to attempt the journey. They are men and women with guts who know they are risking their lives. The all have military backgrounds, and all are well educated, each one with their own field of expertise. They are all highly gifted and willing, indeed anxious, to explore the universe. The colonel has set up a special program for anyone who thinks that the Long Zero is beginning to exert any influence on his or her body.

But the recruits have no freedom, they all must stay inside the fence and get themselves in shape. They work out daily to the point of physical exhaustion. Of course we have only just begun this training, but we can already achieve more than we ever thought we would be able to. When I am ready, I want to come with you to Drach. Who knows whose child I might bring into the world?"

"You mean it? You would come with me?"

"Why else do you think I would have accepted a cylinder from Mundy? Do you think it was so that I could go off in search of adventures with the recruits, and die in some dark corner of the galaxy? Or to take a bad jump and end up whizzing through space for all eternity? I want to be with you when you leave again... that is of course, if you can wait until I can follow you. Mundy says things will go faster if we keep ourselves preoccupied with our training, rather than sitting around and wondering about the upcoming journey. But he also says that we must steel our minds as well as our bodies to be prepared for anything that may occur."

Hans went back to the fridge got a soda and some cheese, buttered some bread and proceeded to have another small feast. He was indeed feeling much better...even on his best days he had not been what anyone would have called a big eater.

"Except for the group that the Colonel has selected, only Mireille and I will be joining you," said Monaco. "Yes, she is also carrying a cylinder and is already beginning to change. She is determined to go with Augustin."

Hans, who was just about to stuff two pieces of bread into his mouth, turned his head in surprise.

"Yes," said Monaco. "Mireille too..."

"No, no...that's not what caught me off guard," interrupted Hans. "Are you sure that Augustin has decided to return to Drach?"

"It is his most ardent wish. He just hopes that he can survive another journey...he knows only too well that he has to reckon with his age. Apart from that, he is convinced that you will also back."

Hans began to tell her about Mantown, and its surrounding area, with such enthusiasm, that it almost became infectious. He described the forests and the lakes; the hills, the fields of pastel flowers; the amphibians and all the different species of flies.

Time flew by and they finally decided to go downstairs to the dining room. There they found the Observator, his wife Simone, Augustin, and Mireille all sitting around the table. They all leaped to their feet to greet Hans. He was embraced, kissed and patted repeatedly on his bony shoulders. Hans and Augustin laughed at the sight of each other and needed no words to express their happiness. They clasped one another's hands with a strength that would have broken all of Minor's fingers.

After everyone was seated again, they all began talking softly. Flamel stressed the importance of not telling anyone outside this small circle of friends also about Drach.

"The secret of the departure point will be guarded by Philippe and Simone Mundy. Our good Observator has decided to remain here and continue his research. You and I, Hans, will wait until Monaco and Mireille are ready to accompany us. The best thing for us to do in the meantime, is to read as many books as possible that might be important to the people of Mantown."

Hans nodded and attacked the food that had been set before him as if he hadn't had anything to eat yet that morning.

"I'm too old to leave everything which is dear to me," said the Observator. "My place is here, in Helgen. There is much to do and besides, the Colonel needs me.

I'll spend the time that you are still here with me wisely. To be honest with you, I cannot even imagine life without you. I have had a terrific run with Augustin, and Mireille and Monaco have become my closest friends. And Hans, well Hans holds a very special place in this old heart, and I will always keep in mind that one of you might return... someday..."

After the communal breakfast, Hans and Monaco went outside for a walk. The compound was bustling now, what with barracks and soldiers all over the place, which were not here when Hans had left. He headed over to have a look at the table of the Brotherhood. It was still Philippe Mundy's old workroom, but there were people there whom he did not recognize. Stephan Weckmann, the doctor, wanted to take him immediately to another room to examine him, but Hans insisted he be allowed to relax and just look around for a bit. When he went back outside Brendel came up to him and told him that Carandini should expect to be spending a long, long time in prison.

"It's a miracle that Albert Roth, my man who was shot, wasn't killed. He's in intensive care, but I've just received word that he'll pull through. I imagine that there are a lot of people in Italy who will breathe a sigh of relief when they hear the news that Carandini is not coming back."

He looked Hans up and down, slowly shaking his head.

"First Flamel and now you... You are as lean as a rake! What are you doing to yourself?"

"Don't worry about a thing, Brendel," laughed Hans. "All I have to do is eat some more!"

He finally could not escape from Dr. Weckmann any longer and was confronted by an entire team of doctors whose sole purpose was to examine him. They weighed him, took blood, his heart and respiration were checked, and then he was attached to an assortment of machines that performed a battery of other tests upon him. It struck him oddly that not one of these people asked him anything about what he had been doing. And later that day, when having a conversation with the Colonel, he also said or asked anything about Hans' activities.

Hans knew what Kelly had said to Flamel:

"The fact is...I am your guest, and I am very grateful that you let us join you, for what happens here concerns the entire world. Thanks to you we are on the verge of new breakthroughs in science, and everyone is happy to be working with Philippe Mundy.

We had only one big concern...

We were afraid that Carandini would be given an opportunity to sneak in a couple of his men. He was a danger to all of us. Our power extends only so far, Hans, but now that we finally have him, he will disappear behind thick prison walls."

Hans suspected that the Colonel knew something was being kept secret from him. He was an acute man who could see the finished puzzle before all the pieces were in place.

He poured Hans and himself a drink and then subtly tried to tempt him into giving something away.

"It still strikes me as strange that the Brotherhood of Helgen lived and worked here such a long time ago. I have seen the photo album that belonged to Paolo Carandini. No one has a clue where all those people went. You occasionally hear about a collective suicide among certain cults and sects, but in this case no one ever found a corpse, and there is nothing else to indicate a mass suicide. Anyway, they took their most important secret with them, wherever it is they went..."

He looked up at the ceiling.

Hans raised his glass and said:

"To your health, Colonel!"

Colonel Kelly emptied his glass with one swig and said:

"Come with me, Hans, and I'll show you where the men and women who carry the steel are training. Your girlfriend and Mireille will be among that group. I hope to have some people ready soon who can also take a place inside the circle."

Before they left, the Colonel stopped, and looking Hans directly in the eye, said:

"I have all the confidence in the world that things will go well with the experiments. But what are we supposed to do after that? Even the Observator cannot, or will not, give me an answer when I ask him what will happen to those people who undertake this journey."

"There is a good chance that anyone who leaves will never return," said Hans. "It will be always be a perilous enterprise, and I wonder if anybody should really be doing these kinds of things at all..."

"I guess we'll see soon enough," sighed Kelly. "For the present however, we have our work cut out for us examining these little flies and their origins."

"The flies," thought Hans, keeping his mouth shut.

He simply nodded and opened the door.

They went to another barracks, where the young would-be travellers were training. It was a complete gym, with any kind of equipment one could want...and Dr. Weckmann. Much of the training was based on weightlifting, and all exercise routines and progress were strictly monitored and recorded. A muscular man in his early twenties was working out with a pair of dumb-bells and having a great deal of difficulty getting them off the floor. He had raised them about one inch off the floor and had to drop them again. With a broad grin on his face Hans walked up to him and took off his jacket. He was wearing a short-sleeved shirt under it and the man raised his eyebrows cynically when he saw Hans' skinny arms.

Hans stooped, reached for the dumbbells, and with one fluid motion swept them both over his head and held them there for a while before placing them gently back on the floor.

"One day you'll be able to do that too," he said to the justifiably surprised young man. "And the strangest part is, that it's not just the training that will make it possible. You train your body to get into better physical condition and to rid yourself of all your extra energy...but it is something quite different that will build up your inner strength. I have never done any weight training in a gym...all I've done is walk."

He and the Colonel proceeded on, looking for Monaco, when from behind him, Hans heard someone say, their voice full of admiration:

"You must be Hans Winters..."

Chapter 14: The Leaving

Augustin Flamel surpassed even himself in his latest theatrical offering...he and his apprentice, Hans Winters, bewildered his audience with their feats of magic. What seemed to stir the crowd's imagination the most was the finale, because of its inherent and apparent simplicity.

Flamel and Hans both stood at the side of the stage and juggled big, colorful balls. More and more balls materialized and floated low over the audience, who were allowed to hold them and examine them. The balls felt rubbery to the touch and were covered by a shiny, transparent coat. They seemed to have almost no weight whatsoever. Both illusionists held a ball above their head and slowly ascending, floated majestically over the heads of the audience, drifting higher and higher, until they reached the ceiling.

It became obvious what would happen next, and anyone who had been lucky enough to grab a ball, would not even think about parting with it.

Back on stage Flamel asked everyone to hold the balls tightly and those who did were levitated out of their seats, arranged in a long row, and floated around the theatre. To guard against accidents, Hans and Augustin did not allow them to fly too high...just high enough to be very astounded, and perhaps just a little frightened, to find themselves travelling in this fashion. Anyone who wanted to experience it was encouraged to borrow a ball from someone who had already flown. At some performances

Hans held a ball under his arm, floated over the seats, and selected to fly with him to the highest points of the theatre. Sometimes there were more than a hundred people floating through the theatre at the same time. Everything was being recorded for eventual television specials, so the press was always welcome, and they never stopped talking about what they experienced at Flamel's show.

Meanwhile, back in Helgen, the flies were being extensively examined. They were not only edible, but they were healthy to consume as well. They contained all the vitamins and minerals a human being needed. The only thing everyone agreed on was that they were able to extract water from the air, but it remained a mystery as to how they were able to divide like cells using the power of thought. They were fed to the Colonel's recruits with the end result of them being better able to adapt to the Long Zero. Augustin and Hans had been forced to roam the world over vast distances for many years, attempting to come to terms with, and control, this new power they found within them. If these new disciples maintained their current progress, they would be ready to make the journey in less than two years' time.

Hans and Augustin did all they could to help prepare them, and when they were ready they took them to that far-away world where little creatures swarmed, and above which multiple moons tumbled around in an eternal pursuit. The novice travellers had gone completed all the phases of development, and had suddenly come to understand the meaning and the wonder of Astra.

Sic itur ad astra - this is the road to the stars!

The Observator had his twenty little objects fully under his control and had learned how to best keep them safely under the table, in the temple of Janus, encouraging them to transfer their powers into the steel.

Augustin made several journeys with Mireille, and Monaco accompanied Hans. They sat all sat beside each other on the rocks of the strange world and looked up at the starlit sky with its tumbling satellites.

And they learned to cope with the pain and fear they were forced to endure on these journeys.

"Going is nothing compared to leaving," Hans told Monaco over and over. "Only then will you actually know what it means to go through hell."

Flamel sold his property in Helgen to Patrick Kelly's group, and donated the balance of his considerable wealth to organizations that had proved that they were working to improve life on Earth. Hans also had accumulated a lot of money that he could not take with him. After intense consultation with Kelly, he set up a foundation that would seek a method of using the balls to generate nutrition for the world.

Hans and Monaco shivered and could not help but cry, when Flamel and Mireille went into the mountains one night, knowing that this would be the last time. The time had come for them to say goodbye to everything they had known before; to everything they had become.

They decided to take a car and drive through France and Monaco.

They wanted to see Cannes and Nice again, to stop and look at the Mediterranean, to roam the old familiar streets and boulevards, and sleep in the same little hotel in Nice where they had such a wonderful time together.

Pierre Pirenne walked them up to a barn where he had several cars stored. He gave them the keys to a comfortable French car. Pierre proudly wore a very expensive gold watch and two diamond rings that were presents from Carlo Dordoni, the Ghost of Genoa, as an expression of his joy and gratitude at the disappearance of his rival, Andrea Carandini.

"I know you are very busy with terribly important things back in Austria," he had said, "but I don't want to become at all involved in that. I have become fairly important and powerful since having been saved from Carandini, and I owe it to you. Anyone associated with Flamel can always count on my affection, help and protection."

Hans and Monaco had both read hundreds of books. The history of the Earth was indelibly imprinted on their memories. Time after time he told her about the journey to Drach and prepared her for the worst.

"It will seem like the hour of your death, sweet Monaco, and you will be alone."

"I am not afraid," she had assured him. "For I know where I will end up."

They made love in the small hotel room in Nice, took a swim in the warm sea, and enjoyed sumptuous meals. They sat at a gambling table and won a fortune, and immediately gave it away to an elderly Belgian couple, who had never seen so much money.

Little things, like buying a newspaper, sitting in the sun, shopping, even taking a shower -

they all became very special events to them, because they knew that they would soon be leaving this familiar world behind.

Watching a sunrise or sunset, feeling the wind on their faces, watching a cloud pass by, a walk through busy streets, a drive in the country, going to a movie, discovering an unread book, listening to music, it all was very melancholy, for they loved the earth more and more; this was their home, this is where they were born. They knew very well that everything here would change quickly, thanks to the things that would be discovered in Helgen. The Brotherhood of Helgen had shown the way and Augustin Flamel and his people had followed their tracks down new, uncharted paths.

A new era was dawning.

They returned to Helgen and spent their last night with the Observator and Simone Mundy...the evening was marked by much silent staring and a growing feeling of excitement. While it was still dark out the Observator drove them away from the compound and dropped them off at the roadside.

They climbed up the mountain until they reached the spot where the Brotherhood had made their circle. They undressed and put their clothes in a bag that the Observator would collect later.

Monaco concentrated and Hans watched as she disappeared.

He straightened himself and stared into the darkness. He heard the wind rustle and saw the star-spangled sky. He filled his lungs with the cool, oxygen rich air, and then kneeled on the same spot upon which Monaco had rested just a moment or two before. He was healthy and strong and did not dwell now on the terrors of the journey. He just wanted to follow Monaco and start a new life with her on Drach. She wanted to go with him when he set out on his voyage of discovery...travelling on a hangstring attached to two flies as they tried to solve some of the riddles that lay beyond Mantown.

He was seized by panic for a moment, when initially he could not focus hard enough on the Long Zero. Then he caught hold of what was inside of him and once again became the demigod who could go wherever he pleased.

Hans slipped away and his journey began.

Colonel Patrick Kelly stood in his office in one of the barracks at Helgen. He opened a drawer in a steel filing cabinet and took out a thick envelope. Philippe Mundy was sitting in an easy chair with a glass of wine in his hand. The Colonel had invited him over for a drink.

"It will not be difficult to find someone who can impersonate Augustin Flamel," said the Colonel. "I even have someone in mind who could pass for Winters. We will announce that they will no longer be appearing in theatres, and that they will be devoting themselves completely to their work in Helgen."

The Observator raised his black eyebrows and scratched his beard.

"We both know they will not be coming back again, Philippe. The same goes for Mireille Robin and Louise Vernet, who we've grown to know and love as Monaco..."

Still Mundy did not react. He took a small sip from his glass and placed it on an end table.

"Being a military man, I always want to know what is happening, I want to be in control of every situation and not be surprised... I don't like them at all. Andrea Carandini doesn't know it but his meddling here was the direct cause of an interesting discovery. Do you remember a couple of years ago, Augustin Flamel and Hans Winters had left us? And I was afraid they would fall into Carandini's hands? I wasn't so off base considering Hans ended up walking straight into his arms. And when Albert Roth rushed to his rescue, he almost paid for it with his life. You were working hard at the table of the Brotherhood that day and the new concrete roof had just been completed, making the building virtually soundproof. You could not hear the little helicopter flying above you with two of my officers on board. I had given them orders to take a good look at the surrounding area and take photos of it..."

This finally got Mundy's attention and he leaned forward in his chair. The Colonel opened the envelope and took a pile of photos out.

He handed one of them to the Observator, who already knew what he was about to see.

One area of the surrounding countryside had been photographed in exceptional detail and on a bare rock outcropping a circle was visible.

"I happen to be in real good shape," said Kelly. "I like to train along with my men every now and then, and take long walks. A walking tour through the mountains is very relaxing for both the mind and body. I went out searching for the spot where the circle is. It took me a long time, but I am a determined man. I finally discovered the correct location and found that the circle in question had completely disappeared. Do you know what I have done, Mundy? I have commandeered all the negatives of these photos and the one belonging to this photo in particular...well, that I cut into a thousand pieces."

He took the photo back from the Observator and began to tear it up.

"A truly enormous responsibility rests upon your shoulders, Observator."

Kelly had never called him that before. He sat down opposite him and raised his glass of wine up to him.

"Perhaps it is good for you to know that I am sharing this responsibility with you now. It is very possible that the fate of the Earth is in our hands."

The Observator drank, nodded and put his glass down on the table again.

"I don't know if I should be relieved or afraid, Colonel," he said. "But I do know that you and I have much to talk about..."

THE END

ABOUT THE AUTHOR

Koos, a 'Dutchy' with spunk and an inexhaustible drive and fathomless imagination, is one of the most prolific authors of sci-fi and children's books in The Netherlands. His novels, All-Father and Wolf Tears, earned him the moniker, the Dutch Stephen King.

He wrote his first sci-fi novel, Adolar, in one weekend when he was 18 years old and the manuscript was published shortly thereafter.

Koos has published over 70 books, both children's books and novels, hundreds of comic scripts, and he has worked as a copywriter. He is currently working on several screenplays and new novels.

To read more about Koos and his work visit his website at www.koosverkaik.com or follow him on Facebook at https//www.facebook.com/koos.verkai

www.ingramcontent.com/pod-product-compliance
Lightning Source LLC
LaVergne TN
LVHW010639110826
845149LV00014B/2887

* 9 7 9 8 9 9 3 7 0 9 2 4 6 *